What ot

Compelling. Suspenseful. Inspiring. These three words and so many more came to mind when I was reading about Carla in Sue Cass's latest novel, *Dawn's Light*. Sue's creative narrative allows the reader to *see* and *feel* the story as it unfolds. An intense page turner from beginning to end, *Dawn's Light* draws the reader in from the first few words and takes you on a ride that will leave you trying to catch your breath in some parts while cheering out loud in others. Thank you, Sue, for taking us on a ride that is sure to be enjoyed from beginning to end.

—Angel B. Pennyman
Experience His Freedom Ministries Founder

Dawn's Light is a riveting story of the power, grace, and healing of God in the midst of real spiritual warfare. Sue Cass shares godly wisdom in making sense of powers and principalities from a biblical worldview. A wonderful read and a valuable life lesson.

—Steve Wood. Sr. Pastor
Mount Pisgah U.M.C.
Atlanta, Georgia

Sue Cass has written this poignant novel, *Dawn's Light*, which literally captivated me as I began to read it. She has skillfully woven a mixture of romance, intrigue, Christian values, and subtle tactics of Satan. She also reveals the awesome long-suffering and compassionate love of God the Father through the provision of His Son, Jesus Christ. The Father's heart of love, redemption, and restoration is clearly revealed in this novel. I highly recommend this book!

—Bill McKinnon, Pastor
World Outreach Church
McRae, Georgia

Dawn's Light

Dawn's Light

SUE CASS

TATE PUBLISHING
AND ENTERPRISES, LLC

Published by Tate Publishing & Enterprises, LLC
127 E. Trade Center Terrace | Mustang, Oklahoma 73064 USA
1.888.361.9473 | www.tatepublishing.com

Tate Publishing is committed to excellence in the publishing industry. The company reflects the philosophy established by the founders, based on Psalm 68:11,
"The Lord gave the word and great was the company of those who published it."

Cover design by Junriel Boquecosa
Interior design by Honeylette Pino
Author photo credit: Olan Mills

Published in the United States of America

ISBN: 978-1-62994-076-2
1. Fiction / Christian / Suspense
2. Fiction / Mystery & Detective / General
13.11.22

Dedication

Martha McKinnon,
My sister in Christ and friend extraordinaire.

Love you bunches,
Sue

Acknowledgment

All praise, honor, and glory
to God, through His Son,
my Lord and Savior,
Jesus Christ.
Without Him this book
would not be possible.

So many times the words "thank you" are just not enough to express the love and gratitude I feel for some people the Lord has brought into my life. Dr. Clifford Garrison is one of those people. These past twenty years of being friends have been a blessing that can't be described. You have helped me through my own struggles, supported whatever ministry the Lord has called me to do, and given valuable advice, counseling, and direction in many areas to me as well as many other people. I am so blessed to have you as a friend. We've walked a long and twisting path over the years and I thank you for always being there. God bless you, my friend, and thank you for your insights in areas of writing this book.

I do not believe we meet people by accident. It was no accident that the Lord saw fit to place this wonderful lady in my life some fifteen years ago. Martha McKinnon keeps me on my toes, won't let me wallow in the down sides of life, her laughter is infectious, her love for the Lord runs deep. Much thanks, my dear friend, for all your help during the process of writing this book. What a blessing you are to me and God sure knew what He was doing when He brought you into my life.

I want to thank all those at Tate Publishing who have helped me through yet another novel. The Lord knew he was leading me to people who care, want my book to be the best it can be, and are professionals in what they do. Thank you all for your patience, kindness, and guidance through this process.

Thank you to all who have been praying for me through this process. May God continue to bless you.

Blessed is he whose
transgression is forgiven,
whose sin is covered.

—Psalm 32:1

Other books by Sue Cass:

Pursuit

Seek My Face

Sacrifices of a Saint

Laying Down My Net—A Walk of Faith

Prologue

Carla braces against the wind as she faces the water looking out over the sea. Black, ominous, boiling clouds roll threateningly toward the shore. The sky has suddenly turned black, replacing the sun. The wind is hurricane force, whipping and bending the trees as easily as if they are straws. Pushed to almost the breaking point, their arms sweep the ground. Their trunks lean menacingly, as though being shaken by the strong arms of a giant. A few have been ripped from the ground.

The roar of raging waves fills the air. Crashing against the beach with such force, they leave grooves, holes, then suck the fine sand back out into the gaping mouth of the sea. Their rage cannot be tamed. Their fury is bent on destruction.

The few seagulls that have braved the wind are whipped about like loose paper picked up from the street. They're being thrown up, around, down, and can't seem to get a foothold on where to go or how to get there. One bird is driven down, down, down. With every ounce of strength it has, it fights to keep from hitting the ground like a bomber nose diving toward earth with deadly results. At the last second before impact, it swerves, just missing the branch of a large tree and lands in the dirt beneath a wall with the words "But the earth helped the woman, and the earth opened its mouth and swallowed up the flood which the dragon had spewed out of his mouth" written on it. Dazed, the bird stands, ruffles its feathers and staggers toward an empty barrel.

"Run!" people scream in terror. "It's a tsunami!" a man hollers as he runs as fast as he can toward the hotel. The waves roar toward shore, threatening man, beast, and life. Anything in their path will be gone in the blink of an eye, never to be seen again.

Carla grabs her five-year-old daughter's hand as the little girl screams, "Mommy!"

"Come on, honey, we have to run as fast as we can."

The little girl tries but the sand seems to imprison her feet. The torrents of rain burn their eyes, raindrops so large they feel like small pebbles pelting their face, bare arms, and legs. Carla stumbles. "Mommy!" the little girl screams as she trips and Carla drags her across the sand.

"Lord, help us!" Carla screams as she stumbles again while swooping up her daughter into her arms.

Stumbling again, she almost drops her daughter as people rush past her. A woman slams into her, almost knocking her to the ground. She cusses at Carla and continues to run frantically. Mothers yelling for their children to hurry up, children crying in fear, screams are heard and the roar—the roar of the monstrous waves grows louder. Slowly, methodically, like an army of giants, these twenty- and thirty-foot high waves march closer and closer as people frantically try to get out of their path. Nothing will stop them. These monsters have a mind of their own.

Carla runs holding her daughter tightly in her arms. A huge wave roars up behind her and just as it's about to swallow her whole, Carla's eyes fly open and she bolts upright in the middle of her bed. Gasping for air, she hugs herself in the dark of her bedroom. Her body is covered in sweat and her heart is racing. Realizing she is grasping a wad of blankets tightly, she loosens her grip. *It was only a dream!* she thinks, relieved. Her heart finally slows and she lies back down.

Chapter 1

Small shops line the quiet streets of Ivy. Their window fronts display the usual beachfront items for the tourists that come in the hot summer months. "Bill's Variety Store" sits on the corner of Elm Street. Styrofoam surf boards lean against the outside wall with bathing suits rustling in the wind on their hangers. Long beach robes dangle from a string that stretches between two poles. A few pots and pans, picnic baskets, sunglasses, snorkels, and air mattresses are displayed in the window.

Next door is an opening in the side of the building with a sign hanging above the opening: "Pizza your way." The aroma of freshly baked pizza waifs through the air, leaving passersby to think about lunch. Across the street is a small grocery store with shelves lined with items most tourists might like. Soda and beer is in the cooler along with juice and milk. A small freezer holds assorted ice cream. A rack stands near the front door with every kind of candy imaginable. A display case has magazines and books. On the center shelf of aisle three tubes and bottles of sun lotion and sunscreen are almost gone. The three gas pumps lined up in front of the store appear to be from the 1940s. The tourists love pulling up to them and pumping their gas from these quaint pumps. Most are surprised they work.

A dress shop, with mannequins dressed in bright summer dresses and shorts and halter tops stand in the window advertising a sale discount, sits on Myrtle Street next to a small post office. The owner was told location was important so when the small building became vacant, Mildred thought it would be perfect due to the traffic in and out of the post office. It's done well.

"The Happy Oyster" is a seafood restaurant and is always a favorite for lunch and dinner. Hanging across one corner of the ceiling is a large fishnet with various shells trapped within its ropes. An oyster bar lines one wall. A large swordfish hangs on one wall with the worn oars of an old fishing boat nearby. Several round tables fill the room. If one is looking for a quiet atmosphere to enjoy their meal, this is not the place. The Happy Oyster is always filled with the clinking of dishes, conversation, and laughter.

"Marty's" is the local fast food restaurant with charcoal hamburgers, French fries, and milk shakes to die for. Susan's Craft Store offers children's craft lessons and Martha's Christian Bookstore has a wide variety of novels. Down by the dock, Art's scuba diving shop offers lessons for a nominal fee. The sign reads: "See the real world of fish for $35.00 an hour. Professional instructors available."

Christ Lives Church is a non-denominational church nestled within the hibiscus, palm trees, and oleanders off Main Street but near the center of town. The church was built when the town was established and was damaged severely in 1940 when the one hundred five-mile-per-hour winds swept down the coastline and through the town. It was rebuilt and much of what could be salvaged was used in its rebuilding. The old wooden pews are lined with comfortable cushions and the stained glass windows that were not totally shattered once again line the walls. The steeple was found some three miles away but now sits prominently back in its place at the front of the roof. Old Pastor Rex, as people called him, has retired and the new pastor is still getting acquainted with the locals. There's True Gospel Baptist Church at the edge of town, Holy Hope United Methodist is down the street six blocks, and further to the north is the St. Peter's Catholic Church.

Ivy was established as a small seaport town in the late 1800s and many of its residents congregated here leaving their busy lifestyles in the big cities. The old timers are mostly gone but their children and grandchildren have carried the town. It's no longer a seaport with the large ships docking off its shores. A few fishing boats are seen out on the sea but those are from the "Ivy Fishing Expedition." Tourists are welcomed onto the medium-size fishing boats for a day of fishing the deep blue waters. Their catch is cleaned, filleted, and packed in ice for their trip home.

The Holiday Inn, Hyatt Regency, and Comfort Inn hotels line the shimmering beach. When people began learning about Ivy being a beautiful quaint oceanfront town with pristine beaches, they began coming by the droves. Originally, there was only one small hotel. When the big hotels began moving in, the "Seaman" went out of business and was eventually turned into a rental shop for beach chairs and lounges with a bar and grill in the back. McDonald's, Wendy's, and Burger King all tried to put a franchise in town but the city council flatly turned them down after every family in town raised holy cane. "We don't want them here!" the people screamed and signed petitions. Taco Bell, Denny's, and IHOP got the same reception, leaving Wanda's Café safe from closing.

The homes with the sandy beach at their backdoors have mostly been refurbished. Most now are built on stilts in case the tide comes too close. Hard lessons have been learned so when anyone decides to build, it's either far back from the water's edge or on stilts. Of course, there's no guarantee the water will not rise, rushing through a living room in a storm. The residential areas are away from the main part of town. Some are within walking distance.

Most residents depend on the larger towns for their workplaces and shopping. Ivy is their retreat from the world of chaos. The local business owners have left that world and rest comfortably in the knowledge that their chaos only lasts for a summer.

As with any small town, everyone knows everyone and the gossip flies, the businesses are family owned and run, and everyone knows everyone else's business. Kids and grandkids are expected to carry on the tradition or hopefully so. Some have left for the "bigger world" and never return but others have returned and raised their families where they themselves grew up. Carla is not one of them. She's only been here six months.

* * *

Upon entering Bill's Variety Store, the air conditioning is a welcome relief from the searing heat outside. This is an unusually hot summer for this part of the country and both residents and tourists alike welcome the cool waters of the Atlantic Ocean.

Carla and her five-year-old daughter walk down the narrow aisle looking for the small plastic pail Missy wants for digging in the sand when they go to the beach. Bill waves from behind the counter. "Hi Carla, how are you and Missy doing today? It's sure hot out there."

Carla smiles. "Hi Bill. We're doing fine. You got that right, it's really hot today. Missy and I are headed for the beach and she needs a little bucket and shovel."

"That sounds like fun."

Walking around the counter, he approaches the two and leans down in front of Missy.

"And how are you today, Missy?"

"Fine."

"Are you heading for the beach?" Bill asks.

"Yes," Missy replies.

Standing back up, Bill points down the aisle. "You'll find some buckets at the end of this aisle. They even have a little shovel attached."

"Thank you," Carla says as she takes Missy's hand. "Tell Mr. Bill thank you, Missy."

Missy whispers "Thank you" as she pulls her mother toward the buckets.

Missy picks out a pink bucket with pictures of fish swimming around its circumference. The little shovel is attached with a nylon string. "Mama, can I have some candy?" Missy asks as they turn to go to the checkout counter. Carla smiles down at her daughter. "I think we might be able to arrange that," she replies while walking toward the counter.

Carla had not noticed before the clothes hanging on a rack next to the aisle. She suddenly bumps into the rack, almost knocking it over. Grabbing the rack pole to keep from falling and tipping it, her eyes suddenly fill with tears. Rows of men's Army fatigues, swim trunks, T-shirts, and towels are lined up on the rack. Apparently, Army fatigues are the latest craze and Carla can't get away from them fast enough. She quickly straightens the rack and almost runs to the counter wanting to escape the memories.

"Are you okay, Carla?" Bill asks. He's witnessed the accident and her tear-filled eyes have not escaped his notice either. Carla swipes at an escaped tear, sets the bucket on the counter, and answers, "I'm okay. Just clumsy today, I guess."

"Mama, can I have some candy now?" Missy asks.

"Now, just what kind of candy would you like, Missy?" Bill asks with a big grin, hoping to lighten the situation.

Pointing to a bowl with lollipops, Missy grins broadly. "I want one of the red ones, Mr. Bill."

Bill grins and reaches into the bowl, pulling out a bright red packaged lollipop and hands it to her. Carla pays for the items and as they step back out into the heat, Bill thinks, *God love her. She's had a hard time since her husband died.*

* * *

Walking slowly along the side street toward her home, Carla smiles as Missy swings her new bucket, sucks on her lollipop, and skips along happily. Carla bought the small house after a friend had brought her to Ivy as a place to "drown her sorrows in the Atlantic ocean." She had rented a house for one month craving the solitude and wanting to make a new start but not knowing where. Her love for the ocean and all the amenities drew her to stay. Her friend, Meg, had talked her into looking at houses for sale and Carla fell in love with the small two-bedroom home nestled back from the main part of town but close enough to be able to walk to town and the beach.

* * *

Entering the small front yard, Carla stops. *I think Mike would have loved this place. He always loved the beach,* she thinks, looking at the flowers she's planted along the front of the house. The rose bush has buds of pink and the hibiscus has bright red flowers. Missy had planted a small Rose of Sharon as her part of the gardening and it's grown by leaps and bounds in the short time they've been here. Looking at the small Rose of Sharon, Carla can't help but smile, remembering that Missy learned that Jesus loves flowers in her Sunday school class and immediately named her Rose of Sharon "Jesus."

"Are you sure that's what you want to name it?" Carla had asked her at the time.

"Yes!" Missy answered emphatically. "The teacher said Jesus loves flowers and when I see it I think of Jesus loving my flower."

Carla didn't argue.

* * *

Entering the front door, Missy has already run to her bedroom to don her bathing suit. The living room faces the street with a large picture window that is covered with blinds and sheer drapes. A sofa, TV, coffee table, armchair, and recliner fill the room. Framed pictures of her and Mike taking their wedding vows, one of Mike in his Army fatigues, Mike holding Missy as an infant, and Missy in a ballerina tutu hang on one wall. A hand-stitched "Jesus is the Lord of this home" is framed and hanging near the door.

The kitchen is off to the left with a small dining table next to a window that overlooks the backyard. It has all the modern conveniences because the previous owner had just redesigned the kitchen and added new cabinets and appliances. A small laundry room sits off the kitchen in its own alcove.

Carla's bedroom has its own bath, which she is grateful for. Missy's room is across the hall from the main bathroom and is decorated with ballerinas dancing across the walls. A small toy chest sits on one side of the room and dolls lean against pillows stacked on the twin-size bed.

The back patio is protected from the sun by a roof that stretches the full length of the back of the house. The long covered patio was what really attracted Carla to the house. She loves being outside and with the large yard with the privacy fence she knew Missy would be safe and she would have the enjoyment of the outdoors while watching her without having to sit directly in the sun. The swing set was a Christmas present to Missy this past Christmas from her grandfather. "Pa-pa" and Carla's older brother, Rick, helped Carla move from Atlanta to Ivy.

Her father was as heartbroken about Mike's death as was Carla. He loved Mike like his own son and when Mike was killed in Iraq it tore at the hearts of the entire family. Pa-pa wasn't happy about Carla moving down south but it was a choice he knew she had to make on her own. He just hoped it was the right one.

* * *

The sea air always gives Carla a sense of a fresh beginning each morning as she sits on her back patio sipping her morning coffee and listening to the birds chirp. She can hear the seagulls squawking as they dip and dive riding the wind's currents. Missy seems very happy and Carla doesn't have to worry about her playing in busy streets. She'll be starting school in the fall and Carla needs to begin thinking about what she'll do for the rest of her life. Being a widow is a huge adjustment and Carla isn't sure just how to cope with everything right now. It's been less than a year since Mike's death and people are already telling her, "You're still young. You'll fall in love again." Carla wants to scream at them but instead says nothing.

Missy runs full speed down the hall, "Mama, I'm ready. Can we go to the beach now?" She has her beach towel thrown over her shoulder with the end of it dragging the floor and her new bucket with the shovel clattering inside as she runs toward her mother.

"I need to put my swim suit on and then we can go." Carla replies.

"I'm going to build a big castle!" Missy exclaims as she holds her arms out wide, showing her mother just how big the castle will be.

Carla laughs, "That's a pretty big castle you have planned. Are you sure you can build one that big?"

"You bet I can! It's going to have windows and everything."

"Wow. That sounds nice. Hold on while I go change."

Missy plops down on the edge of the couch. "Hurry please."

Carla laughs and goes to change.

* * *

Once at the beach, Missy begins digging in the sand. With the blanket stretched out on the sand, a beach umbrella, and a small ice chest with water, Carla sits watching her daughter digging a big hole in the sand. *Oh, Mike, I wish you were here to see your daughter. She looks so much like you. She loves the water just like we do and I'm thankful for that.*

Missy hollers, "Can you see how big my castle is getting, Mama?"

Carla is pulled from her thoughts. Ever since bumping into the rack of fatigues, her mind has wandered back to memories of her husband. They met her first year of college and fell in love almost immediately. She was a business major and he was studying law. They married six months later.

Carla was twenty years old and Mike twenty-two. It was difficult for them with both going to school fulltime and the everyday expenses of living and their college fees. They were living on a thread, but the Lord provided for them along with her father helping occasionally. Their hopes and dreams were about to come true as they looked forward to graduation in another year. Unexpectedly, Carla discovered she's pregnant and the financial situation became even more critical.

Their small one-bedroom apartment was barely big enough for the two of them and now with a baby on the way they weren't sure what to do. Many nights were spent discussing their options and praying. "Honey, I talked to a recruiting officer today with the Army and he said that the Army will pay for the rest of my education. He said you'd get the medical attention you need too. It would only be three years and that's not very long." The discussions continued for weeks. It seemed Mike was bound and determined to fight for his country. "If you join the Army, you won't be here for the birth of our baby," Carla would argue but he always had an answer. Mike finally convinced her that joining the Army could be the answer and through many tears and more discussions, she finally gave in.

* * *

Mike went to basic training at Fort Benning, Georgia, and came home on leave for one week before being shipped to Iraq. Only by God's grace was he able to be home for the birth of their child. Most of the next two and a half years Mike was at war and she was raising their daughter alone. Missy barely knew her father and when Carla finally graduated it was only her brother and father that were able to attend.

When it was time for Mike to be discharged, the war escalated and he was reassigned. He would not be discharged for at least another six months to a year. Carla was devastated. He was allowed to come home for two weeks on leave. Then he would return to Iraq. It was the last two weeks she would ever spend with her beloved husband. One week after arriving back in Iraq, Mike's jeep was blown up by a roadside bomb, killing him and two other soldiers instantly. Carla's world suddenly turned upside down.

* * *

"Mama, come look!" Missy hollers, waving the pink shovel in the air. Seagulls are scampering about the sand as a woman sitting nearby tosses bread crumbs out to them. Carla slowly stands and walks to where Missy has wet sand piled high. Patting the wet sand into place, Missy is forming her castle and Carla sits down beside her in the sand. "Oh honey, that looks beautiful."

"Can you help me? It's getting really big."

Scooping up a handful of sand, "Where do you want me to start?"

Smacking the shovel against one side of the castle, Missy replies, "You can start right here!"

The lady feeding the seagulls watches as Carla and Missy spend the next hour shaping and molding the mansion castle. It's become a *mansion* because Missy has continued to add additions to it. What began as one large pile of wet sand has been transformed into what Missy has described as another bedroom and a kitchen and living room. "The queen has to have a kitchen," Missy explains.

Mother and daughter work diligently as the woman watches intently. Each time Carla happens to glance in her direction, she quickly looks away but then continues to watch them.

"Missy, maybe we better go in. It's getting pretty hot and I don't want you to get sick," Carla says, rising to her knees.

"Oh Mama, can't we just finish my castle?"

"It looks pretty finished to me. If you make it any bigger we'll have to move into it." She laughs.

Missy laughs while picking up her bucket and shovel. "Okay. Can I get in the water first?"

"Sure. Let's rinse your pail out while we're at it."

Taking the pail and shovel, Missy runs toward the water. Seagulls scatter and Missy laughs as she splashes in the shallow ripples and jumps the small incoming waves.

The woman watches.

* * *

Picking up their towel, folding the umbrella, and grabbing the handle of the ice chest, Carla looks toward the stranger and sees she's still watching them. The woman suddenly turns her head away and a shiver snakes down Carla's spine. Slowly, she and Missy walk toward the woman. The woman picks up a book and pretends to start reading. Her sunglasses hide her eyes but Carla senses something isn't right. Stopping in front of the woman, Carla looks at her. The woman looks up, "Can I help you?"

Carla hesitates for just a moment. "I noticed you were watching us. Do I know you?"

The woman sets her book in her lap and before answering reaches down picking up her water bottle. "Yes, I was watching you. Your little girl is adorable."

Glancing down at Missy, Carla can't shake the feeling there's more to this woman watching than admiring her daughter. "Thank you. I don't think I've seen you before. I'm Carla. Do you live here in town or are you just visiting?" Carla asks cautiously.

"I'm just visiting. I'm Nancy, by the way. Nancy Burns." Turning her attention toward Missy, she asks, "And what is your name, pretty one?"

Missy slides closer to Carla's side before answering. "Missy."

"That's a pretty name but I'll bet that's short for something. A nickname, maybe?"

Missy looks up at her mother and says nothing.

The woman smiles broadly and exclaims, "I'll bet that's short for Melissa! Am I right?" Carla doesn't like the direction this conversation is going and takes Missy's hand. "We need to be going. It was nice meeting you, Nancy. Have a good day."

"Wait!" the woman rises from her beach chair.

Carla steps back, not knowing what the woman is going to do. All of her instincts are screaming to get away from this woman and get away now!

"Okay," the woman confesses. "I know who you are. I'd just like to get acquainted, is all. Maybe we can visit for a few minutes."

"I don't think so," Carla replies, wrapping her arm around Missy's shoulder and holding her close against her side. "We really need to be going." Taking a few steps, she suddenly stops and turns toward the woman. "Just how do you know who I am?"

The woman turns, picks up her book, towel, and plastic water bottle. "I just know," is all she says and walks away briskly, leaving Carla and Missy standing next to the empty chair.

* * *

Carla can't seem to shake the bad feeling she had talking to Nancy at the beach. She doesn't recall ever seeing her before. *She did say she doesn't live in Ivy. So how does she know me?* Carla thinks as she washes a pan from dinner. Missy is busy coloring and watching cartoons on TV. *What is it about her that gives me the creeps? Maybe I'm just imagining things. No! I still get the shivers just thinking about her.*

* * *

The next day, there's a knock on the door. Missy runs to answer it. Opening the door, she looks up and there stands Nancy smiling down at her. "Hi Melissa," Nancy says. Missy doesn't answer her and turns her head toward the living room yelling, "Mama, the lady from the beach is here."

Carla has just stripped the two beds of their sheets and is walking down the hall with her arms filled with the dirty sheets and pillowcases she's about to put in the washer. Her long blonde hair is pulled back in a ponytail. She's barefoot, and the shorts she's wearing are ragged cutoff jeans. Holding the sheets tightly against her chest to hide the shiver that suddenly courses through her body, she quickly walks toward the open door.

"Hi Carla," Nancy says, standing near the open door. Carla notices for the first time the woman isn't as tall as she is and on the plump side. Her hair is dyed red, the slacks she's wearing are tan, her sleeveless blouse hangs below her waist, and again her sunglasses cover her eyes. Carla learned many years ago when her mother was suffering from breast cancer that the eyes are the window to our soul. Her mother would try to hide the pain and suffering she was enduring in the last stages of the horrible disease that took her life. Carla would see the pain in her eyes as she'd sit next to her bed holding her mother's hand. Watching one's eyes became important to Carla. It helps her read people.

"May I come in for a moment?" Nancy asks without removing her sunglasses.

"Ah, I'm kind of busy right now." Adjusting her arms around the sheets and gesturing with her chin, Carla continues, "As you can see, I'm in the middle of doing laundry. This really isn't a good time."

"But I'll only be a minute."

Don't let her in! "I'm sorry but I don't have time to visit right now, maybe some other time."

Carla can tell by Nancy's body language she isn't happy with her answer. The woman stiffens for just a second then relaxes just a bit. The smile she displays strikes Carla as phony as a three dollar bill and another shiver streaks up her spine.

"I'll come back another time and maybe we can talk then." Nancy turns and starts down the walkway.

"Wait!" Carla exclaims. "How did you know where I live?"

The woman stops and without turning around says, "I just know," then continues to the sidewalk.

Carla closes the door and walks toward the laundry room with Missy right behind her.

"Mama, what did she want?" Missy asks.

"I don't know, honey."

"I'm glad you didn't let her in."

Carla stops walking and turns to Missy, "Why is that?"

Missy shrugs. "I don't like her."

"But you don't know her. How can you not like someone you don't know?"

Missy shrugs again. "She gives me the willies!" and runs to the back door.

Carla places the sheets in the washer and while dumping the laundry soap in, she thinks, *Missy isn't the only one who gets the willies! I think I'll call Dad and see if he has any ideas about what to do about this. I don't know who this woman is, how she knows me, but it's going to stop right now, right here!*

Once the sheets are washed and in the dryer, Carla decides to sit outside while Missy is swinging and playing. Dialing her father's office on her cordless phone, she waits while the phone rings. Just as she's about to hang up, his secretary answers, "Hello, Dr. Anderson's office. Can you hold please?"

"Yes," Carla answers as music softly comes on the line. Taking a sip of her iced tea, she waits and waves at Missy when Missy waves to her while sliding down the slide in her swing set.

"Thank you for holding. How can I help you?"

"Hi, Patty. This is Carla. Is Dad busy?"

"Oh, hi, Carla. It's been kind of a mad house around here today but let me find him."

"No, that's okay. If he's busy I don't want to bother him."

"It's okay. Let me see if he can talk." The music fills Carla's ear once again.

A moment later, her father answers, "Hi, honey. How are you? Is Missy okay? You okay?"

"Hi, Dad. Yes, we're fine. You're busy so I can call later if that's okay."

"I'm never too busy for my little girl. What's up?"

"I just need to talk to you about something but it can wait. Can I call you at home tonight?"

"Sure but if it's important we can talk now. I'll just make the next guy wait a few more minutes." He chuckles.

"No. I'll call you tonight."

"Are you sure? You sound troubled. What's going on?"

Carla feels guilty about disturbing her father when she knows he's busy. "It's nothing really. I'll call you tonight. Bye, Dad."

"Bye, honey."

When Missy sees her mother is off the phone, she runs to her and asks, "Mama, can we go to the beach?" She takes a drink of her mother's iced tea.

"Only if we stay for an hour," Carla replies.

"But that won't give me time to build another castle."

"But it will give you time to play in the water. I have things I need to do so if you want to go that's my terms."

Missy barrels into the house and down the hall toward her bedroom, hollering, "Okay."

* * *

Carla's home is only four blocks from downtown and the beach access is directly across the street from the main thoroughfare. Carrying the beach blanket and beach towels, she takes Missy's hand as they cross the street. Stepping onto the sand, she's glad they have flip flops on. The sand is hot! Looking around the beach area for a place to stretch out their blanket, Carla suddenly sees a familiar face. Sitting in a wooden beach chair, book in hand, sunglasses in place, Nancy turns to look at them. She lifts her hand to wave but Carla ignores her and grabs Missy's hand and walks briskly toward an area down the beach that is vacant of people. *What's she doing here!?* Carla thinks as she almost drags Missy alongside her. "Mama!" Missy cries as she tries to jerk her hand free. Carla suddenly lets go of her, realizing she's practically dragging her daughter through the sand. Turning and looking back, she feels she's put enough distance between her and Nancy to feel comfortable.

* * *

A wave sneaks across the water as Carla takes hold of Missy's hand. Carla sees the wave and knowing it's going to smack them, she waits. Missy is giggling and jumping up and down in water up to her waist. Carla knows what Missy's reaction will be and smiles broadly. The wave suddenly washes over them, covering Missy, sending her wiggling and floundering in the water. She pops her head up and laughs hysterically. Carla lets go of her hand as Missy swipes at the water running down her face. Giggling, Missy begins jumping up and down again.

"I think we need to go now," Carla says, guiding Missy toward shore.

"Oh, Mama, do we have to?"

"Yes. Remember I said we couldn't stay longer than an hour and we've been playing longer than that."

Disappointment shows on Missy's face but she knows if she fusses about it her mother won't let her come the next time she wants to.

They each dry off and begin walking across the sand. Carla looks in the direction where Nancy was sitting but the beach chair is empty.

"Can I get a lollipop on the way home?" Missy asks as they start to cross the street.

"I think that can be arranged."

The bell above the door rings as Carla and Missy enter Bill's Variety Store.

"Hi, Carla. Hi, Missy. It looks like you two have been swimming." Bill greets them from behind the counter.

Missy runs forward and states, "We have and a big wave almost drownded me."

"Drown, Missy, not drownded." Carla laughs.

"Well, you sure must be a good swimmer because here you are right in front of me," Bill laughs. "What can I do for you?

Missy points at the jar of lollipops and states happily, "I want a red one please."

Bill reaches in the jar and hands her a red one while Carla reaches into her shorts pocket for change.

Turning to leave, Carla suddenly and un-expectantly bumps into Nancy, who has been standing behind them without their realizing it. "Oh!" Carla exclaims.

"Hi, Carla," Nancy replies.

A shiver runs down Carla's spine. "Excuse me," Carla flatly states, trying to move around her.

Nancy steps in front of her, blocking her way. "Is it all right if I come visit about three o'clock? I'd still like to get acquainted."

Carla feels anger rising and looks at her pointedly. "No, it isn't. I don't want to be rude but I don't know who you are or what you want and I'd prefer you not come to my home again."

Nancy doesn't seem fazed in the least by the confrontation and smiles. "I just want to get acquainted. Become friends." The smile suddenly disappears and anger flashes in her eyes. "We will talk, Carla. Now or later!" She then stalks to the door, leaving the bell ringing loudly.

Bill has stood perfectly still with his hands pressed on the counter top. Carla stands staring at the door and Missy is busy sucking her lollipop. Carla turns to Bill with a questioning expression, "Do you know that woman?"

Bill seems as shocked as Carla at the verbosity of the woman's statement. "She's been in a few times but I don't know much about her. You know her?" he asks.

Carla is dumbfounded and almost stutters as she finally replies, "I met her once at the beach the other day. She said her name is Nancy and the next day she showed up at my house. She says she knows who I am but I've never seen her before, other than at the beach the other day."

Bill rubs his chin and looks directly at Carla. "There's something about her. I don't mean to talk about my customers, Carla, but there's just something about her I don't like. You be careful, you hear."

Carla nods. "Thanks," and she and Missy leave the store.

* * *

Carla's father can't get the short conversation with Carla out of his mind so when the phone rings that evening he grabs it, hoping it's Carla. "Hello."

"Hi, Dad. Is this a good time to talk?"

"Yes, honey. You've been on my mind all day. Are you okay?"

"Yes. Well, yes and no."

"What do you mean? Talk to me. Tell me what's going on."

Carla isn't sure how to start and hesitates for a long moment then finally says, "Dad, there's a woman I met at the beach the other day and it's really getting weird."

"What do you mean?"

Carla begins telling him about Nancy and how she had watched her and Missy at the beach, said she knows her, and then shows up at her house, and then the incident at Bill's Variety Store. Her father listens intently.

"I'm not sure what to do, Dad. She said, 'We *will* talk eventually,' and the way she said it kind of scares me."

"Did she say what she wants to talk to you about?"

"No, but I really haven't given her a chance to. Every time I get near her, I get shivers up my spine. Missy even said she doesn't like her and gives her the willies."

"Oh. That's not good. You know children are very sensitive to things."

"I know and that bothers me too. What do you think I should do?"

"Do you think she's dangerous? Does she act like she wants to harm you or Missy?"

"That's just it. I don't know. She acts friendly then suddenly she's not."

Her father is quiet for a long moment then says, "The next time she approaches you, ask her what she wants. But, honey, be somewhere where other people are around. I don't think I'd let her come to the house."

"Oh, I won't let her in the house!" Carla exclaims.

"Just see what she wants and then we can go from there."

"Okay."

They talk for a while longer about his practice, what she might be planning for when Missy starts school in the fall, and things in general.

"I need to get Missy's bath and get her ready for bed, Dad. Thank you for your advice and I'll let you know what happens."

"Okay, honey. You be careful. We just don't know what this woman is up to. Call me anytime. Love you."

"Love you too. Bye."

Chapter 2

Missy runs to the window, pulls back the sheer curtains and peers outside. "Mama, it's *still* raining!" she exclaims in exasperation. "Is it ever going to stop?" she asks as she plops down on the couch.

It's been raining for three days and Carla as well as Missy is ready for the sun to come back.

"I know, honey. There isn't anything we can do about it. We just have to wait until the Lord sees fit to shove the sun back out."

"Oh, Mama, God doesn't push the sun."

"Sure He does. He likes to play ball so He uses the big ole sun to roll around." Laughing, she knows Missy isn't buying it.

"No He doesn't. You're making that up."

"Yes, I am, but it's a nice thought, isn't it? Jesus playing ball?"

Missy giggles. "Can we play Candyland since it's still raining?"

"Sure. I'll finish ironing this blouse while you get the board."

"Okay." Missy runs to her room.

* * *

In many ways, Carla feels blessed by the steady rain. She has feared Nancy would show up at her door or be at the beach every time they decided to go. With the rain, she's not had to worry about Missy wanting to go. Today has been some catching up on things around the house and now it's time to play a board game with her daughter, hoping to lessen her boredom.

* * *

Two days later, the rain has let up but has not stopped totally and Carla needs to go grocery shopping. She decides to go to the Publix twenty miles away to stock up. Pushing the cart along the meat counter, she suddenly senses someone watching her. She turns and looks around the store but sees no one suspicious and resumes her shopping. Her nerves are on edge the rest of the time and she tries to hurry through the aisles picking up cereal, bread, milk, cookies, vegetables, fruit, and whatever else is on her shopping list. Standing in the checkout lane, she once again senses someone watching her but again sees no one.

Missy insists on helping to push the cart to the car and while holding on to the cart, she suddenly gasps as they approach the car trunk.

Carla looks down at her and says, "What?"

"The beach lady is over there," Missy says, pointing.

Carla whirls around. "Where?"

Missy points toward some cars several cars away. "Over there."

Carla looks and looks but doesn't see her. "Are you sure it was her? I don't see anyone."

Missy nods and says, "Ah huh. It was her, Mama. She had red hair."

Carla hurriedly places the groceries in the trunk, slams the trunk lid, and straps Missy in. "Mama is she following us?" Missy asks from the backseat.

Dear Lord I hope not. "I don't know, Missy. Maybe it was some other lady with red hair."

"No. It was her! She was standing between the cars looking right at us. I know it was her! I'm scared Mama," and Missy begins crying.

Carla starts the car and slowly backs out of her parking place. Looking in the rearview mirror as she pulls forward, she sees Nancy step out from beside a car and watch them leave. Cold chills cover her body but she says nothing about it to Missy. Instead, she tries to comfort her.

* * *

Arriving home, Missy helps Carla carry the bags of groceries into the house. She's stopped crying but is still scared and runs to her room and jumps on her bed, hugging two of her dolls close against her chest.

Dear Lord, what are we going to do? This has really gotten out of hand and now Missy is scared half out of her wits and it's really starting to scare me too. Please, Lord, send your angels to protect my daughter and me. In Jesus' name. Amen. Carla's prayer is heartfelt as she puts the groceries away.

"Missy, can I come in?" Carla asks, knocking on Missy's bedroom door.

"Yes."

Carla opens the door and sees Missy hugging her dolls and walks over to the bed and sits down on the edge. "Are you okay, honey?" Carla asks. Reaching over, she moves a strand of Missy's long brown hair away from her face.

Missy begins to cry. "I don't like that beach lady."

"I know, honey. But she's not going to hurt us."

"How do you know? She goes everywhere we go. Can't you make her stop?"

"Honey, I'm trying. Remember I wouldn't let her come in the house and I won't talk to her."

"But she still follows us."

Carla scoots close to Missy and takes her in her arms. "Honey, remember God has his angels watching over us. He's not going to let anything happen to you and neither am I."

"But what if he's busy and doesn't see her?"

Carla chuckles. "He's *never* too busy to take care of his children. He knows where she is and what she's doing just like he knows where we are and what we're doing."

Missy sniffles and replies, "Oh. Then He'll make her go away?"

I sure hope so! "Let's just trust Him to keep us safe. Okay?"

"Okay."

Carla scoots off the bed and returns to the kitchen.

* * *

The rain continues and it seems it will never stop. Missy is getting "cabin fever" and about to drive Carla up the walls. *Please Lord, make it stop raining before this kid drives me nuts!* Carla prays as Missy runs through the house for the fifth time. Just as she's about to shout for Missy to stop, the doorbell rings. Her thought immediately goes to Nancy. Missy skids to a stop and then bolts toward the door. "Missy! Don't open it!" she shouts. The doorbell rings again and sucking in a breath Carla walks to the door. Peeking through the peephole she gives a loud sigh of relief and opens the door. "Hi, April. Come on in."

April lives three houses down and has a daughter the same age as Missy. April is five feet eight inches tall and weighs about 125 pounds. Her long brown hair reaches her waist. She normally wears it pulled back with a headband and lets it flow down her back but today she has it in a ponytail. Her jeans look starched and the T-shirt she's wearing has a large sunflower covering her chest. April's tan speaks of many hours on the beach and several times she, Carla, and the girls will go together.

* * *

Missy shouts, "Hi Jenny. Come and see my new doll." She grabs April's daughter's hand and begins running toward her bedroom, not giving Carla time to even tell Jenny hello.

"Thank God for small miracles." Carla laughs.

"What? You mean she hasn't been an angel these past five days of entrapment?" April laughs.

"You saved her hide from being strangled by ringing our doorbell. We haven't had rain like this in who knows when," Carla says as they walk toward the kitchen.

April pulls out a chair as Carla asks, "Would you like some coffee?"

"Coffee sounds good if you have some made."

"It will only take a minute," Carla says as she takes a can of coffee out of the cabinet above the coffee maker.

"So how have you been?" April asks.

"Oh, pretty good, I guess. Busy trying to hide from a woman that's been stalking us mainly." Carla nervously laughs. She's wanted to talk to April about it but just hasn't had the time to call her.

"What? What woman? When did this start? Why didn't you say something?"

Carla starts laughing. "Wow, slow down. I'll tell you all about it. Let me go check on the girls while the coffee brews. I'll be just a minute."

Carla goes to Missy's room and taps on the door and opens it without being invited in. The girls are sitting on the floor in front of Missy's dollhouse that she's pulled from the closet. Each girl has a doll and is chattering away pretending it's the dolls talking. "Need anything?" Carla asks. "Can we have some cookies?" Missy asks. She points to the dolls and continues, "The girls are hungry."

"Sure." Carla walks back to the kitchen.

"Are they okay?" April asks.

"They're fine. They're playing with the dolls and want some cookies." Laughing, she reaches for the cookie jar and holding four cookies up, "The dolls are hungry."

April laughs and Carla takes the cookies to the girls.

Carla has poured each of them a cup of coffee and returns to the table.

"Tell me everything!" April demands.

Carla takes a sip of her coffee, sets the cup on the table, and takes a deep breath. "Well, it started about two weeks ago. Missy and I were at the beach and I noticed this woman kept watching us."

April nods, not taking her eyes off Carla. Carla launches into the full story, telling her about the beach and Bill's Variety Store. When she says, "She even showed up at my door and said she wanted to visit!"

April gasps and asks, "Did you let her come in?"

"No! Of course not! She wasn't happy about it either." Carla exclaims. Lifting her cup, she takes another drink of coffee before continuing. "I don't know how she even found out where I live! When I asked her how she knew where I lived, she just answered, 'I just know.'"

"That's creepy!" April states.

Carla continues. "She said her name is Nancy Burns. I'm beginning to wonder now if that's even her real name. She's just creepy! I get shivers just thinking about her." Carla grabs both of her arms and starts rubbing the goose bumps that have risen. "She really gives me the willies!"

"Go on, go on. What else has she done?" April presses.

Carla begins again telling about the grocery store and Missy getting so scared. "Oh and I called my dad and asked him what he thinks I should do. That was before we saw her at Publix."

"What did he say to do?"

"He thinks I should ask her what she wants. But he was adamant about my not letting her in the house and to be sure there are plenty of other people around when I confront her."

"Hmmm, I don't know if I'd do that. I mean, if I did, I think I'd want others right there with me."

"You may be right. I just wish I knew what this is all about! It's crazy! I've never seen this woman before in my life! Would you like more coffee?"

April reaches her cup across the table, handing it to Carla. Carla takes both cups to the counter and while pouring the coffee says, "I've been praying about this and I've just decided I'm going to let the Lord take care of it. He said He is our protector, so let Him protect!"

"He does have a big army of angels, that's for sure." April responds.

Carla returns with the coffee and sits back down. Both seem to be in their own deep thoughts for several moments. April finally looks directly at Carla and says, "Do you want me to have Alex check on you off and on? You know he will."

"Oh, April, that's sweet of you but I don't want to bother your husband. He works so hard and he doesn't need to be worrying about me."

"Well, if that crazy woman comes here again you grab that phone and all six feet four inches and 240 pounds will come blasting through that door."

Carla can't help but laugh. Alex is a very large and very muscular man with not an inch of fat anywhere on his body. He was honorably discharged from the Marine Corp two years ago and is still full of the Marine brawn. April has told her in the past she's really grateful he has the gym, otherwise, she doesn't know what she'd do with him. Alex owns and manages Muscles Galore Men's Gym in town and owns another one in a neighboring town that a long-time Marine buddy manages. April hit the ceiling when he mentioned reenlisting so he decided it was in his best interest to become a family man and decided against reenlisting and quickly became a business man.

"I better go see what the girls are up to," Carla says, standing up.

"We need to be going. Alex is taking me out to dinner tonight so I need to get hold of my sitter. She'll be home from work any minute," April states, shoving her chair against the table. "Jenny? Come on, we need to leave." She hollers.

Jenny walks down the hall, "Oh Mama, do we have to? We were having fun."

"Hey, I have an idea." Carla interrupts. "Why not bring Jenny over and let her spend the night since you haven't lined up the sitter yet?"

"Are you sure?" April asks, surprised.

"Sure. It's not like I have anything better to do on a Friday night. They'll have fun."

"Oh that would be great!"

The girls are clapping and looking at April expectantly.

"I guess I don't have to ask you if that's okay by you," April says to her daughter. Turning her attention back to Carla, "If you're sure it's okay, I'll have her here at five. I'll feed her before I bring her over so you don't have that to worry about it."

"Five is fine," Carla replies. "Don't worry about dinner. We're having pizza."

The girls squeal and as they all walk to the front door, the girls are chattering faster than a magpie about what they'll do and the toys Jenny should bring. As Carla and April step out onto the front porch, Carla touches April's arm and glances around to see if the girls are within earshot. "Why don't you pick her up about noon?" Carla whispers. "That way you two will have some free time." She blushes slightly.

April bursts out laughing and says, "Gotcha. Great idea!" Then reaches over and hugs Carla. "We'll see you about five then. Come on, Jenny. Let's go home."

Halfway to the street, April turns, glances at Carla standing on the porch, then jumps up in the air clicking her heels together and yells, "Yeee haaaa."

Carla bursts our laughing.

Chapter 3

"Time to wake up, Missy," Carla yells from the kitchen. "Time to get ready for church." Carla places a bowl, a spoon, and a box of cereal on the table and walks to Missy's room. Touching Missy's shoulder, she shakes her gently and Missy groans.

"Come on, honey. You need to get up," she says.

Missy throws the covers back, yawns loudly, and scoots to the edge of the bed. "Is it still raining?" she asks as she yawns again.

"No. The sun is out."

Missy's eyes pop wide open and jumping up, she runs to the window. "Oh boy, can we go to the beach today?"

"It's Sunday. We're going to church this morning. Come on and eat your breakfast," Carla replies while making the bed.

Carla pulls into the parking lot of the Christ Lives Church and parks. Missy jumps out of the car and runs toward some children that are standing near the front door with their parents. Carla reaches across the seat and picks up her Bible. *I hope Pastor John gives an uplifting sermon today. I really need it!* she thinks, walking to the church entrance. Greeting some of the women as she steps inside, Carla looks forward to the service. Even though she doesn't attend every Sunday, she feels peace each time she enters the church. She turns to look for Missy and not seeing her, she immediately walks back outside. Missy is giggling with two other little girls and Carla walks over to them and says, "Hi girls. It's time to go to your Sunday school class."

"Hi, Carla," Mrs. Norton says. "How are you?"

"Oh, hi, Mrs. Norton. I didn't see you standing there. I'm good. How are you?"

"Oh I'm just peachy."

Carla looks up at the sky and replies, "I'm sure glad it's finally stopped raining!"

"Oh me too! I thought we were going to drown! I don't remember it raining for five days in a row before. It's really been crazy weather lately."

"It sure has. Missy and I were really getting cabin fever."

"Oh me too. Well we better get in there. I think they'll be starting the music soon." Mrs. Norton states as she starts toward the door.

Carla leaves Missy at the door of her Sunday school class after speaking to her Sunday school teacher for a moment.

"I'll be back to get you right after the service, Missy, so don't leave."

"I won't, Mama," Missy replies.

Carla returns to the sanctuary and takes a seat. The praise band members are walking onto the stage with their guitars and horns. One young man sits down behind a large set of drums and a pretty teenage girl steps up to the keyboard.

A middle-age man walks to the podium and begins by saying, "Welcome to the house of the Lord. Good morning."

The congregation echoes, "Good morning."

"Before we start, there are a few announcements we need to be aware of. First, we ask that you pray for the Michaels family. Mr. Michaels went to be with the Lord yesterday. Funeral arrangements are still being made so we'll get you that information as soon as possible."

Mrs. Leary is sitting next to Carla and leans over whispering, "Oh, he was such a loving man!"

The man continues, "Next Sunday, we're having a picnic right after church at the Fish Pond so we hope everyone will bring a dish and have a great time. Bring your swimming suits. Praise God it stopped raining!"

Everyone laughs and someone in the back row shouts, "Hallelujah!" The drummer gives a loud drum roll.

The man continues, "I think that's about it. The rest of the announcements are in your bulletin. Oh, the women's group meeting is canceled for Tuesday night." He leaves the stage and the praise band begins playing.

The congregation stands and as they sing, Pastor John walks onto the stage. When the song is finished, he steps forward and says, "Let's pray." Everyone bows their heads and he begins praying, "Lord, oh Lord Almighty, how we praise you. We bless your Holy Name, oh God. We thank you for this beautiful day and we thank you for your mighty word. Give me your words, Oh God, so this message you have given me will bless the hearts who hear it. It's a hard lesson, Lord, but you know what your sheep need to hear. Speak to our hearts, Lord, and open the ears of everyone here to hear your truth and open our hearts to receive it. In Jesus' name, Amen.

* * *

Pastor John Greely is a handsome fifty-two-year-old man. His dark wavy hair with a touch of gray at the temples is trimmed neatly. His brown eyes sparkle and he always has a ready smile. The tan slacks and blue short sleeve shirt fits nicely on his six-foot-tall slender body. He, his wife, and three young children came to Ivy four months ago. He's begun making some changes in the church as most newly appointed pastors do. There's been a little flak from some of the older members that have been used to the way things have always been. With an attitude of

"If it ain't broke, don't fix it," he's had to maneuver around some strong opinions. For the most part, most people like and have accepted him already. Many are open to new ways, new ideas, and his sermons have been hard hitting and making people aware of those things that many preachers don't like to talk about. He definitely is not a "feel good" preacher! The kind of preacher that won't speak of sin and repentance but tell the people what they want to hear. This has caused some raised eyebrows but he firmly stands on the belief that if we do not ask for forgiveness and repent of our sins, we will not be forgiven and if we are not forgiven we will not enter the kingdom of heaven. After all, that is exactly why Christ died on the cross.

Pastor John opens his Bible and states, "Open your Bibles to Revelation 12. I'm going to read verses one through four and please follow along or listen closely. It will also be on the screen."

Bible pages rustling can be heard throughout the sanctuary as he patiently waits for the people to find the scripture. Carla opens her Bible and, being familiar with many of the scriptures, takes a deep breath. She silently prays, *Lord, help me to hear what you want me to hear.*

The pastor begins reading. "Now, a great sign appeared in heaven: a woman clothed with the sun, with the moon under her feet, and on her head a garland of twelve stars. Then being with child, she cried out in labor and in pain to give birth. And another sign appeared in heaven: behold, a great, fiery red dragon having seven heads and ten horns, and seven diadems on his heads." Pastor John stops reading and says, "A diadem is a crown." He then resumes reading. "Verse four. His tail drew a third of the stars of heaven and threw them to the earth. And the dragon stood before the woman who was ready to give birth, to devour her Child as soon as it was born." Pastor John bows his head and prays, "Lord, thank you for your word. Let your truth prevail and bless this reading. Amen." A slight rustle ripples through the congregation as Bibles are set aside or closed.

Pastor John stands looking out over the people for a moment, saying nothing. He makes eye contact with various people then takes a deep breath and states loudly, "Ladies, listen up! Gentleman, listen up! This is important." It suddenly becomes so quiet that if a pin were to be dropped it would easily be heard by everyone. "As we know, this is Mary being described and is about to give birth to Jesus. Satan is the dragon. Because of his pride, God kicked his fanny out of heaven and all those angels that followed him went with him. They're called demons. And believe me, folks, there's a lot of them!" Pastor John stops and takes a sip of water then continues, "Satan, the devil, is *very* patient! He waits, he watches, and he waits some more for the perfect opportunity to attack. He's standing there, waiting for the Christ child to appear. You ladies know how long labor can take. You gentlemen have worn holes in the hospital carpets pacing the floor for hours waiting for that child to make its first cry." Laughter ripples through the room. Pastor John smiles and says, "Been there, done that. Three times!" The laughter grows louder.

He continues, "Satan is not after just Jesus. He is after *your children*, too! He's after *my* children and he won't give up!" He states emphatically. Carla sits up straighter in her chair and is listening intently. Pastor John jams his index finger toward various sections of the sanctuary as he shouts, "He wants your child, and your child, and your child!" He hesitates for just a moment and more softly says, "And mine." The tension in the room is palpable so when someone suddenly sneezes it sounds like someone has set off a bomb. Pastor John continues, "Oh yes, the devil is out there. He's stalking your child!"

Carla gasps loudly and quickly covers her mouth with her hand. *Oh, dear God, is that what is happening? Is the devil after my baby?*

Pastor John stares out at the people and says, "Drug pushers! Pedophiles, pornography, girly magazines, atheists. What else, church? Think about the violence in this country everyday. Think about what's on the Internet. That isn't God at work, it's the devil!" he shouts. He takes a deep breath and continues, "Gangs infiltrating every city in this country, for crying out loud! Did you know that right here in the great state of Georgia that we have the largest human trafficking in this country. Oh yes! Hear me people!" he shouts. "Atlanta, Georgia, is the largest sex trafficking city in this country according to what I heard on the news the other night! Two-year-olds are ripped from their yards. Teen girls are snatched off the street, boys are stolen off their bikes, for the sole purpose of being sold for sex!"

Carla is almost in tears. Her heart is racing, she's shaking, and her mind is in a whirl. *Oh my God, oh my God. Are you telling me Nancy wants Missy? She's going to try to steal her and sell her? Oh my God, oh my God, help me. What are you telling me, Lord? Tell me what to do!* Carla can barely breathe and Mrs. Leary touches her hand. "Are you okay, Carla?" she asks with concern showing in her voice. Carla doesn't answer. *Oh dear God, tell me what to do. Please, Lord, protect my baby.* "Be still and know that I am God." The Lord gently whispers.

Pastor John is still speaking but Carla barely hears his words. Mrs. Leary looks over at her again and whispers, "Carla, are you okay?" Carla is pulled from her thoughts and merely nods slightly. Pastor John is saying, "If you aren't watching what your child is doing on the Internet, or if you're allowing your kids to hang out at two in the morning, or you know someone is abusing your child and you do nothing, you're in the devil's camp! Hear me, church, you're in the devil's camp! Get on your knees. Get before God Almighty and pray. Pray He, in all His mercy, will forgive you and *repent!* God is merciful. When we ask for forgiveness He gives it." The pastor stops and reaches for his cup of water that's sitting on the edge of the podium and takes a sip. Heaviness hangs in the air. There's a sense that the people are afraid to breathe too hard. Nerves are tingling and heads are lowered. Pastor John stands waiting. Silence permeates the sanctuary.

Pastor John takes a deep breath and smiles broadly and says, "Hey, but there's good news! There's *great* news! Satan is defeated! He was defeated at the cross! The Lord reigns! Hallelujah!" he shouts, and the sanctuary bursts into whistles, clapping, and shouts of "Amen." People stand clapping and praising God. The praise band bursts into song and everyone sings, "My Jesus, my Savior, Lord, there is none like you. All of my days I want to praise the wonders of your mighty love." At the end of the song, the pastor continues, "If you haven't asked the Lord Jesus into your heart, now is a good time to do it. If you want to pray asking for forgiveness, now is a good time to do it. The altar is open and I'll be up here to pray with any who would like me to pray with them. These are the last days' church. We don't know the minute or hour or day the Lord will take us home. Are you ready? Are you right with God? Come, lay your burdens at His feet. Those who would like to leave may do so quietly so as not to disturb those praying. Come." Several people start walking forward and kneeling at the altar in prayer. Tears are being shed, confessions made, and a line of people form waiting to pray with the pastor.

Carla can't seem to stand so stays seated as people leave their seats. Some go forward to pray, and some leave the sanctuary to mingle outside.

Mrs. Leary stands looking down at Carla. "Carla, are you okay? You're as white as a sheet," she whispers.

Carla tries to smile and says, "Yes, I'm okay. Thank you."

"Are you sure? Maybe you need to sit for a while. I can sit with you if you aren't feeling well."

"No, no. That's okay. I'm okay. I need to go get my daughter."

"Okay, if you're sure. I hope you aren't getting a bug." Mrs. Leary turns and walks toward the door.

Carla takes a deep breath and shakily stands. Holding onto the back of the pew, she makes sure her legs will hold her up then slowly walks toward the hall that leads to the children's Sunday school classrooms.

Near the end of the hall is Missy's Sunday school room and as Carla approaches, she hears loud voices from within the room. Most of the children have already left but three women are standing just outside the door holding their child's hand. "Excuse me" Carla says as she steps between the women to enter the room. She steps inside the door and suddenly screams, "Get away from my child!"

Nancy spins around, letting go of Missy's hand. Missy is crying hysterically and runs to Carla. "She's *my child!*" Nancy screams.

Missy is clinging to Carla with a death grip and Carla has to pry her hands lose. "Missy, go over to Mrs. Green for a minute," she says. Mrs. Green is standing near the door and reaches out her arms indicating for Missy to come to her. "Nooo, Mama," Missy cries and Carla takes her by the shoulders gently and says, "Please, Missy. Go to Mrs. Green. It's going to be all right." Mrs. Green walks over and gently guides Missy to the door as Missy howls.

As soon as Missy is out of sight, Carla screams, "You crazy woman, that is my child and don't you dare ever touch her again!" and lunges for her. She grabs her hair and pulls as hard as she can. Nancy is screaming, "She's my kid, not yours," and fights back. Someone yells, "Get the pastor," as Carla and Nancy rip at each other. Carla is almost crazy with rage. *Human trafficking, the devil wants your child, child sex* flows through her mind and as each thought makes its presence, she hits Nancy all the harder. Suddenly, a voice booms within the room, "That's enough!" A giant of a man grabs Nancy by the shoulders and another grabs Carla, separating them. Nancy is screaming vulgarities and fighting to get loose. Someone slams the door closed leaving the two women, three men, and the teacher in the room. Carla is breathing so hard she may hyperventilate and Nancy is being firmly told to shut up.

Pastor John sternly says, "Now what's all this about?" Both women start talking at the same time. Pastor John holds his hand up, "One at a time! Carla?"

Carla takes a deep breath and glares at Nancy. "That woman has been stalking me and my daughter for weeks now and I came in here and she was trying to take Missy."

"She's not your daughter, she's mine!" Nancy screams.

"You're crazy!" Carla yells.

"Your baby died and they gave you my daughter by mistake and I want her back!" Nancy yells.

Oh dear God, we have a Solomon situation here! "Ladies, please! Maybe we should go to my office and discuss this." The pastor says. *Lord, don't let them go at it again, please.*

"Fine!" Nancy says, jerking her arm out of the giant's grip.

"Maybe that's best" Carla says.

Outside the door, a group of people have gathered and as the two women and three men come through the door, they part to let them pass. Missy is still crying and runs to her mother, grabbing her around the waist. Carla turns her body in a protective manner to keep Missy out of Nancy's reach. "Shhh, honey, shhh. It's okay."

"Mama, she tried to steal me," Missy says through her tears. "She told the teacher I was her daughter and she wouldn't let go of my hand." Missy starts to cry harder and Carla picks her up and hugs her close.

"Shhhh, I'm here now, honey. It's okay. Shhhh."

Carla turns to Pastor John with tears in her eyes and says, "I'm taking my daughter home if you don't mind."

Pastor John looks at her compassionately and says, "Okay. Can we meet tomorrow morning and talk about this?"

"Sure," Carla replies.

The other "giant" leans down and whispers to Carla, "I'll walk you to your car." Carla whispers a thank you and starts to walk down the hall.

Nancy screams, "She's not yours! I'll get her back. Just you wait and see."

The pastor waits until Carla is down the hall and out of sight then turns to Nancy. Her face is red with anger and he gently says, "I'm the pastor. Are you new here? I don't think I've seen you before."

Nancy glares at him and says, "Are you kidding? You wouldn't catch me dead in one of your stinkin' churches!"

Pastor John is a little taken aback by her fury but covers it well. "Are you willing to meet with me tomorrow afternoon so we can talk about this?"

Nancy bursts out laughing, then snarls, "There's nothing to talk about, preacher boy! She's mine and that's final! I'll get her back. Mark my words!" and she stomps off down the hall toward the entrance.

Chapter 4

"Hello," Carla's father says into the phone.

"Dad, its Carla." Carla suddenly bursts out crying.

"Carla? Honey, what's wrong? Take it easy, honey. Tell me what's wrong. Is Missy okay?"

"Ye– yes she's okay." Carla tries to stop her tears and is having a difficult time of it.

"Oh good! Tell me what's wrong, honey? Is it that woman you told me about?"

"Yes. Dad, she tried to steal Missy!" Carla bursts out crying again.

"Oh my gosh! Dear God, are you sure Missy is okay? Carla, stop crying please and talk to me."

"Hold on." Carla lays the cordless phone down on the table and snatches some tissue from the box. She blows her nose and picks up the phone. "Dad, it was awful," she says.

"Honey, start from the beginning and tell me everything."

Carla starts by telling him about seeing Nancy in the parking lot at Publix and how scared Missy was.

Her father mumbles, "The woman must be crazy."

"We came home and then we were doing fine but only because it rained for five days and we couldn't get out. Missy was driving me crazy because she was so bored but we did okay. I was scared Nancy would come to the house again but she didn't and then we went to church Sunday and…" Carla bursts out sobbing.

Dr. Anderson patiently waits for her tears to subside.

"That's when Nancy tried to kidnap her." Carla chokes out.

"Right there in church?" he asks incredulously.

"Yes! She was in her Sunday school class and I was in the service. The pastor gave a sermon that just turned me upside down and inside out. He was preaching on the devil and how he tries to get our children. And it was like the Lord was telling me that's what all of this is about. Nancy is the devil and wants to steal my baby!" She bursts out crying again.

"Okay, honey, calm down. Take it slow. What happened?" he soothes.

"Hold on." Carla blows her nose again then continues, "When I went to get Missy from her Sunday school class after the service, I walked into the room and Missy was screaming and crying hysterically and Nancy had her by the arm and wouldn't let her go. I just lost it, Dad!"

"Where was the teacher? Was Missy alone with her?" He asks angrily.

"The teacher was there but this woman is crazy, Dad! There wasn't anything the teacher could do really, except try to stop her from taking Missy. That's what she was doing when I walked in."

"So what happened?"

"I screamed at Nancy to let Missy go and I guess she was so shocked to see me that she let go of Missy and Missy ran to me. I was able to get Missy to go with another mother outside the room and, dear Lord, forgive me, I attacked Nancy! I just went ballistic!"

"You *attacked* her? Carla, what'd you do?"

"I pulled that ugly red hair of hers until I had fistfuls of it and I beat on her as hard as I could and I was screaming, and biting, and kicking and—"

Her father bursts out laughing and is laughing so hard he almost drops the phone.

Carla whispers, "It isn't funny, Dad."

Trying to stop laughing, her father chokes out, "You go, girl!" and roars laughing again.

His laughter causes Carla to start giggling and within moments both are laughing together.

When they're both able to contain their laughter Carla says, "She said Missy is her daughter, not mine. That mine died and they gave me hers by mistake."

"Honey, that's crazy! This woman is really off her rocker!" he exclaims.

"She swore up and down she isn't giving up. She swore she's getting Missy back."

"So,"—Dr. Anderson starts laughing again—"who broke up the fight?"

"Someone must have run and got the pastor because all of a sudden these two really big men grabbed us. One grabbed her and the other grabbed me. It's a good thing, too, or I may have killed her."

Dr. Anderson has a picture in his mind of his feisty daughter beating the tar out of Nancy and can't seem to get that picture out of his mind. Carla hears another chuckle over the phone line then her Dad asks, "Are you okay? Did she hurt you?"

"I have a couple of scratches on my arms but that's all. I'm fine."

"Good. So what happened next?"

"The pastor was with the two men and he asked us what was going on. Every time I tried to say something, Nancy would start screaming. Then he suggested we go to his office and talk about it and when we walked out the door Missy was crying hysterically and ran into my arms. The pastor let me bring her home if I'd come to his office and talk about it later."

"Is she okay now?"

"No. She's calmed down enough to where she isn't crying but is afraid to go out of the house and she's sleeping with me."

"Dear God. Carla, I want you to come home! You're not safe there with that woman still around!"

"I've been thinking about that. Not about moving back to Atlanta but coming home for just a short time until I can get settled down a little."

"I'm not talking about a short time, honey. I'm talking about permanently!"

"Dad, she'll just find us! If she found us here she'll find us there. No, I love it here and so does Missy. We'll come home for a while but I'm not moving back."

"Okay, okay. I just want you safe."

"I know and I won't do anything to jeopardize Missy. I've talked to Pastor John and he's been very understanding. He's suggested I go to the police. He didn't say it outright but the way he spoke when I met with him the next morning he feels like she's the devil too."

"She certainly sounds like it. She's crazy, we know that for sure. Honey, I'm going to call your brother and run all this by him right after we hang up. I'll call you in the morning so hold off going to the police until I call, unless she shows up or does something else! Is there someone that can stay with you and Missy?"

"We're okay. Rick can't do anything. He doesn't have any jurisdiction down here."

"Honey, he's a detective! A darn good one, I might add, and he can investigate this woman and see if she has a criminal background. Did she say where she's from?"

"No. But she did say she's only visiting Ivy."

"Wait a minute. Did you say she said they gave you her baby?"

"Yes."

"Missy was born in Atlanta so this woman must be from Atlanta."

"You're right! I hadn't thought about that. Of course, I haven't thought about anything rational about this whole thing."

"Okay, let me talk to Rick and I'll get back with you. What'd you say her name is?"

"Nancy Burns. But I don't know if that's even her real name."

"Rick can find out, I'm sure."

"Thanks, Dad. We'll be fine and if it's okay with you, we'll leave Saturday to come there."

"You could leave tonight as far as I'm concerned!"

Carla laughs and says, "I love you and thank you."

"I love you too, honey. Give Missy a kiss for me and you lock every door and window in that house and don't open them for anyone! I'll talk to you in the morning. Bye Honey."

"Bye, Dad."

* * *

The next day, Carla is talking to April on the phone, telling her what happened at church. "I can't believe that woman would walk right into the church and try to snatch her!" April says incredulously.

"I can't either but who knows what crazy people will do," Carla replies.

"You can't stay there alone! You and Missy come and stay with us for a while. We have plenty of room."

"Thank you but we'll be all right. I talked to Dad Sunday night and we're going to go home for a while until we can settle down a little."

"That's good. When are you leaving?" April asks.

"We're going to leave Saturday early." She laughs then continues, "Dad wanted us to leave Sunday night."

"Well, why didn't you? Get your butts out of dodge!" April laughs.

"I need to get the rest of the laundry done and go to the bank and, you know, line things up with the mail and all that kind of stuff."

"How long do you plan to be gone?"

"I don't know, a few weeks maybe."

"How can I help? Is there something I can help you with? Do you need groceries or anything?" April asks compassionately.

"No. If I need anything I'll just go to Bill's Variety. I pretty well stocked up a week ago."

"Carla, I know you can take care of yourself but if you're going to go anywhere, will you please let Alex go with you? That woman is obviously dangerous. She won't mess with you if my hunk of a husband is with you."

"Oh, April, that's not necessary but I appreciate the offer though. Alex has more to do than to babysit us, but thank you."

"Okay, let me put it this way, my dear friend. You are *not* going anywhere without him! You need to think of Missy's safety now."

"For crying out loud, I am!" Carla snaps.

"I know, I know. I know you are. I'm sorry. I'm just really concerned about what that crazy woman might do and you may not be able to stop her by yourself and you sure can't count on strangers to step in. Look at how many stories we've heard about people standing by while a woman is beaten to death and do nothing. Please reconsider."

Carla is silent for a long moment then says, "Maybe you're right. I sure didn't expect her to show up in church. Maybe Alex can go with me to the post office and the bank and a couple of other places I need to go. I can do all my errands in one day and that way it won't tie him up except for a few hours."

"Thank you, Jesus!" April states loudly. "What day do you think you'll want to go do your errands so I can tell Alex?"

"Well, today's Tuesday, how about Thursday? That will give me time to get the house cleaned, laundry finished, etc."

"That's fine. I'll tell Alex and call me Thursday morning early. He can pick you up. Is Missy any better?"

"No, not really. I asked her if she wanted to go to the beach tomorrow and she screamed, 'No!' She's scared to death Nancy will grab her again."

"You may need to get her into counseling."

"I know. I've been thinking about that. There are some good ones at home so while we're there maybe she can see one then. We'll just have to see."

"Okay. Well, I need to go. Carla, if you need anything will you promise to call me? I'm here for you, I hope you know that."

"I do, April. You're a good friend and I love you. Thank you and I will call."

"Okay. Bye."

"Bye."

* * *

Carla has been busy cleaning house, doing laundry, setting clothes aside for packing. Missy has mainly been watching TV and playing quietly in her room. Her usual bubbly personality has been trampled on and fear has been her companion since Sunday. She doesn't want to play with either of her favorite board games, Candyland or Hi Ho Cherio. Any mention of Nancy and she runs to her room, jumps on her bed, and hugs dolls close to her chest. She won't play outside unless Carla is right there within a few feet of her and forget the joys previously experienced on the swings and slide. The child is living in terror and Carla isn't sure what to do. She wants to take Missy for counseling but they'll be leaving in a couple of days for Atlanta. In the meantime, they've become prisoners in their own home.

* * *

Thursday morning, Alex pulls into Carla's driveway ready to take Carla and Missy to run their errands in his big four wheel drive Chevy truck with its oversized tires. Missy has ridden in it before and always gets excited about "riding way up in the sky." Opening the door, Alex picks Missy up and lifting her above his head, he says, "Okay, squirt, here we go," and lowers her inside on the seat. Missy giggles. Alex helps Carla in and Carla scoots in close to Missy. Alex jogs around to the driver's side and gets behind the wheel squishing Missy between him and Carla. Missy suddenly feels very safe.

The first stop Carla asks Alex to make is at the bank and when Carla goes into the bank, Missy and Alex wait in the truck out in the parking lot. They can see the front door from where they're parked. Alex has left no stone unturned. He deliberately parked where he can see Carla walk in and back out. "So, squirt, how are you today?" Alex asks as they wait.

Missy looks down at her hands, "I'm fine."

"Are you sure?" Alex asks softly as he places his muscular arm on the back of the seat behind Missy.

"Yeah, but I'm still scared, Uncle Alex." Alex really isn't her uncle but everyone agreed Missy could call him that since the families have gotten so close.

"What are you afraid of, squirt?" Alex asks gently. Of course, he already knows the full story. Alex loves this child as much as his own and anyone who would try to harm her has a very real death wish as far as he's concerned.

Missy glances up at him and quickly looks back down at her hands.

"You can tell me, Missy. It's okay," Alex coaxes.

"I'm scared the beach lady will steal me again," Missy whispers.

Alex lays his big hand on Missy's shoulder and wiggles her shoulder a little. "Hey, as long as I'm alive, nobody is going to steal you or hurt you! Do you hear me, squirt? I'm not going to let anybody grab you."

Tears well up in Missy's eyes. "But you aren't with me all the time. She might break into my house and steal me." Missy starts crying.

"Come here, honey." Alex picks her up and sets her on his lap wrapping his arms around her. "Aren't you and your Mom leaving Saturday to go stay with your grandpa for a while?"

Missy nods yes and swipes at a tear.

"Well, while you're there, then the police can be looking for her and arrest her. Then when you come home she'll be in jail and you won't have to worry."

"But what if they don't find her?" Missy says looking up at Alex.

"Oh, they'll find her! Your Mom, grandpa, and Uncle Rick will make sure of that!"

"Maybe Uncle Rick will shoot her!" Missy exclaims.

"Oh now, we don't want to think like that. Here comes your Mom."

Missy crawls back to her place on the seat as Carla struggles to climb up in the truck cab. Alex reaches across the seat taking Carla's hand and giving her a jerk. She almost flies across the cab. Missy starts laughing and Alex winks at Carla.

"I'll only be a minute" Carla says when they pull into the parking lot at the post office.

"Take your time," Alex says and parks in front of the door.

Missy is sucking on a lollipop the bank teller gave to Carla. News has traveled fast and sympathetic looks are given wherever Carla has stopped. "I hope they get that woman. Do you know who she is?" people have asked Carla at the last two businesses she's entered. "No and I'm sure something will be done" Carla replies and then quickly changes the subject.

Alex has the radio playing softly while he and Missy wait in the truck when Missy suddenly shouts, "There she is!" and almost chokes Alex climbing up his side and grabbing him around the neck.

Alex throws his arms around Missy hugging her tight and asks, "Where, Missy?"

Missy is crying and points to the dress shop next door. "Over there!"

"I don't see anyone, honey. Do you still see her?"

Missy clings to Alex and has dropped her lollipop. "She ran into the store."

"Okay, honey. Calm down. I'm not going to let her hurt you. It's okay."

Carla steps out of the post office and suddenly Nancy steps out of the dress shop and stops in front of the door looking at Carla. Missy screams, "That's her!" and Alex suddenly lets go of Missy and reaches for the door handle. "Stay here!" Alex demands.

Carla sees Nancy out of the corner of her eye and stops in midstride and faces her. Every cell and muscle in her body jumps into fight mode. She says nothing as she glares at Nancy. Nancy hollers, "I'll get her back!" and when she sees Alex stride around the front of the truck she turns and runs the opposite direction. Alex says nothing but gently places his hand in the middle of Carla's back guiding her to the truck door. He helps her in and Missy immediately grabs hold of Carla, crying. Carla hugs her close and soothingly says, "It's okay, honey. She's gone. It's okay."

Alex enters the truck, starts the engine, and when Carla glances over at him she sees his jaw muscles flexing. His eyes are like steel. He glances over at Missy and reaches over and rubs her back. "Hey, squirt. It's okay. She's gone now and she isn't going to hurt you." Missy sniffles. Carla relaxes her hold on her and asks, "Can you sit between us now?" Missy nods yes and scoots down between Alex and Carla. Carla sees the lollipop and picks it up, handing it to Missy. "Do you want your lollipop?" Missy shakes her head no and scoots as close to Alex as she can without crawling up in his lap. Alex places his hand on her knee and smiles down at her then pulls out of the parking lot.

* * *

Pulling into Carla's driveway, Alex doesn't shut the engine off but turns to Carla and says, "Go get a bag for you and Missy. You're staying with us tonight." Carla starts to reply but Alex cuts her off. "That's not a request, Carla!" Carla nods and says, "I'll be right back." Missy stays in the truck with Alex while Carla enters the house. Alex sits staring straight ahead, tapping the steering wheel with his index finger and Missy sits quietly beside him.

Chapter 5

The drive to Atlanta and then on to Gainesville has been a tiring six-hour drive. Carla has had to stop for gas and Missy has had to go to the bathroom several times. Carla calls her father on her cell phone. "Hi, Dad. We're almost there. Should I stop and pick up something for dinner? Do you need anything?"

"No, honey, Berta has dinner in the oven and we're just waiting on you."

"Okay. We should be there in about thirty minutes."

"Just come on in. See you in a little bit. Bye, honey."

"Bye."

* * *

Carla was a sophomore in high school when her mother got sick. As the disease progressed, her mother wasn't able to keep up with the normal everyday duties of running a home. Her husband had hired Berta to help out when the children were small. But by the time Carla's mother passed, Berta was in full charge of keeping the home clean and doing most of the cooking. Dr. Anderson had a full schedule with his practice even though he made every effort to be home with his teen children and to partake as much as possible in their activities. He considers Berta a Godsend and has offered to hire a full-time housekeeper to help her but she adamantly refuses any help. She became a surrogate mother to Carla and Rick.

* * *

Carla pulls into the long winding driveway that is lined on each side with crape myrtles. The trees are in full bloom and she can smell their fragrance as she slowly approaches the two-story house. She pulls onto the cement pad at the side of the house and parks. She's turned the engine off but doesn't immediately get out of the car. Instead, she sits looking out over the backyard. The groomed lawn flows to the water's edge. Lake Lanier spans out as far as she can see like a picture postcard. She can see boats scooting across the water in the distance.

Her father's twenty-four-foot pontoon boat is nestled beneath the dock roof with Rick's sixteen-foot ski boat rocking gently next to it. The house sits on three acres of land. Professional landscapers keep the grounds looking picture perfect. Shrubs, azaleas, and a weeping willow tree are strategically placed and wild dogwoods line one side of the property. A large fountain with an angel standing tall in the center has her head bowed in prayer. The fountain is positioned in a specially designed flower garden in memory of her mother. Forget-me-nots are in full bloom around its base. Their small blue flowers are abundant, enhancing the statue base and flowing over the rock wall that contains them.

Carla sits quietly as the memories flow through her mind. *Rick and I sure had a lot of fun diving off that dock. I remember how Mom used to holler for us to come in and we'd always holler we didn't want to. We never could get enough of the water and swimming. Oh, the parties we've had here in high school. Then Mom got sick and—* Missy interrupts her thoughts asking, "Are we going in, Mama?" Snapping out of her reverie, Carla grabs the door handle, "Yes. Come on."

* * *

Carla and Missy pass by the heated swimming pool and enter through the sliding glass doors on the back patio. When Carla and Missy enter the kitchen, Berta drops the knife she's chopping celery with at the kitchen island and runs to them, "Oh thank God, you're home!" she exclaims. She hugs Carla tightly then leans down and hugs Missy. She looks into Missy's eyes and says, "Oh my sweet little girl. Are you hungry?"

"Just a little," Missy says.

"Well, dinner will be ready soon. Would you like a cookie for now?"

"No, thank you. I'll wait for dinner."

"Okay. I'll bet you're tired though. Why don't you take your things up to your room and I'll call you when dinner is ready." Berta suggests.

Berta turns to Carla and suggests the same thing. "Thanks, Berta, but I think I want to talk to Dad for a minute first. Do you know where he is?"

"He's in his office, I think. I have ice tea made if you'd like some."

"Thank you, I think I will have a glass. Missy, take your things to your room and I'll be up in a little bit."

Missy picks up her child-size suitcase and the doll she brought in with her and heads for the winding staircase. Carla watches as Berta pours her a glass of tea.

* * *

Carla's childhood home was specially built when Dr. Anderson and her mother, Rose Mary, married. Five bedrooms, five and a half baths, den, office, formal dining room, large kitchen with all built-in appliances and an eight-foot-long island in the center were just starters. The vaulted ceilings with exposed beams were something Rose Mary wanted and a large living room with a rock fireplace. Dr. Anderson wanted a den with a fireplace as well as a full basement for "puttering." It seemed an awfully large house for the newlyweds but Dr. Anderson said he wanted it for the large family they planned to have and didn't want to have to be moving all the time to larger homes to fit their needs, plus having Lake Lanier in their backyard was a bonus he couldn't pass up.

Of course, a medical student couldn't afford a home like this but his very generous father said he'd pay to have it built if he promised to finish medical school and become a surgeon. Dr. Anderson readily agreed. It wasn't a difficult decision to make since he'd always dreamed of becoming a heart surgeon like his father since he was a boy.

Rose Mary was pregnant soon after their honeymoon but had a miscarriage and the next three pregnancies resulted with the same sad ending. When she was finally able to carry Rick full term, they were overjoyed and Carla followed two years later. Then the doctors told her she and the child would be at great risk if she got pregnant again.

* * *

Carla walks down the long hall to her father's office. The door is open so she taps on the doorframe then enters. "Hi, honey, I didn't know you were here or I would have come out to greet you." Her father says as he walks around his desk to give her a hug. He holds her for a long time and when they separate he sees tears in her eyes. "Come on, sit down," he says as he gently guides her to the oversized chair near his desk. He sits down in the chair next to hers. "I'll bet you're exhausted from that long drive."

"I am pretty tired. If Missy hadn't had to go to the bathroom every five miles it wouldn't have taken so long. Then the ball game must have just let out and you know what that means trying to get through downtown Atlanta!"

"Oh my! You did hit it at the wrong time of day. I'm surprised you're not still tied up in traffic but I'm glad you're here now safe and sound."

"Yeah, me too. Dad, I need you to do something for me as soon as you can if you don't mind."

"What's that?" he replies.

"I think I need to get Missy into counseling. She's really having a hard time with everything and I'd like to do it as soon as possible. Do you know, or know of, a good child psychiatrist?"

"I've already been thinking about that and I've been asking around. Everyone I've talked to seems to think Dr. McDaniel is very good. She's been in practice for several years and everyone says the kids love her. She's here in Gainesville. I'll give you her phone number."

"Oh thank you! That's great. Thank you for checking into it before we even got here."

"Honey, when you told me she wouldn't leave the house, sleeping with you, and scared to death all the time, I knew she was going to need some help getting through this. Is she any better?"

"No. We saw Nancy stalking us when we went to the post office and now she's even more terrified. I'll tell you about that a little later." Carla stands up and says, "I think I'm going to go lay down. I'm really beat. Would you ask Berta to call me when dinner is ready?"

"Sure, honey." Dr. Anderson stands up and gives her a hug. "Get some rest, honey, you're dragging."

* * *

Carla holds Missy's hand as they enter Dr. McDaniel's waiting room. Missy hesitates for a moment, looking around the room then takes a seat while her mother talks to the receptionist. Dr. McDaniel is approximately five feet three inches tall. One might mistake her for the ordinary grandmother about to sit in the rocking chair on the front porch with a glass of ice tea instead of being a well-known child psychiatrist. She's almost the spitting image of Ms. Bee on the *Andy Griffith Show* on TV. With her rosy cheeks, wide smile, twinkling blue eyes, and her gray hair pulled back into a bun at the nape of her neck, she steps through a door and smiles brightly. Reaching out her hand to shake Carla's, she says, "Hello, I'm Dr. McDaniel." She looks at Missy and smiles, "You must be Missy. How pretty you are."

Turning to Carla, she says, "Please come this way," and leads them down a short hall. They enter into a room that has a child-size table and chairs, a toy box, and various toys scattered about the room. "Please sit down," she instructs them, pointing to a couch and four chairs on one side of the room. Missy scoots close to Carla as they sit on the couch.

They chat for about five minutes then the doctor asks Missy if she'd like to play with a toy while she talks to her mother. Missy picks out a dark-haired doll. "We'll be right here in the next room, Missy, and we'll be right back," the doctor says. She and Carla enter her office and Carla begins telling her about meeting Nancy on the beach and the following events. Dr. McDaniel listens intently and asks few questions.

When she's heard the full story and how Missy has reacted to all the events, she says, "I think we should meet three times a week to start off and then see how well Missy progresses and go from there. How long do you think you'll be in town?"

"I'm not sure right now. Maybe a month but it could be longer. It just depends on how things go with Missy, what might be put in the works about Nancy, and well," she hesitates, "just a lot of things." Carla replies.

"I understand. Let's see how Missy responds and go from there for now."

They return to where Missy is sitting quietly on the couch holding the doll close to her chest and slowly and methodically stroking the doll's hair.

"Missy, your mother and I have talked and she's told me all about this Nancy woman." Missy stops stroking the dolls hair and hugs it tighter. "Would you like to come back tomorrow and we can talk about how you feel about all of this?" the doctor asks.

Missy glances up at her mother and Carla nods her head yes. Missy looks at the doctor and softly says, "I guess so."

"Oh, that's wonderful," the doctor exclaims. "I'm sure we have a lot to talk about. I'm looking forward to seeing you tomorrow then."

"Thank you," Carla says as she takes Missy's hand and they leave.

* * *

Arriving back at her father's house, Carla sees Rick's car in the driveway. Missy jumps out of the car and runs into the house. "Uncle Rick!" she yells and runs into his waiting arms. He grabs her up and twirls her around in a circle laughing. "Hey, kiddo, how are you?" he asks then stands her on the floor.

"I'm fine," Missy says, giggling. "Are you going to take me for a boat ride?" Missy excitedly asks him.

"No, not today. I have to work but maybe this weekend. How's that sound?"

"That long? We can't go tomorrow?" she says, disappointed.

"No, I'm afraid not. I'll tell you what. I'll try to get off work early and maybe we can go before Saturday. Now I can't promise that but I'll try."

"Oh boy. Will you try real hard?"

"I sure will." Rick says, laughing.

"Missy, you need to go change clothes, honey." Carla says as she sets her purse on the table and walks over to give Rick a hug. "Hi, big brother. It's good to see you."

Rick releases her but holds her by the shoulders and looks deep into her eyes. "You look like heck. It's been rough from what Dad has told me."

A weary smile crosses Carla's face and stepping back from Rick, "Thanks a lot. Yeah, it's been pretty rough."

Rick glances around to see if Missy has left the room, then says, "I did some checking, Sis, and you have a real nutcase on your hands." He points to a thick file sitting on the counter. "I brought some of what I found out and we can talk about it later. Dad's still at the office and said he'd be home about six. I want him here to hear this too. I'm glad you decided to come home."

Carla gives a long deep sigh and says, "Yeah, I am too. Missy and I met the psychiatrist today that Dad recommended and I'm really hoping she can help Missy. The poor kid is terrified and all this has to stop somehow."

"It will, don't you worry about that! I have some things already in the works but we'll talk about that later."

Missy runs into the kitchen wearing shorts and a T-shirt and asks, "Mama, can we go swimming? Uncle Rick, will you go swimming with me?"

Carla looks at Rick and grins broadly. "I don't think you're going to get out of this."

Rick laughs and puckers his mouth into a pout and running his finger under his eye as though he's wiping a tear away, says, "Oh, I wish I could, Missy, but I need to go do some things. I'll be back this evening but you have fun while I'm gone."

"Oh okay. But can I go swimming, Mama?"

"Sure. Let's go find our bathing suits. I'll beat ya' upstairs," she challenges. "I'll see you later, Rick," she hollers as she races Missy to the stairs.

* * *

The rest of the afternoon is spent in the pool. Carla gets out drying herself off and taking a seat on the patio she calls April.

"Hi, April. It's Carla," she says when April answers the phone.

"Oh, hi. I've been thinking about you. How are things going?"

"Pretty good. We met Missy's psychiatrist and I really like her already. I think Missy will like her too."

"Oh that's great! I'm so glad you were able to find someone."

"Yeah, me too. Dad checked around before we even got here and a lot of people recommended her."

"That's good."

"So how are things at home? How are you?" Carla asks.

"Oh, we're fine. Jenny keeps asking when Missy is coming back. She really misses her."

"I'm sure Missy misses her too."

April hesitates for a long moment. Carla finally asks, "April, is something wrong?"

"Ah. Well, I wasn't going to say anything."

"What?"

"I might as well tell you." Carla says. "Alex has been checking on your house since you've been gone. You know, just keeping an eye on things."

"I appreciate that."

"Carla, he found a note taped to the door yesterday. Since he knew you weren't going to be back for a while he read it."

Shivers zip down Carla's spine. "What did it say?"

"Now please don't go ballistic on me."

"April, what did the note say?" Carla demands sternly.

"It said, 'You can't hide forever. I'll find you and my kid.'"

"Oh my gosh! I can't believe this! How did she even know we left?"

"Maybe she saw you putting suitcases in the car or something. I don't know."

Carla's hands are shaking. "Do you still have the note?"

"Yes. Alex said we need to keep it for evidence if she's ever caught."

"Not *if* but *when*!" Carla says angrily.

"Mama, can I get a sandwich?" Missy interrupts.

Carla covers the mouthpiece with her hand and replies to Missy, "Dry off and go ask Berta if she'll fix you a *half* of a sandwich. We'll be having dinner soon."

She turns her attention back to April on the phone. "I'm sorry. Missy wants a sandwich. Please keep that note in a safe place so it doesn't get lost."

"Oh, I put it in the safe for safekeeping! Carla, do you know what you're going to do about her?" April asks with concern in her voice.

"No, but Rick was here when we got home and he said he's already got some things in the works, whatever that means. He said, and I quote, 'You have a real nutcase on your hands,' and pointed to a thick file he brought with him."

"Well, we already knew she has to be crazy!"

"Yeah. We're going to talk about this tonight after dinner. Rick wants Dad to hear everything and I do too."

"I can't wait to hear what he tells you. This is really scary!" April says.

"Well, listen. I need to get out of my wet bathing suit. Dad will be home soon and I need to see if I can help prepare dinner. I'll call you in a few days. Tell Alex thank you for watching the house for me. I love y'all."

"I will. Love you too. Give Missy a hug for me. Bye."

"Bye."

* * *

It's been a tiring day and Carla has told Missy to eat her sandwich and suggests she take a nap afterwards. Missy isn't an argumentative child so she does as she's told and after talking with Berta a few minutes, Carla slowly climbs the stairs. Before going to her room, she quietly slips into Missy's room to check on her. She reaches for the blanket and slowly slides it across Missy's sleeping body. She stands looking down at her daughter for a moment. Missy's brows are crinkled as she dreams.

Carla slowly lowers herself to the floor beside her bed. Kneeling next to her bed, she places her hand gently on Missy's leg and begins praying. "Father, I come to you in Jesus' name. Thank you for being our heavenly Father. Thank you for your grace and mercy. I praise you, Lord. I come to you with a heavy heart, Father. You know what we have been going through these past couple of months. You have kept us safe. Even when Nancy had a hold of Missy, you kept her from being hurt. Lord, she's scared but you said in your word to bring the little children to you. I'm bringing Missy to you now, Lord. I'm giving her fears to you and asking you to heal her. I'm asking you to bar the enemy from doing any more harm to my little girl. Lord, I don't know why Nancy is doing this. You said in First Corinthians 4:5 that you will bring to light what's hidden in darkness and you'll expose the motives of men's hearts. Lord, please show us Nancy's motives. They're evil obviously, but why? Why Missy? Help us, Lord, to understand and guide us in what to do. Thank you, Father, for keeping her safe. Give her your peace, Lord. In Jesus' name. Amen." Carla has tears streaming down her face as she stands. Wiping the tears with her hand, taking a deep breath, she turns and walks to her room.

* * *

A gentle hand is felt on Carla's shoulder, awakening her, "Dinner's ready" Berta says softly. "Would you like me to wake Missy?"

Carla yawns and sits up on the edge of the bed. "No. I think I'll let her sleep awhile longer."

"Okay, I'll keep some dinner warm for her."

"Thank you"

Berta walks back downstairs as Carla splashes water on her face.

Dr. Anderson and Rick are already at the table when Carla enters the dining room.

"Hey there, sleepy head," her father says. "Did you have a good nap?"

Carla pulls a chair out and sits down at the table. "I think I died!" she replies.

"Where's Missy?" Rick asks.

"I'm letting her sleep a little longer. She's been having nightmares and keeping us up all night."

"Poor kid. Is she still sleeping with you?" Rick asks.

"Since we've been here, no, which is good. I think she feels pretty safe now."

"That's good" her father states.

Berta sets a large bowl of green salad on the table. "I'll be back with the chicken in a minute. Go ahead and start." She says as she turns toward the kitchen. Dr. Anderson says a short blessing over the food and they begin their meal. Baked chicken, scalloped potatoes, asparagus with hollandaise sauce, and steaming buttery rolls are soon set before them. Their conversation is light. Each knows that after dinner it will be anything but light so all avoid the topic of Nancy. Rick is telling them about an incident at work when Missy appears in the door yawning. "Can I have some dinner too?" She asks. "I'm hungry!"

"Come and sit by Pa-pa" Dr. Anderson says, pulling out a chair next to him. Rick grins and says, "Hi, kiddo. Did you have a good nap?" Missy rubs her eyes, yawns, nods her head yes, and climbs onto the chair. Carla begins fixing her a plate. When the cake and ice cream has disappeared and all four are expounding on how good the food was and how full they are, Missy asks, "Can we go for a boat ride, Uncle Rick?"

Rick looks at Carla, then his watch, and asks, "What do you think, sis? You wanna go for a quick spin around the lake?"

Missy looks at Carla expectantly. "Can we, Mama, can we?"

"There's gas in the tank and it's still early. We could buzz around the lake for maybe an hour." Rick says.

Carla laughs and looks at Missy. "We can go for a quick ride. That's all, Missy. Uncle Rick, Pa-pa, and I have some things we need to talk about."

"Oh boy!" Missy shouts. "I'll put my swim suit on."

"No swim suit, Missy. We're only going for a ride."

Missy stops, "But—"

"No buts, Missy. Get a jacket. It will be chilly out on the water." Carla says sternly.

"Okay," Missy hollers as she tears out of the room and up the stairs. The three adults sit laughing then Rick goes out to uncover the boat and make the necessary preparations.

"Are you coming, Dad?" Carla asks.

"I don't think so, honey. I've got some paperwork I need to do. You three go ahead and have fun. I'll be here when you get back."

"You could use some fun too." Carla replies.

"Not tonight. I have four surgeries lined up and I need to get this done. You go ahead."

"Okay. We'll be back in a little bit." Carla says. "Missy, come on!" she yells.

Windblown, happy, and laughing, the three return from their speeding around the lake. During the week, there aren't many boats on the lake and much to Missy's delight, Rick opened it up full throttle and sped across the open water while Carla held Missy standing between her legs and her arms wrapped tightly around her waist. Missy screamed, laughed, and shouted, "Faster, Uncle Rick!" Rick would glance over at her, laugh, and shout, "Hold on!" each time he was going to make a turn. It was a "joy ride" Carla and Missy needed badly.

* * *

Entering Dr. Anderson's office, Carla takes one chair, Rick takes a seat next to her with the Nancy file in his lap, and Dr. Anderson sits behind his desk, sliding the computer screen to the side. A large bookcase takes up the entirety of the wall behind his desk. Framed pictures of the family—Carla and Mike during their wedding, Carla and Missy sitting on the patio, Rick in a police uniform that was taken before he became detective, Missy in her pink tutu in the Arabesque ballet position, and a picture of his beloved Rose Mary smiling while she holds a bouquet of red roses he gave her on their last anniversary—are dispersed among the many classic books and a few medical books. Dr. Anderson has always been a fan of authors such as Charles Dickens and Oscar Wilde. His collection includes an 1884 *Adventures of Huckleberry Finn* by Mark Twain, a 1929 *All Quiet on the Western Front* by Erich Maria Remarque, *To Kill a Mockingbird* by Harper Lee, and *Withering Heights* by Emily Bonte, to name just a few. A file cabinet sits in one corner.

Rick looks at Carla and says, "Are you ready for this?"

Carla takes a deep breath and replies, "Yes."

"Let's pray first," Dr. Anderson says and bows his head and begins praying. "Father, we ask for your presence here with us as we learn about this woman. Guide us and show us the way we are to go. In Jesus' name, Amen."

Rick opens the file and begins. "Well, as I stated before, you have a real nutcase on your hands. I did some digging after Dad told me what was going on and Nancy Burns is not her real name."

"I wondered about that," Carla says.

"Her real name is Carol McPhee. Nancy Burns is just one of her aliases."

"Dear Lord, what are we dealing with here?" Dr. Anderson says.

Rick glances at his father then continues, "This is not the first abduction she's tried. It's her third."

Carla gasps and their father shakes his head.

"Let me go back to what I've learned so far. Another guy in the department is helping me with this. He remembers her from some time back."

"Has she ever been arrested?" Carla asks.

"Yes, but let me start from the beginning. From a transcript that I was able to get from her first arrest—"

"She's been arrested more than once!" Carla exclaims.

"Sis, just calm down and let me go through this."

"I'm sorry," Carla apologizes. "Continue."

"From the transcripts from the first court hearing Nancy, as you know her, was fifteen years old and got into a wrong crowd.

She got into Wicca, Satan worship, witchcraft, Ouija boards, all kinds of demonic stuff."

"Ouija boards. That's just a game!" Carla says.

"No, honey, it's not. It's an instrument of the devil," her father interjects.

"Is that why you wouldn't let us have one when we were kids?" Carla asks her father.

"Yes. I didn't tell you then. You were too young to understand. But it is no game. Go on, Rick. Forgive me for interrupting."

"Apparently, they're popular again because I saw some toy store advertising that they have them the other day." Rick says, then resumes his report. "When she was seventeen, she got pregnant. Just before she turned eighteen, her baby was still born and because she was so messed up mentally from all the satanic stuff and her being underage, her parents had the baby cremated immediately. She never saw it."

"Oh, dear God!" Carla gasps.

"Apparently, she was really messed up mentally and was convinced that her baby was still alive."

Dr. Anderson whispers, "Lord, have mercy."

"Anyway," Rick continues, "she continued with her occult activities and according to her testimony," Rick flips through the pages of the transcript and runs his finger down a page, "and I quote, 'The Ouija board said my baby never died. It's in the hospital nursery.' So she went to the hospital and got caught trying to steal a baby."

"How far did she get?" Dr. Anderson asks.

"Not far. She tried to convince the attending nurse that she was the mother but the nurse wasn't buying it and the police were called in. She was arrested for attempted kidnapping and got two years' probation with the understanding she'd get psychiatric help."

"In other words, a slap on the wrist!" Carla states.

"She didn't have a record and apparently it was a sympathetic judge," Rick replies.

"So what about the other arrests?" Carla asks.

"She changed her name, dyed her hair—hmmm, let me look, oh, black—and moved to another state."

"They weren't checking on her?" Carla asks incredulously.

"They did for a little while but the system is full of murderers and they just let her slip through the cracks I guess."

Carla looks at him sternly and says angrily, "So she's out there causing all sorts of pain to others and they did nothing!"

"Honey, calm down," her father says. "Let him finish."

Rick flips through his notes and continues, "A year later, the police get a report that a woman and her little girl are being stalked. The police begin investigating and learn it's Nancy. Only this time, her name is Mary Jones. It took them a few months to run all this down and they were finally able to arrest her when she grabbed a little girl at a Walmart."

"And?" Carla asks agitated.

"She got three years in the state pen."

"So how did she zero in on Missy?" Dr. Anderson asks.

"We're not sure about that yet. Bill is checking some more things out."

"So what are we supposed to do?" Carla asks.

"I think you need to get an attorney, honey." Dr. Anderson stands up and stretches.

Carla looks at him. "I can't afford an attorney. The insurance from Mike is almost gone and I'm planning on looking for work when Missy starts school."

Her father walks over to her and stands looking down at her. "Carla, you need an attorney to deal with this and you don't have to worry about the money. I'll pay for it."

Carla stands up and facing him replies, "Dad, you gave me the money for the house in Ivy, you've done so much already."

"You're my daughter and that's my only grandchild. You need to be protected and not just from physical harm. You'll need an attorney when she's caught. Let me do this for my granddaughter and you."

"He's right, sis. You need a good attorney and I know just who to get."

Carla hugs her father and says, "Thank you. I better go see what that granddaughter of yours is up to."

Dr. Anderson looks at his watch and says, "It's almost ten and I have rounds to do at the hospital. I better get on the stick."

Rick stands up holding the file. "Oh man! I gotta get home. There's a good cop show coming on!"

Everyone laughs and goes in different directions.

Chapter 6

Larry Dunn strides into his office and is surprised to see Rick sitting across from his desk thumbing through one of his law books. "Hey, Rick. What a surprise. I haven't seen you in a while. How are you?" he asks, reaching out to shake Rick's hand.

"I'm good. Yeah, it has been a while. I hope you don't mind Sara letting me come in." Rick says, holding the law book up. "I wanted to look up something. Hope you don't mind."

"No, that's fine. Something on one of your cases?" Larry asks.

"Curiosity, mainly."

Larry leans against the edge of his desk and asks, "So what can I do for you?"

"I'd like to talk to you about a situation my sister and her daughter have found themselves in. Is this a good time? Maybe we can meet for lunch or something if it's not."

"What kind of situation?"

"Stalking, attempted kidnapping."

Larry whistles and walks around to sit behind his desk. "That's pretty serious stuff."

"Yeah it is," Rick replies.

"How about meeting for dinner? I'll be in court all day."

"That's fine. That will give us time to catch up too. Where do you want to meet?" Rick asks as he places the law book back on the shelf.

"Why don't we meet about six at Longhorn's? I've been craving one of their steaks."

"Sounds good to me. I'll see you there. Thanks." Rick says and leaves Larry's office.

* * *

Rick calls Carla, "Hey, sis, I'm meeting with my friend the lawyer tonight. Is there anything I don't know about that I need to tell him?"

"Well, be sure to tell him Missy has been in counseling from all of this and has been doing really well up until yesterday."

"What happened yesterday?"

"We went to the North Georgia Outlet Mall shopping and we were in one of the stores when Missy grabbed me in a death grip and started crying. She said she saw Nancy."

"Did she? I mean, was Nancy there?" Rick asks concerned.

"No. What happened was she saw the back of a woman with red hair going around the corner of some of the displays and thought it was Nancy because of the red hair."

"So what'd you do?"

"I picked her up and walked around to the aisle where the woman was. I wanted to see her for myself. It wasn't Nancy but Missy is still scared."

Rick takes a deep breath and sighs loudly. "Poor kid. This has really scared the heck out of her. When does she see the counselor again?"

"Tomorrow," Carla replies.

"Okay. Anything else I need to tell Larry? Oh, his name is Larry Dunn. You may remember him. We chummed around a good bit in high school. Great guy and smart!"

Thinking for a moment, she says, "I don't think so. Well, maybe. Oh, I don't know, Rick. This whole mess has me going nuts."

"It's okay. No big deal. I'm meeting him at six and I'll tell him the whole story and we'll see what he says," Rick states.

Carla is silent for a moment then asks, "Rick, do you really think I need an attorney? I haven't done anything wrong. *She's* the devil that's after my child!"

Rick chuckles then says, "Yes, sis, you should have an attorney. When she goes to trial you'll need someone to represent you. Larry is the prosecuting attorney. He'll probably be the one prosecuting her."

"But it didn't happen up here. We were in Ivy," Carla says.

"Carla, let's just see what he says and go from there. We'll take it one step at a time. Okay?"

"Okay. Thanks. I just wish it was over and we could go home and forget all this!" she states emphatically.

"I know," Rick replies.

"Oh! I almost forgot! My neighbor is checking on the house and found a note taped to the door last week. It was from Nancy."

"What did it say?"

"'You can't hide forever. I'll find you and my kid.' Something like that."

"Do you still have the note?"

"April has it. That's my neighbor. It was her husband that found it and she said they kept it for evidence."

"That's great. I'll be sure to tell Larry."

"Dear God, will this never end? I just want it to be over!" Carla states with tears forming in her eyes.

"I know. It's going to be okay. We'll get her and she'll spend many years behind bars. This is serious stuff and it's her third strike. There's no telling what else we may dig up before then. Just hang in there. It's going to work out and then you can put all of it behind you."

"I suppose you're right. Thanks."

"I know I'm right! I gotta go. I'll talk to you in a few days. Give Missy a hug for me. Hang in there, sis. I'll call you. Bye."

"Bye." Carla hangs up the phone deep in thought.

* * *

That evening, Rick meets with Larry at Longhorn's and while looking over the menu, Rick asks, "So what kind of case are you trying?"

"Oh, just some simple open and shut deal, an attempted robbery in a woman's home." Larry starts laughing, takes a sip of tea and continues. "The poor sucker who tried to rob her broke in and was met looking down the barrel of a three fifty-seven! Grandma wasn't messing around and held him there until the cops came." Laughing even harder, he says, "She was preaching the Bible to him the whole time."

Rick chuckles, "How old is she?"

"Eighty-four and the sweetest little ole lady you ever want to meet."

"Yeah, until you break into her house," Rick says, laughing.

They each order their favorite steaks and during the meal, Rick tells Larry about Nancy, how Carla met her, the stalking, showing up at her house, the fight, and finally the note.

Larry listens closely then asks, "Does she have the note?"

"Yes. Her neighbor has it."

"Good. Be sure they don't lose it. It will be needed in court," Larry says while chewing.

Rick picks up his glass of ice tea and says, "The problem is, this is all taking place in Ivy. Carla and Missy are just here for a while trying to get settled down from everything. They aren't staying. Dad wants them to move back here but Carla refuses. She really loves it down there and I guess I don't blame her, lots of painful memories here."

"What do you mean?" Larry asks then stabs another piece of meat.

"Her husband was killed in Iraq. I guess she just needed to get away from the area. Kind of ease the pain, I guess."

"That's understandable. I'm sorry to hear that. That's tough."

"Yeah it is, but Carla is tough and she loves Missy more than life itself." He grins broadly. "Nancy doesn't realize just how lucky she is to still be alive. Carla beat the crap out of her in that Sunday school room. Talk about Mama Bear protecting her cub? Carla would die for her kid! It took two big guys to pull them apart." Rick laughs.

"I know what you mean. I've had a few of those cases. Her living in Ivy isn't that big of a problem. Of course, I can't take the case if it's tried down there but I know a good attorney down there. I could always talk to him. Of course, it would make it a whole lot easier if Nancy tried something up here." Larry states.

"From what we're learning about this woman, I wouldn't put it past her. She's been in trouble in other states and then came back here. We haven't been able to figure out how she chose Missy though. But we will."

Larry continues eating and Rick changes the subject. "So, you ever get married? Dating? What's going on in your life, Larry?"

Larry glances over the top of his glass as he takes a drink then sets his glass down and looks down at his empty plate. Placing both hands on his stomach, he leans back and says, "Oh that was good! Nah, I'm still single. Just haven't found the right one, I guess, and too busy being married to the law for much dating. What about you? Married with a dozen kids by now, I suppose."

Rick bursts out laughing and says, "No. I'm still a bachelor too. Carrying a badge and gun, the hours, well, you know women. They want their guy home safe and sound. Came close once but she said she couldn't live worrying about me getting killed all the time and she walked to greener pastures."

Larry nods understanding, "The perils of being in law enforcement."

The two men talk for a while longer, pay their check, and leave, going to their cars. Standing next to their cars in the parking lot, Larry says, "Call me, Rick, if anything happens. For now, there isn't anything that can be done until you catch this woman. Tell Carla I'll be happy to talk to her when the time comes but for now, like I said, not much can be done."

"I appreciate that. Hey, it's good seeing you again. We need to get together more often. Maybe we'll buzz around the lake sometime. I have a ski boat docked at my dad's on Lanier. You still like to water ski?" Rick asks.

"Oh man, I love to water ski! I still have my slalom. I've been wanting to get a boat but I just don't have the time any more to really put it to use."

"Well, come and enjoy a day at least. How about this weekend? Come on up to dad's and we can spend the day on the lake. It'll be fun." Rick states, excited.

"Now that sounds like a deal. I'll call you Thursday or Friday. By golly, I think that's a great idea! Thanks, Rick. I'm going to take you up on that offer and I'm already looking forward to it."

Rick slaps him on the shoulder and says, "Great! I'll talk to you later then," and enters his car.

* * *

Carla has been helping Berta in the kitchen Saturday morning while Missy is watching cartoons on TV. Rick strides into the kitchen and asks, "Where's Dad?"

Carla turns and replies, "He's at the hospital. One of his patients isn't doing very well and he said he wanted to go check on her."

"Oh. I guess I'll catch him later," Rick replies and starts to leave the room.

Missy has heard his voice and comes running in. "Hi, Uncle Rick. Can we go for a boat ride today?"

Rick laughs, gives her a big hug, and says, "A friend of mine is coming this morning and we're going to be going out in the boat. If your mom says you can and it's okay with him then we can take a spin around the lake."

"Mama, can we?" Missy asks excited.

"That's up to Uncle Rick and his friend. I doubt they'll want a little girl hanging out with them all day."

"Uncle Rick?" She pleads.

"I don't think Larry will mind if we ride for a little while but your mom is right. You can't spend the whole day in the boat, kiddo."

"Not the *whole* day. But can I go for a ride?"

"That's fine with me but let's see how Larry feels about it," Rick replies.

"Oh, it's Larry that's coming?" Carla asks.

"Yeah. He loves to water ski and I invited him up for the day."

"Will you teach me how to water ski, Uncle Rick?" Missy asks expectantly.

Rick laughs and looks at Carla. "Now, *that's* definitely up to your mom!"

"Can he, Mama? Can Uncle Rick teach me to water ski too?"

"You don't have any skis." Carla says.

"We can get some."

"Let's think about this for a while. Right now you need to go make your bed."

"Okay." And Missy runs upstairs.

"That's quite the kid you have, sis."

Carla beams with pride. "Yes, she is."

"How do you feel about her learning to water ski? She loves the water and we were pretty young when we learned."

"I don't know. I haven't really thought about it but you're right, she does love the water."

"Well, I could pick her up a pair of kids size doubles if you want," Rick replies.

Hesitating, Carla says, "I'm not sure, Rick. She's still pretty young."

"Not that young and maybe it will help with her insecurities. I just won't buy red ones." He laughs.

Carla smiles halfheartedly. "Let me think about it."

The doorbell rings. Rick says, "That's probably Larry. I'll get it."

Opening the door, Rick greets Larry. "Hey, Larry. Glad you could make it."

"Yeah, me too. It's been a while since I was here. The place hasn't changed much." Larry says.

"Come on in. Would you like a cup of coffee or anything?"

"No thanks. I'm good."

Carla walks into the living room, "Hi, Larry. It's good to see you again. When Rick told me you were his lawyer friend I couldn't remember you at first. You haven't changed much."

"Just older. It's good to see you too after all this time. I'm sorry to hear about your husband. Rick told me."

"Thank you."

"Well, listen. We need to go uncover the boat and fill up the gas tank if we're going to tear up the lake today," Rick says.

"It's good seeing you again, Carla. Maybe we can talk later," Larry says as he and Rick walk toward the door.

"Oh she's coming too. We need a spotter and Missy will never forgive me if she doesn't get to ride in the boat. I hope that's okay." Rick says to Larry.

Larry couldn't be happier. He'd never said anything to Rick or Carla but in high school he had a serious crush on her but was too shy to ask her out on a date.

"Oh, that's great. No, I don't mind at all," Larry grins.

"You didn't tell me I was going too," Carla says to Rick.

Rick laughs and says, "Well, now you know. I can't watch Missy, spot, and drive all at the same time so it stands to reason you'd be going. You will, won't you?"

"Of course if I want to live in peace with my daughter." Carla laughs.

"Okay. We're going to run down to the station and fill the gas cans and we'll be ready to go in about thirty minutes. Can you and Missy be ready then?" Rick asks.

"Sure. We'll come down to the dock." Carla replies and leaves the room.

Missy screams and hollers, "Go faster!" as Rick pulls Larry behind the boat. Larry is jumping the wakes from other boats and turning circles around on his ski while flying across Lake Lanier's cool waters. Suddenly, Carla hollers, "He's down," and Rick looks back then spins the boat around in a large circle heading back to pick Larry up. Carla has her arm raised high in the air warning other boaters that there's a skier down. Missy shouts, "He's down," and does the same. Rick and Carla burst out laughing.

Pulling the boat up slowly beside Larry, Rick says, "Ready to go again?"

"No, I think I've had enough for a while. I don't think my legs will hold out much longer. It's been too long. I'm out of shape," and hands his ski up to Carla. She lowers the ladder and Larry climbs into the boat.

Missy asks suddenly, "Can I try? Can I try?"

"No honey! The ski is too big for you. You have to learn on two skis first and you don't have any."

"Oh, Mama, I can learn on one," Missy says, disappointed.

"No. You have to learn on two skis first, honey. Then you can learn to ski on one."

Larry quickly adds, "She's right, Missy. It's really hard to ski on one ski if you've never skied before."

"Okay. But can we ride fast some more?" Missy asks hopefully.

Rick bursts out laughing and states, "You're a real little thrill seeker, aren't you? Pull in the rope and let's go."

Larry pulls the rope in and as soon as it's clear, Rick shoves the lever forward and the boat bursts across the water. Missy bursts out laughing.

* * *

Berta has fixed chicken salad sandwiches with chips and ice tea and brings it out to the pool where Missy is splashing in the pool and Rick, Carla, and Larry sit at the table in the shade of the large umbrella talking and laughing.

"Come on, Missy. Lunch is ready." Carla says.

Missy crawls out of the pool and asks, "After lunch can we go out in the boat again?"

Rick grins and says, "I think we've had enough for today. What do you think, Larry?"

"Oh, I could go one more round if you don't mind."

"Yeaaah!" Missy screams. Everyone laughs and digs into their sandwiches.

Another hour is spent buzzing around the lake again. By the time the four come in Missy is exhausted and half asleep, Larry's legs are shaking from the constant pressure on his legs while skiing, and Rick and Carla are ready to call it a day.

Carla starts to pick Missy up, who has now fallen asleep on the couch to carry her upstairs. Larry says, "Let me do that," and gently picks Missy up carrying her behind Carla upstairs and gently lays her on her bed. Carla covers her and stands looking down at her. Larry stands beside her and whispers, "She's really a sweet little girl, Carla."

Carla smiles and turns to him. "Do you have any kids?"

"No but I love kids and she's as cute as a button."

Carla walks to the door and they go back downstairs. She, Rick, and Larry talk for a short time.

Larry stands and says, "Listen, I really enjoyed today. Thank you for inviting me, Rick. I had a great time! I better get going. I have some briefs to deal with before Monday."

Rick stands, "Hey man. It was great! We need to do this more often. It's like old times. Next time, maybe Carla can drive and you and I can ski together. That would be fun."

"Yeah, that would be fun. Let's plan on it. I need to get out more." He looks at Carla and grins, "And Missy can be our spotter."

Carla bursts out laughing, "She would too!"

Rick interjects, "Yeah. Did you see her raising her arms up when you fell? She's something else!"

Larry laughs as they're walking to the door. "Yeah, I did. I thought it was really cute. Well, it was good seeing you again, Carla. Call me any time if something comes up."

"I will, Larry. Thanks again." Larry and Rick walk out to his car.

Larry stands quiet for a moment then looks at Rick. "Ahhh."

Rick starts laughing. "You still have that crush on her, don't you ole boy!" Rick says.

"Is it that obvious?" Larry says as his face turns beet red.

Rick turns serious. "Larry, she's not ready. It will be a year at the end of the month when her husband was killed and it's not going to be a good time for her. She really loved Mike and she's just not ready to start dating. Take it really slow, guy, if you're thinking about asking her out."

"Thanks, buddy. I appreciate you telling me. I don't want to do anything that will make her uncomfortable."

"I'll see you later." Rick says and Larry gets in his car and pulls away.

Rick turns and walks down to the dock. *Larry's a really nice guy and he and Carla would make a good couple but I don't know. I sure hope he doesn't blow it. It's obvious he has something going for her*, Rick thinks as he sets the empty gas cans on the dock and stretches the canvas cover over the boat.

* * *

Carla has met with Dr. McDaniel and they've decided Missy is doing so well that once-a-week counseling should be okay for her at this point. “If something arises though, you be sure to call me and get her back in here immediately,” Dr. McDaniel states.

“I will. I’m just so happy she’s done so well.” Carla replies.

“I am too. She’s a brave little girl, tough too.”

Carla laughs and says, “Not when she sees red hair!”

“She’s getting better with that. She understands now that not everyone with red hair is going to hurt her.”

“I’m happy to hear that. Thank you for all your help. Missy really likes you. I think she might even miss coming to see you,” Carla says as she stands to leave.

Dr. McDaniel laughs and says, “Oh, all the kids love me.”

“I can see why. Thank you again and we’ll see you next week,” Carla says and leaves.

While Carla was talking to Dr. McDaniel, Dr. Anderson called Rick from his office.

“Hi, Rick. It’s Dad. Have you got a minute?”

“Sure. What’s up? You don’t usually call me at work.”

“I think we have a problem.”

“What kind of problem?” Rick asks cautiously.

“I came home late last night and there was a note in the mailbox along with the rest of the mail.”

“Oh no. Not Nancy!”

“Yes. I haven’t told Carla yet. You know Mike’s death anniversary was a few days ago and Carla has been in tears for the past few days. Berta has been trying to keep up with Missy but now with this, I don’t know, son. It could push Carla over the edge. I’m really worried about it. I’d like for you to be here when I do tell her. You know more about how to handle this stuff than I do and you know she’s going to be pretty upset.”

“What’s the note say?” Rick asks with an edge to his voice.

“‘I know where you are now and I’m coming to get my kid!’”

“Oh crap!” Rick exclaims. “What time are you going to be home?” He asks.

"Why don't you come about eight? That way Missy will be in bed. We don't want her seeing her mother upset any more than she already is or knowing this witch is in town."

"You're right. I'll see you about eight and, Dad, don't say anything to Carla before then."

"No, I won't. Thanks, son. I'll see you then."

"Okay. Bye."

Rick immediately calls Larry and tells him about the note. "I'm going to get right on it and find out how this crazy woman found her!" Rick says angrily.

"Probably the Internet," Larry replies. "Heck, you can run anyone down on there."

"Yeah, probably, but I'm going to find out and get this woman if it's the last thing I do!"

"Now, calm down, buddy. You getting all hot under the collar isn't going to help Carla."

"Yeah, yeah, I know. She's just gone through so much and I hate it she's having to deal with this now. Especially when she's grieving Mike's death all over again." Rick replies, trying to calm down.

"I'm sure it's tough for her but like you said, 'She's tough.' She'll be okay. Give her time. Do you want me to come out tonight and be there when she's told?"

"Oh thanks but I don't think that will be necessary."

"I'll come if you want me there," Larry states emphatically.

"Thanks but I think Dad and I can handle it. I'll call you if I have to arrest her for murder." Rick laughs.

"I hope that doesn't happen!" Larry laughs. "Call me tomorrow and let me know how I can help."

"It may be a couple of days before I know anything definite. Me and Bill will work on this twenty-four seven if that's what it takes. At least we know she's in town now."

"Rick, you might consider having someone with her and Missy if they go out shopping or anything. Nancy knows where she's at now and will be watching." Larry cautions.

"I've already thought of that and I'm going to talk to one of the gals in the department as soon as I hang up. She can become Carla's new best friend or at least watch from a distance. This *is* going to stop!"

"Good! I'll talk to you later then. Stay cool, Rick. Carla needs a cool head now."

"You're right. Thanks."

* * *

Carla has given Missy her bath and after kneeling beside the bed with her during their prayers, she tucks her in and kisses her goodnight. Looking down at her before leaving the room, Carla thinks, *Oh, Mike. She looks so much like you. Just look at those long lashes and that sweet face.* Her eyes well up with tears but she manages to smile as she walks into the kitchen. "She's all tucked in now," Carla says to Berta and her father.

Her dad smiles, nods, and says, "All that swimming today must have worn her out."

Carla laughs and replies, "She's a regular fish. I remember how much we loved to swim and play in the lake but I think she has Rick and I both beat in that department."

Rick walks through the door and Carla looks surprised. "Speak of the devil, what are you doing here so late?" she asks Rick.

Dr. Anderson answers before Rick can, "I asked him to come, honey. We need to talk. Let's go in my office."

A shiver runs up Carla's spine as she follows her dad and brother down the hall. "You need to sit down, honey," Dr. Anderson says.

"Dad? What's going on? Are you okay?" Carla asks, fearing her father has bad news about his health. "Are you sick?" she asks, sitting down in the armchair. Rick sits down next to her and looks intently at his father.

"No, honey, I'm not sick." He reaches down and slides open the drawer of his desk and pulls out the note he found in the mailbox.

Rick sits quietly and Carla sucks in her breath when she sees the note in her father's hand. Tears immediately begin sliding down her cheeks and she groans, "No. Not her! Not Nancy. She couldn't have found us!" and she breaks into heart-wrenching sobs. Her father rushes around his desk and kneels down in front of her. She throws her arms around his neck and sobs into his shoulder. Rick has seen a lot of heartache in his line of work but can't help tearing up as he places his hand on his sister's arm. They let Carla cry until she's finally able to pull away from her father and wipe the tears. Dr. Anderson stands up and reaching over to the corner of his desk, he retrieves a box of tissues and hands it to her.

Blowing her nose and wiping the tears away, Carla is finally able to speak. "How—how did she find us?" she asks through sniffles.

Rick swipes at his tears, clears his throat, and answers, "We suspect through the Internet."

"Why Rick? Why is she doing this to us? Why my Missy?" She blows her nose again waiting for an answer.

"We located her parents today. Maybe they have some answers. We called them today and they're willing to talk to us so we're going to see them tomorrow. They live in Athens."

"Honey, Rick is doing everything possible to stop this woman," her father adds.

Carla starts crying again and taking a deep breath, she says, "I know. I know you are, Rick."

"Sis, listen to me." Rick places his hand on her shoulder gently. "Try to stop crying. I need you to hear me. Okay?"

Sniffling and blowing her nose, Carla says, "Okay."

"I talked to one of the women officers today that's a friend of mine. She and I went to the captain and I told him what was happening. He's given her permission to be your new best friend."

Carla looks at him, puzzled. "New best friend? You mean like a bodyguard?"

"Yes. Well, kind of. She's going to stay here at the house with you and if you go anywhere she's going to be with you but at a distance." Rick explains.

Dr. Anderson releases a long sigh. "Oh, son, that will be great! I was hoping you could arrange something like that."

"But won't Nancy know she's a cop?" Carla asks.

"No. She'll be in street clothes like everyone else and because she won't be right beside you when you're out it won't be obvious she's with you. She's good, sis. She's done this several times as undercover."

"But doesn't that make Missy like bait? No, I won't do it!" Carla says emphatically.

"You're not listening!" Rick says strongly then continues more softly. "Nobody is bait! I said *when* you go shopping or out anywhere, she'll go, too. You can't stay cooped up in this house hiding forever."

"Oh!" Carla replies then laughs. "If dad doesn't mind, we could stay cooped up until you catch her."

"I don't think so. Missy would drive you crazy." Rick laughs.

"Honey, listen to Rick. He's going to catch this woman and then you and Missy can move on with your life." Dr. Anderson says.

Carla sighs and replies, "I know. I just wish it was over."

"Honey, do you think you can keep Missy from knowing what's going on?" Dr. Anderson asks gently.

"She's going to want to know who this woman is that suddenly moves in. She's smart and it's not going to be easy."

Rick interjects, "I thought maybe we could tell her she's our cousin and just here visiting."

"That might work." Dr. Anderson says.

"Yes. I think that might work. What's her name?" Carla asks.

"Becky. Becky Martin."

Carla sits quietly and Rick looks at his father and nods. Dr. Anderson gives him a thumbs up and they all sit quietly for a few minutes.

Rick stands up and turns to Carla. "Are you okay? Are you okay with this plan?"

"No, I'm not okay but I will be." Carla takes a deep breath and stands. "When is Becky coming?"

"Tomorrow. She'll be here about noon she said."

Dr. Anderson walks around his desk to Carla. "It's going to be okay, honey."

Rick looks at Carla, reaches out and suddenly hugs her. "Sis, I'm going to catch her," he whispers next to her ear. Carla starts crying again. Rick releases her and says, "I need to get home. I'll call you tomorrow and see how things are going."

Dr. Anderson reaches out and Rick starts to shake his hand but his father pulls him into a hug. "I love you, son, and thank you for all you're doing for your sister and Missy." Tears have welled up in his eyes and he releases Rick.

"I'll talk to you tomorrow," Rick says and turns quickly to leave as he wipes a tear from his own eyes.

Berta appears at Dr. Anderson's office door and taps lightly. "Telephone, Carla." Neither she nor her father had paid any attention when the phone rang a couple of times and went silent.

"Who is it?" Carla asks.

"She said her name is April."

"Oh, that's my neighbor in Ivy. I'll take it in my room. Thanks, Berta." She quickly turns to her father and says, "Thanks, Dad. I'll see you tomorrow," and gives him a hug.

"Try to rest, honey. It's all going to work out."

"I will," and Carla runs upstairs. "Hi, April." Carla says into her cordless phone as she plops down on her bed then suddenly starts crying.

"Oh dear God. What's wrong, Carla?" April asks frantically.

Carla wipes her tears, "She found us! April, she found us!" and bursts into sobs.

April waits until Carla can get her tears to stop and asks, "How? When?"

Carla begins telling her about her father finding the note.

April interrupts her and asks, "What did it say this time?"

"I don't know. I just lost it when dad pulled it out of his desk. I didn't even ask and I don't think I even want to know at this time." Tears stream down her face. "Hold on. I need some tissue," she says.

When Carla returns, April asks, "So what are you going to do? What is your brother doing? Has he learned anymore?"

Carla wipes the tears, takes a deep breath, and tells her everything that Rick said and how an undercover policewoman is coming to stay with them and go everywhere with her and Missy.

"Oh, I'm so glad!" April exclaims.

"I guess I am too. Rick had just left when you called." Carla starts crying again and finally states, "I'm just so sick of this! I want to come home to my little house and build sandcastles with Missy on the beach, and—" She breaks down sobbing again.

April waits and when the sobs turn to hiccups, she says, "Carla, would you rather talk about this some other time? You're obviously very upset and I may not be helping with all my questions."

"Do you mind? This is just such a shock. I was even thinking about maybe coming home in another week. I can't hide forever," Carla says.

"I don't mind at all. You have a lot to deal with right now. How's Missy?" she asks.

"She's fine. She doesn't know Nancy is here and we're not telling her."

"Oh that's good! Honey, try to get some rest. I'll call you in a day or two."

"Okay. Thanks. I'm sorry," Carla says and begins crying again.

"I'll talk to you later," April says and hangs up.

Carla stretches out on her bed and cries herself to sleep.

Chapter 7

Becky Martin has been an undercover policewoman for seven years and very familiar with these child abduction cases. She's greatly respected among her colleagues and even though she has a great sense of humor and looks like the everyday country girl, those that know her know she's one to be reckoned with when it comes to children. She and Rick have worked together on cases before and dated for a short time until they both realized it wasn't going to work out and parted friends.

When Rick came to her about Carla and Missy's situation, she readily agreed to help out. She pulled up the latest photo she could find of Nancy and with computer enhancement placed various colored hair and hairstyles on the photos of Nancy she now carried with her.

Stepping out of the taxi in front of Dr. Anderson's house, she retrieves two suitcases from the backseat. She pays the driver, thanks him, and walks to the front door and rings the bell. Carla opens the door and Becky whispers, "Act surprised." Carla is surprised! Standing on the doorstep is a petite woman dressed in jeans, tennis shoes, a T-shirt, and a long dishwater blonde ponytail hanging out the hole in the back of a baseball hat with the Braves embroidered across the front. Carla exclaims quickly,

"Becky! I didn't know you were coming? When did you get in?" and throws her arms around Becky, hugging her.

Becky laughs and shouts when Carla releases her, "Surprise cousin!"

"Come on, come on in," Carla says, glancing around the front yard.

They step into the foyer and Becky sets her suitcases down. Missy walks up and stands beside Carla. "Who's that, Mama?"

Carla moves Missy forward a step and says, "This is your Uncle Rick and my cousin, Becky. She's come to visit for a while."

Becky leans over and smiles at Missy, "Hi. You must be Missy."

Missy shies away a tad then says, "Hi."

"It's good to meet you, Missy. I hear you love to swim."

Surprised, Missy says, "Who told you that?"

Carla and Becky laugh and Becky replies, "Your Uncle Rick, of course."

"Oh. He takes me for boat rides too."

"Oh I know. He's told me how you love to ride in his boat."

"Where do you live?" Missy asks.

"Honey, why don't we let Becky come in and maybe you can show her to her room with me. Then you can get acquainted."

Carla closes the front door and starts to pick up one of Becky's suitcases but Becky reaches for it first. "I'll get it," she says and smiles. "Just lead the way."

The next day, Missy is splashing in the pool while Becky and Carla sit under the umbrella at the table. "Have you and Rick known each other long?" Carla asks.

"Yes, a while. We've worked some cases together." She hesitates then continues. "I don't know if Rick told you but we dated for a short time. With our schedules and all it just didn't work out but we're still good friends."

"That's too bad. Rick's a great guy, even if he is my brother."

"Yeah, he is," Becky agrees.

Becky watches Missy for a short time then states, "Boy, does Rick love that kid! It's tearing him up inside what's happening with all of this."

"Has he said anything more about what he's found?" Carla asks.

"He and his partner visited with her parents and came back with some good information and some documents."

"What kind of documents?" Carla asks as she leans forward and places her elbows on the table.

"Well, for one, they had no idea where her baby was cremated. There wasn't anything in the transcript that Rick had and the hospital refused any information without a subpoena. They now have a copy of the death certificate and a certificate from the crematory."

"Oh wow! That's great." Carla is silent for a long moment and when she leans back, tears have formed in her eyes.

"What is it, Carla? What's going through your mind?" Becky gently asks.

"As badly as I want her caught and put in jail, there's a part of me that feels sorry for her. From what Rick told us about her, I just can't imagine going through what she did."

"I can understand that you might feel that way but you must also realize that she has, and had, some pretty heavy dark stuff going on that was influencing her," Becky states softly but pointedly.

Carla looks over at Missy dogpaddling across the pool. "How does someone get into that kind of stuff? And so young?" she asks, turning her attention back to Becky.

Becky shakes her head and says, "Kids get influenced by a lot of stuff pretty easily. Look how easy it is for pedophiles on the Internet, for example. These kids give out their whole addresses, real names, and even what school they go to and suddenly find themselves meeting some creep thirty years older than them and carried off somewhere."

Carla shivers.

"I don't know how religious you are but I can tell you this. Satan is after anyone he can get! Especially kids and if a kid can be sucked into believing his crap, excuse me, he's going to do all he can to keep them," Becky states flatly.

"Rick said she was heavy into the Ouija board and even Satan worship," Carla replies.

"Yes, she was, and still is, from what we've learned. The Ouija board is where she thinks the devil communicates with her. Anyway, that's what her parents told Rick and his partner. They refused to allow it in their house and so she moved out and moved in with a bunch of Satan worshippers. They haven't spoken to her since."

"Dear Lord!" Carla exclaims. "Well, she was right about one thing. That thing is of the devil! This whole mess convinces me of that."

Suddenly, Becky hollers at Missy, "Can you dive off the edge, Missy?"

Berta steps out of the sliding glass doors onto the patio and hands Carla the cordless phone, "Rick's on the phone."

Carla talks to Rick for a moment, assuring him Becky got there and had a good night and everything is fine. Moving the phone away from her ear, she says, "He wants to talk to you," and hands the phone to Becky. Becky says hello and then walks away from the pool and stands near the end of the house speaking to Rick. Carla goes over to the edge of the pool and sits down dangling her bare feet in the water.

Becky comes back with a concerned look and lays the phone down on the table. Carla stands up and walks over to her and whispers, "What's wrong?"

Becky looks at her and then glances over at Missy in the pool then back to Carla and whispers, "The cops just got a call from one of your neighbors saying there's someone that's been riding real slow back and forth by this house. The husband went out to check and when whoever it was saw him, sped off. He didn't have time to get a plate number."

Berta sticks her head out the door and announces, "Lunch is ready."

Carla quickly says, "Missy, come on. Lunch is ready."

Becky whispers, "Perfect timing."

Missy climbs out of the pool and asks, "Miss Becky, did you see me swimming?"

"I sure did!" Becky says, smiling.

"Get dried off, honey, and go upstairs and get out of your wet bathing suit then come down and have lunch."

Missy grabs the towel her mother is handing her and quickly dries off and runs into the house.

"You think it's her, don't you?" Carla asks Becky before they enter the house.

"That would be a safe guess," she replies and steps into the house.

* * *

Carla has prayed for safety over her child and her family and that the Lord would help Rick and the officers to find Nancy and put a stop to this madness. Every night, as she listens to Missy's prayers, she is saying her own. Tonight is no different and as she crawls in her bed after a night of discussion with Rick, Becky, and her father, she once again asks God for his divine intervention. *Lord, what should I do?* Carla asks near the end of her prayer. A whisper of a voice, filled with love and compassion answers, "I love you, My child, and I want you to go to church Sunday." Carla thanks the Lord and falls soundly asleep.

* * *

During breakfast the next morning, Carla is deep in thought. Missy is her usual exuberant self and asking if she can go swimming and can they go buy her some skis so Uncle Rick can teach her to ski. Carla barely hears. "Mama! Can we go buy some skis?" Missy exclaims.

Carla is jerked out of her thoughts and answers, "What? Oh. Yes, Missy, I guess we can go buy you some skis but not today."

Becky looks at Carla as she sets her cup of coffee down and says, "You're a million miles away. Care to share?"

"May I be excused?" Missy asks.

"Yes, honey. Take your plate to Berta please."

When Missy has left the room, Carla looks at Becky and replies, "I was praying last night and the Lord said He wants me to go to church Sunday."

"We can do that." Becky responds.

"I haven't been back to church since Nancy tried to take Missy from her Sunday school room."

"Then maybe it's time you face those fears. God has a reason for telling you to go and I know I wouldn't mind going. I don't get to church as often as I'd like to."

"I'm still a member at one here. We'll go there."

"That's fine. What time is their service?" Becky asks.

"They have one at eleven. I think that's the one dad goes to. Maybe he'll go with us."

"That would be nice but I won't be riding with you. When you are out at the car getting ready to leave, I'm going to be standing in the doorway waving in my PJs and will holler 'Bye' in a hoarse voice, like I'm sick. That way if Nancy is watching and wants to follow she'll know your cousin is sick. I'll come later."

"But you won't be sitting with us, will you?" Carla asks.

"No, I won't. But I'll be where I can see you and get to you in a split second. You needn't worry. Don't look for me because you won't recognize me." Becky smiles and continues, "Missy will stay with you. If possible, sit near the center of the row so it will make things difficult for Nancy to just grab and run. There will be people she'll have to climb over if she wants to try anything."

"Okay. What about when we leave?" Carla asks hesitantly.

"Keep Missy close to you and if possible hold her hand but act as normal as possible. I'm sure people will want to stop and chat and that's okay, but try not to be out in the open away from a group of people."

"Oh Lord, why are you telling me to do this? We're putting Missy at risk." Carla says as she lowers her head into her hands.

"Carla, it's going to be all right. Nancy probably will be watching but I will be too!"

Carla looks up at her and is silent for a long moment. "I just—"

"You just what? Spit it out, Carla. What are you afraid of?"

Carla continues to look at Becky then softly says, "Becky, I don't mean any disrespect but you're a tiny little thing."

"And you don't think I can protect Missy." Becky finishes Carla's sentence.

"I'm sorry. Nancy is mean. She's the devil! She isn't big but she's bigger than you and believe me, she's strong! I found that out for myself!"

Becky bursts out laughing. "I'm sorry, Carla," she says finally. "I don't mean to laugh at your fear. Believe me when I tell you that I *can* handle Nancy, or anyone else that gets in my face."

"What do you mean?" Carla asks.

"I have a black belt in judo and I'm proficient in several of the martial arts. I have a black belt in jiu jitsu, tae kwon do, and aikido and a brown belt in krav maga. I have brought three-hundred-pound men to their knees in tears."

Carla's eyes have grown huge. "You? But you're so little!" she exclaims.

Becky bursts out laughing again. "Big surprises come in little packages, as the saying goes."

"No wonder Rick said you were going to be my new best friend! Holy cow!"

"Do you think you can quit worrying now?" Becky smiles.

"Boy, am I glad you're *my* new best friend! Yeah, just make sure it's her you tackle and not me." Carla laughs.

* * *

Sunday morning, Carla dresses for church and even with the reassurance that Becky will be there and is quite capable of dealing with Nancy should she show up, she's still nervous. Because of Becky's five-feet three-inch height and one hundred five pounds, Carla isn't one hundred percent convinced of Missy's safety. Her father won't be able to attend due to a dying patient that he wants to be near so it will be her and Missy attending. Becky has told her yet again not to look for her because she won't recognize her and to act as natural as possible.

"Missy, come on. It's time to leave," Carla hollers down the hall. "Okay, I'm coming," Missy yells back and suddenly appears at the top of the stairs. Missy has on a frilly brown skirt and white short sleeved shirt. Her hair is combed back into a ponytail that her mother helped her with earlier. Carla has decided to wear slacks and a long sleeve light cotton shirt thinking, *if I have to fight I won't get my arms scratched this time.* With the same thought, she slips her feet into a pair of shoes with flat heels.

Becky, clad in pink pajamas and a terry cloth robe, walks partway to the car with them, coughing and blowing her nose. In a hoarse voice, she bids them goodbye and watches Carla and Missy pull away. She then turns and walks quickly back in the house, closing the door firmly behind her.

Carla's mind is occupied with thoughts of what to do if Nancy shows up at church while driving. *If Becky doesn't get her, I will!* Carla thinks and suddenly gasps as four motorcycles roar past her. A woman riding on the back of one hollers, "Wooooo hoooo!" and Carla just shakes her head and pays closer attention to her driving.

Carla pulls into the church parking lot and it's filled with cars. She was hoping to be able to park close to the front door but instead has to park several rows away. *Lord protect us,* she prays as she takes Missy's hand and they hurry to the church entrance.

Several people are gathered in the narthex chatting and laughing while they wait for the nine thirty service to dismiss.

"Mama, there's Candy. Can I go talk to her?" Missy asks.

"No, honey. I want you to stay with me. Maybe you can talk to her later."

"But I haven't seen her in a long time. Please, Mama."

Carla doesn't release her daughter's hand but walks with her to where her little friend is. While the two girls laugh and talk, Carla is glancing around the lobby. She sees a few people she recognizes, waves hello, but stands steadfast next to Missy. Suddenly, the sanctuary doors are pushed open and the lobby fills with exiting parishioners. Carla grabs Missy hand and says, "We need to go, honey." Missy says goodbye to her friend and Carla leads her into the sanctuary and slides as far to the center of a row of seats as she can near the front. *She'll have a ways to go to the door if I sit here*, Carla thinks as she sits down. Missy sits next to her with a coloring book and box of crayons.

"Can we stand?" the pastor says as he approaches the podium. A large choir stands behind him dressed in their white choir robes and holding their song books ready to sing. The pastor continues after the rustle of people standing quiets. "I feel there is someone in here this morning that needs to hear the prayer the Lord gave his disciples to pray. Let's pray the Lord's prayer together this morning." He begins and all the people pray aloud with him.

> Our Father in heaven,
> Hallowed be Your name.
> Your kingdom come.
> Your will be done
> On earth as it is in heaven.
> Give us this day our daily bread.
> And forgive us our debts,
> As we forgive our debtors.
> And lead us not into temptation
> But deliver us from the evil one.
> For Yours is the kingdom and the

Power and the glory forever. Amen.

Carla has tears streaming down her face as she ends the prayer. *Lord, please do protect us from the evil one. Forgive me, Lord, but I can't forgive Nancy! I know I should but I just can't, not right now.*

"Why are you crying?" Missy asks, looking up at her mother.

Carla glances down at her and gives her a weak smile. "I'm okay, honey."

The choir begins singing "Jesus is Mine" and all join in and three more praise and worship songs are sung.

"You may be seated," the pastor says at the end of the last song. When everyone is settled, the pastor says a hardy "Good morning" and the congregation shouts, "Good morning."

"Oh what a beautiful day it is to be in the house of the Lord!" The pastor exclaims.

"Amen" is heard near the side wall.

"We have just prayed the Lord's Prayer and I think there's more than one of us today that needs to hear this message. The Lord has put a couple of things on my heart to talk about this morning. Let's start with Romans 2:5." He waits as people turn to the scripture in their Bibles.

"Lord, I ask that you bless the reading of your word this morning and give me your words for your sheep. Amen," the pastor prays then continues, "Beginning in verse five. 'But in accordance with your hardness and your impenitent heart you are treasuring up for yourself wrath in the day of wrath and revelation of the righteous judgment of God,' verse six, 'who will render to each one according to his deeds…' Let's stop there. What's an impenitent heart?" He asks the congregation. No one speaks. The pastor continues, "Impenitent means that you've committed a sin and you're not sorry for it. You know you have sinned, you've done it with no regret whatsoever, you don't feel any shame about what you did, and you haven't and won't repent of it! It's someone whose heart is hardened."

Carla is looking down at her hands.

"What did we just read? 'God will give to each person according to what he has done.' If you have committed sin, and we all do, we must repent of that sin. God forgives us when we confess the sin we committed, we repent of it, and that wipes it off the slate." The pastor takes a sip of water, clears his throat, and continues, "Now, what about when someone sins against you? You've done nothing wrong yet someone tries to harm you or gossips about you or says something ugly to you?" Carla is listening intently. "We just prayed asking the Lord Jesus to forgive those who trespass against us and to forgive us our trespasses. Am I right? Did we not just pray that?" Heads are nodding yes and a few have spoken out, "Yes!"

The pastor looks out over the congregation and softly says, "Then *we* must forgive others or God will not forgive us. Mathew 6:15 says, 'But if you do not forgive men their trespasses, neither will your heavenly Father forgive your trespasses.' Un-forgiveness is a sin! We reap what we sow. If we sow forgiveness, we will reap forgiveness. If we sow un-forgiveness, we reap un-forgiveness. We must all be careful that we do not allow our hearts to become hardened because with a hardened heart we are unable to forgive others."

Carla begins feeling quite uncomfortable while listening. Glancing down, she sees Missy busy coloring a picture of a lamb. *You're really beating me over the head with this, aren't you, Lord?* she thinks and tries to turn her attention back to the pastor but her mind is wandering and she's not hearing what he's saying.

"Let's pray," the pastor says in closing. During the offering, Carla wants to leave but remembers Becky said to not be out in the open if possible so she sits through the offering and joins in the singing and soon they're dismissed.

While Carla drives home, she's deep in thought about what the pastor said. She's struggling with what he said about God not forgiving her because she won't forgive Nancy. *Lord, I just can't! I can't forgive the devil and she's the devil as far as I'm concerned.*

She tried to kidnap my baby and is still trying to! How can I forgive someone that evil?

"Mama, can we go buy my skis now?" Missy asks, interrupting her thoughts.

"I don't know if the sporting goods store is open today. Let's go home and have some lunch and I can call and see. If they're open then we can go. Okay?"

Missy pumps her arm and hollers, "Yes!"

Missy and Carla are home about thirty minutes when she hears a motorcycle pull into the driveway. She peeks out her bedroom window and sees a teenage looking girl climbing off the back of a big Harley motorcycle. The girl gives the big burly looking man a high five and yells thanks and heads for the front door. *Who in the world can that be?* Carla thinks as she rushes downstairs expecting to hear the doorbell. The door opens and suddenly she's facing, what she thought was a young girl, Becky grinning broadly and snapping her chewing gun dramatically.

"What in the world?" Carla says as she stands staring at Becky.

Becky bursts out laughing and twirls around in a circle. "How do you like my disguise?" she laughs.

Carla is dumbfounded. Becky is wearing skintight black leather pants, a tight halter top with a leather jacket open down the front, black leather boots, lots of makeup, large round sunglasses cover most of her face, and her long hair pulled back in a ponytail at the nape of her neck.

"You went to church like that?" Carla exclaims.

"Sure. Didn't you see the motorcycles roar past you when you were driving?" Becky grins.

"Oh my gosh! That was you?"

"Yep! I had to get there before you did! I was watching you when you parked and walked in."

"I didn't see any motorcycle guys in church." Carla says.

"You had two sitting two rows behind you and the rest of us was scattered. All cops." Carla is still flabbergasted at Becky's appearance.

Becky grins and says, "I told you not to worry."

Carla shakes her head in wonder and turns to walk back toward the kitchen with Becky following behind snapping her gum and laughing. "I love this job!" Becky exclaims.

Missy comes tearing down the hall and when she sees Becky she skids to a sudden stop. Her eyes are big and she says, "Whose that?"

Becky bursts out laughing again and says, "It's me, Becky."

Missy stands looking at her and tilts her head to the side and says, "Miss Becky? Cool!"

Becky runs upstairs to change clothes and Missy and Carla go to the kitchen and sit at the table waiting for Becky to return before diving into the beef stew and cornbread Berta has ready for them.

"Are you going to call the store?" Missy asks.

"Yes, honey. I'm going to call the store."

"Now?" Missy asks.

"As soon as we're done eating."

Becky comes in and sits down dressed in jeans and a T-shirt. All the makeup has been washed off.

"Mama, can I have some black pants like Miss Becky had on?"

"No!" Carla says sternly. Becky bursts out laughing.

Missy says, "But—"

Carla looks at her sternly, "Don't even go there!"

Missy stays quiet.

* * *

Becky steps out of Carla's car and helps Missy out from the backseat while holding a tissue and coughing. "Just in case Nancy is around she has to continue to think I'm your sick cousin," Becky had explained as they pulled into Kirk's Sporting Goods

Store. Missy runs to the door and tries to open it. Struggling to pull the heavy glass door open, she looks to Becky for help. The three enter the store and Becky wanders off to the right as Carla and Missy stand looking around the store trying to see where water skis are. A man walks up and says, "Can I help you find something?"

"We're looking for kids' water skis. Do you have any?" Carla replies.

"Oh, sure. Follow me. They're right back here."

As they walk toward the rear of the store he smiles at Missy and says, "So, are you the one these skis are for?"

Missy claps her hands together and answers excitedly, "Yes. My Uncle Rick is going to teach me to ski."

"Oh, I'll bet you'll be good at it too," the salesman says. "Here we are. As you can see, there's a good selection," and stops in front of a wall with various size skis hanging.

"I'll let you look while I help this other customer," he says when he hears the door chime. He walks back toward the front of the store.

Missy spots a pair with flowers on them immediately and runs over and stands in front of them. "I want these!" she exclaims.

Becky saunders over to where they're standing.

"Look, Miss Becky, I'm going to get these." Missy exclaims.

Becky is watching a woman who is looking at jackets. She quickly looks at Missy and says, "Oh, those are pretty," and turns her attention back to the woman who has now moved closer thumbing through shirts.

The salesman approaches the woman and asks if he can help her and Becky hears her say, "No thanks. I'm just looking."

The salesman walks back to Carla and Missy and asks, "Have you made up your minds?" Missy points again to the flower-designed skis and says, "I want those."

The salesman takes them down from the wall and places them on the floor. Holding one a little off the floor, he tells Missy to slide her foot in the cup to make sure it's the right fit. She removes her tennis shoe and does.

Looking up at her mother, she squeals, "They fit, Mama! Can I have them?"

Carla laughs and says, "Yes, you can have them, honey."

Missy removes her foot, and while she's putting her tennis shoe back on, the salesman says, "I'll just take them to the counter so you can look around."

Becky steps in front of Missy as the suspicious woman moves closer. Three other customers have entered and as Carla takes Missy's hand and leads her toward the counter, Missy says, "Can I have a life jacket too?"

"You already have one," Carla replies. Carla is paying no attention to Becky or the other customers while she focuses on paying for the skis. Becky has stayed near but is quiet other than coughing and blowing her nose on occasion.

On the way home, Becky is quiet as Missy chatters excitedly about learning to ski and asking about when she can learn? Will Carla call Uncle Rick to come teach her? A dozen other questions follow.

Carla looks at Becky and finally says, "You're awfully quiet."

Becky smiles and says, "We can't get a word in edgewise with the little chatterbox back there."

Carla laughs and says, "Yeah and that's how it's going to be until she can get her little fanny on those skis."

Becky just smiles and looks out the window. Carla pulls in the driveway and sees Rick's truck parked beside the house. "Oh, Rick's here," she says. "I wasn't expecting to see him today," she says as she pulls alongside his truck.

Missy jumps out of the car and runs full speed around the house, past the pool, and into the house hollering, "Uncle Rick, come see. I got some skis."

Carla and Becky burst out laughing and Carla says, "See what I mean."

Carla reaches into the trunk and retrieves the skis while Becky walks toward the back patio. When Becky enters the house, Missy is telling Rick all about her new skis and asking if he'll teach her how to ski today.

Rick looks up at Becky as she enters and says, "Hi. How are things going?"

Becky glances at Missy then to Rick. "Good. We'll talk," she says and leaves the room.

Rick says hi to Carla when she enters then stands staring at the hall where Becky went. Carla looks at him and says, "Hi, I didn't expect to see you here today." Rick doesn't answer her and immediately turns his attention to Missy who is asking him again if she can learn to ski today. "Why don't you go put your suit on while I talk to Becky," He says. Missy shouts okay and starts to run upstairs. Rick hollers, "Missy, I'll be down at the boat in a minute."

Carla looks at him and asks, "Is everything all right?"

"Yeah, I just need to talk to Becky for a minute. Is it okay if I go up to her room?"

Concern shows on Carla's face as she replies, "Sure."

Rick gently knocks on Becky's bedroom door and says, "Becky, its Rick. Can I come in?"

"Sure," she replies.

He opens the door slowly and enters. She's sitting on the edge of her bed studying a picture. Becky looks up at him and says, "It was her. She was at the sporting goods store when we were there to get Missy skis," and hands Rick the picture. The computerized picture shows a woman with brown curly hair and wearing bifocal glasses. She looks nothing like the redheaded woman on the beach.

"You're sure?" Rick asks.

"Positive." Becky replies.

"What made you think it was her when you saw her in the store?"

"I've memorized these pictures. I see her in my sleep and as soon as she walked into the store I knew it was her."

"Did she do anything?"

"No. She pretended to be shopping and would ease her way closer to where Missy was but stopped when I walked over to them."

"Do you think she made you?"

"No. She thinks I'm the sick cousin."

"Sick?"

"Yeah. When they left for church this morning I was coughing and blowing my nose beside the car in case she was watching. Which I think she was from just a gut feeling I got."

"Okay. I better get downstairs or Missy will be having fits." Rick says as he runs his hand through his hair.

"You're going to teach her to ski now?" Becky asks, grinning.

"Oh yeah or we'll never hear the end of it." He laughs and leaves the room.

* * *

Missy is running across the lawn toward the boat while Carla follows behind carrying Missy's new skis and Becky follows her. Missy is in her ruffled bikini and Carla and Becky are wearing shorts and a tank top. Rick grabs a pair of shorts out of his truck and hollers, "I'll be there in a minute," and goes to change clothes.

Carla is behind the wheel in the boat, Becky is sitting facing the back watching as Rick leans behind Missy with his hands on her shoulders steadying her as she squats in the water with her new ski tips pointing skyward. The boat engine is idling. Rick gives Missy a couple of pointers then asks, "Are you ready?" She nods yes and Rick yells, "Hit it." Carla moves the throttle forward and suddenly Missy flies straight up in the air, shooting out of her skis and lands face first in the water a few feet away.

Rick yells, "Not so fast! Barely move it," and wades out to help Missy who's laughing.

Rick gathers up Missy and the skis and helps her put her skis back on while Carla speeds off into a three hundred sixty-five degree turn and slowly comes to a stop where she was. Becky has gathered the rope and tosses it out to Rick. Missy is once again in position and holding tightly to the rope handle. Rick is leaning over, holding her steady and before Rick can say anything, she yells, "Hit it!" Rick bursts out laughing, plops down on his back in the water, and throws water over Missy who is bobbing in the water and waiting for the boat to move forward. Carla and Becky are laughing so hard they have tears streaming down their faces.

Rick rises up out of the water still laughing and when he gets his laughter under control, he yells, "You have to go slow, Carla. Barely move the throttle forward."

Carla is still laughing and yells, "Okay."

Missy and Rick are in position. Missy yells, "Hit it," and even though Carla bursts out laughing again she slowly drives forward watching Missy. Rick runs a few feet splashing behind Missy and let's go of her. Missy screams as she slides across the water a few yards then falls. Carla, Rick, and Becky are yelling praises as Missy bobs in the water laughing.

"Did you see me, Mama?" She yells. "I was skiing!"

Carla slowly circles and Rick swims out to Missy.

"Did you see me, Uncle Rick?" Missy asks excitedly.

"I sure did. Good job! Let's try it again."

Several more attempts are made and finally Missy is scooting across the water, screaming, "Mama, look, I'm skiing!"

Becky is standing in the back of the boat clapping and hooting, "Way to go, Missy." Missy falls and is picked up and pulled into the boat. "Can I go again?" Missy asks even though it's obvious she's tired.

"How about we rest for a bit?" Carla replies.

"Can we ride though?" Missy asks as she plops down on the seat next to Carla. Becky walks forward and stepping between the seats, she picks Missy up, sits down, and places Missy on her lap. Carla looks over at them and smiles broadly. "Hold on," and shoves the throttle forward causing the boat to shoot across the water. Missy bursts out laughing. Rick has changed back into his jeans and T-shirt by the time the women pull up to the dock. They all help cover the boat, store the skis, and walk back to the house with Missy chattering a mile a minute.

Chapter 8

Rick has invited Larry to the lake while talking to him on the phone about the latest event where Nancy was in the sporting goods store. "I'd love to, Rick! Are you sure? I don't want to make a nuisance out of myself."

"Hey, you're no nuisance. I really enjoy having you. I don't get to get out on the lake as often as I'd like and its nice having a friend to do it with." Rick replies.

"I appreciate that. You know I love to ski, so sure, I'll be there Saturday morning early."

"Make it about nine. That will give me time to gas up the boat and be ready to go."

"That sounds good. I'll see you then. Oh, can I bring anything, maybe something for lunch?" Larry asks.

"Nah. Berta is going to be gone this week visiting family so we're going to grill."

"Then I'll bring some beer."

"Nah, that's okay. We have plenty to drink but thanks anyway. Just show up. There'll be plenty of food and drinks." Rick replies.

"Okay, I'll see you Saturday then. How's Carla?"

"She's fine. She doesn't know Nancy was in the store so don't say anything."

"Okay, I won't. See ya later. Bye."

* * *

Over the past week and a half, Carla, Missy, and Becky have gone to the grocery store and even a movie with no incidents with Nancy. Becky is a little surprised, having fully expected to see her somewhere as they shopped or sat in the theater. Becky knew it wouldn't look normal for Missy and Carla to be at the movie without her, being the "visiting cousin," so she sat through the movie with them but paid little attention to it. Her "Nancy antenna," as she calls it, was on high alert.

* * *

On Friday morning, Carla is sitting across the table from her father having coffee when he asks her, "What are your plans for today?"

"I need to get Missy some clothes. She starts school next month so I thought we'd go to North Point Mall and do some shopping."

"Becky's going with you, I hope!" her Dad says emphatically.

Carla grins and says, "Of course."

"Good!"

"She's really nice. I really like her and Missy does too. I can't believe she has all those black belts and she's so tiny!" Carla laughs.

"Rick told me she is very highly trained and believe me, in this case, I'm very glad she is!"

"Oh me too. It's just hard to look at her and try to visualize her 'bringing down three hundred-pound men.'" Carla laughs.

"What little I know about martial arts, it isn't about size so it wouldn't surprise me that she can. I just hope we don't have to see her in action."

Carla laughs. "Yeah, me too."

Becky walks into the room. "Good morning. Is the coffee still hot?"

"Yes. Help yourself," Carla says.

"Good morning, Becky. Did you sleep well?" Dr. Anderson asks.

"Yes, thank you." *Not much.* She replies. She sits down at the table and looks at Carla, "So, what's the plans for today?"

"If you don't mind, I'd like to do some shopping. Missy starts school next month and needs school clothes."

"I don't mind at all! Sounds like fun. Where we going?"

Dr. Anderson stands up and says, "Excuse me for interrupting but I better get on the stick. Sick people are waiting." He smiles.

Carla stands up and gives him a kiss on the cheek. "Have a good day, Dad. We'll see you when you get home."

"Bye, Dr. Anderson," Becky says and he walks out of the room.

"I really like your dad. He seems really nice and I'll bet he's good with his patients too," Becky says, picking up her coffee and blowing gently into it to cool it down.

Carla smiles. "Thanks. He is good with his patients. They all seem to love him and he even prays with some of them if they want him to."

"Wow. That's great."

"Oh, to answer your question, we're going to North Point Mall. Is that okay? Do you think we should go somewhere else?"

"Oh, that's fine. What time do you want to leave? I'll go change clothes." Becky takes another sip of her coffee.

Carla starts laughing.

"What? What's so funny?" Becky asks.

"Are you going in disguise this time? I can't wait to see what you come up with." Carla laughs.

Becky joins in laughing, shaking her head no, then says, "I'm your cousin, remember? I need to be shopping with you and Missy and having a good time."

"Oh, okay. I need to call April. She's left two messages and I just haven't been able to get back to her. How about we leave about eleven?"

"That sounds good. It will give me some time to make some phone calls. Just holler when you're ready." Becky places her coffee cup in the dishwasher and goes upstairs.

* * *

Carla takes the cordless phone out onto the patio by the pool and a cup of coffee and sits down on one of the chaise lounges. Dialing the phone she takes a sip of her coffee as the phone rings.

"Hello!"

"Hi, April. You sound out of breath. It's Carla."

"Oh, hi. I was outside and didn't hear it ringing right away," she replies, panting. "I came running in here. How are you? I've called a couple of times, is everything okay?"

"Yes. Everything is fine. I'm sorry we've just been pretty busy and I wasn't able to get back to you until now. How are you? How are Alex and Jenny?"

"Oh, we're all fine. Alex is still watching your house. He goes every day and checks on it."

"Oh, that's so nice of him. Be sure to tell him I said thanks," Carla replies appreciatively.

"So what's going on with that crazy woman? Is she still hanging around?"

Carla still hasn't been told Nancy was at the Sporting Goods store so she says, "Surprisingly everything has been quiet. No more notes and we haven't seen her."

"Hmmm. That doesn't sound right. If she's so determined, I'm sure she's around someplace. Is the policewoman still with you? I hope!" April asks.

"Yes, she's still here. I don't know April, maybe Nancy has given up."

April is quiet for a long moment.

"You don't think so, do you?" Carla states.

"Well, she just seems so determined. I mean she did hunt you down all the way into Atlanta. I can't imagine someone that determined to just give up."

"Well, I can hope," Carla says wanting to end that part of the conversation.

"How's Missy?" April asks.

"She's doing great! We saw her psychiatrist yesterday and she feels Missy doesn't need to come back unless something happens. It was great news, believe me!"

"That's wonderful! I'm so happy she's been able to overcome her fears."

"She's still leery of redheaded women but seems to be able to control it. She doesn't freak out now," Carla says.

"That's just great! I'm so glad. So do you have any idea when you might be coming home?"

"Dad is insistent that we stay until Nancy is caught. I'm ready to come home now! You know Missy starts school pretty soon and I want her to go to school there."

"Are they any closer to catching her? I mean, you can't stay there forever. Well you can, but I hope you don't," April says.

"Oh I'm coming home, believe me. I want my little house and the sound of those seagulls and the smell of sea air." Tears begin to form in Carla's eyes.

April can hear in Carla's voice she's beginning to get upset so changes the subject. "So what have you been doing that's keeping you so busy, girlfriend?" She laughs.

"Oh, I didn't tell you, Missy is learning to water ski!"

"Really? That's got to be fun to watch." April laughs.

Carla begins telling April all about Rick having Larry over for skiing, Missy wanting to learn, going to buy her skis, and her day of learning. The women are laughing and talking when Missy steps out onto the patio and asks if she can go swimming. "Hold on a sec, April."

"Honey, we're going to go shopping in a little bit so why don't you find something else to do until then?" Carla says.

"But can't I swim until we leave?" Missy asks, disappointed.

"No. We're going to be leaving soon. Are there some cartoons on TV that you want to watch?"

"Oh okay." Missy turns and slowly walks back into the house.

"I'm sorry, April. Missy is bored and wants to go swimming. I better let you go. We need to get to our shopping."

"Oh okay. Have fun." April says. She's silent for a moment then says, "I miss you, Carla. I wish you could come home. Jenny asks all the time when Missy is coming home. We all just miss the heck out of you."

"I miss you all too. Hopefully it won't be long now. Give Jenny a kiss for me."

"You do the same for Missy. I'll talk to you later. Bye." April hangs up and Carla slowly lowers the phone to her lap.

* * *

Carla, Missy, and Becky walk through the mall chatting and laughing with their arms filled with packages. They had their lunch in the food court and then began hitting the stores.

"Oh that's so cute on you!" Carla says as Missy models yet another dress. "Do you like it honey?" she asks Missy.

"Yes, but I like the other one too." She replies, grinning.

"Here, I found this skirt. Try it on." Carla says, handing Missy a skirt clasped to a hanger."

"Come with me," Missy says, taking the skirt.

Becky says with an exaggeration in her tone, "What? You don't like me waiting by the door?"

Missy looks at her and says, "Mama can wait too."

"Honey, I'm looking for other clothes for you to try. Go with Becky. That's the last one I think but I want to look one more time before you get dressed."

"Okay," and she and Becky go back into the dressing room.

Carla had originally planned to go in with her but Becky said, "Let me. You stay with the bags." The way Becky said it and the tone of her voice caused Carla to tell Missy she'd wait and she could model her clothes for her and that was how it was throughout their shopping for clothes.

Becky has had her "Nancy antenna" on the whole time and while she, Carla, and Missy are looking in a store window, she sees Nancy in the reflection. She makes no move to turn around or to alert Carla. They walk away from the window and as they stroll on, Missy is chattering away. In store windows, Becky can see Nancy stopping at various windows on the other side of the aisle but definitely following them. Becky has worn jeans with a light jacket that covers her hips. She hasn't told Carla or let on in any way that she has her set of handcuffs tucked in the back of her jeans waist band.

Last night, she couldn't sleep. She kept sensing that today was the day she would be arresting Nancy. She had no idea what Carla's plans were but just couldn't shake the feeling that today is the day. After tossing and turning most of the night, she prays asking God to guide her and to help her protect Missy and Carla and finally went to sleep about four.

* * *

Carla stops in front of another display window and turns to Missy. "I think that's enough for today. If we think of anything else we can come back tomorrow. What do you think, Becky?" She asks, turning to Becky. Becky has stepped behind Missy.

"Ah, oh yeah. That's fine with me. I'm ready to leave if you are," Becky says. Her mind is strictly on keeping an eye out for any change in movement that Nancy may make.

"Okay, let's head to the car," Carla states and they turn and begin heading for the exit.

* * *

Becky steps to the side placing Missy in between her and Carla.

Later that same night, Missy is modeling all of her new dresses, pants, shoes, skirts, and tops for Pa-pa. "Boy, did you make out like a bandit," he says, grinning. Carla is sitting at the table watching Missy.

Becky has gone outside. She's walking and talking to Rick on her cell phone. "No, we hadn't seen her in almost two weeks. I'm wondering why and suddenly she shows up at the mall."

She listens and suddenly exclaims, "What?"

"She's been stalking another kid," Rick repeats. "From the description given, the kid is Missy's age and has the same hair color and so on. It's almost like she's her twin."

"You've got to be kidding! What's with this woman?"

"I don't know but it isn't good, that's for sure."

"So what happened? Is she now stalking two kids?"

"I don't think so. It turns out the father of the other kid is a cop and he must have scared her pretty bad."

"How?" Becky asks as she continues to walk along the street.

"She made the mistake of trying to peek in the kid's window and Daddy came out shooting."

Becky starts laughing, "I'll bet that made her wet her pants!"

"He hollered 'Police!' but she took off."

"Did he really shoot at her?" Becky asks laughing.

"No, I just added that for a little spice," Rick replies, laughing.

"So now she's back trying to get Missy."

"Yep! Listen, I better go. I'll see you tomorrow. Larry's coming and we're going to go buzzing around the lake."

"Not without Missy you won't," Becky laughs.

Rick laughs and says, "Yeah, I know. The kid is a fish!" He gets serious and continues, "Listen, Becky, stay on your toes. I think Nancy is getting desperate and she'll do anything now."

"I agree. I'll see ya tomorrow."

"Okay. Bye."

* * *

Saturday morning, the house is abuzz. Carla is preparing the ribs, chicken, and steaks for grilling later in the day. Becky is washing potatoes, carrots, and zucchini squash for placing in a steam bag for the grill. Rick is preparing the boat with Missy standing on the dock asking if she can water ski.

"Let's wait and see what Larry wants to do," Rick answers her.

"But he won't mind," Missy states confidently.

"Let's wait and see. Can you hand me that life jacket?"

Missy reaches down and picks up a life jacket off the dock that Rick placed there while cleaning debris out of the boat. "But I know he won't mind. He's nice," Missy insists, handing Rick the life jacket.

"Honey, why don't you go help your mom and Becky. They could really use some help and I'm about done here. Thank you for helping me." Rick says, trying to cover the exasperation he's feeling.

"But I'm helping you, Uncle Rick."

"I know you are and you've been a really big help but I'm all done now."

"Okay. But will you ask Mr. Larry if I can ski?"

"Yes. I'll ask him."

"Okay. Thank you," Missy says happily then turns and runs to the house.

Lord have mercy when that child sets her mind to something! Rick thinks as he stores the oars.

Rick turns when he hears a car pull into the driveway and stop beside his truck. He sees Larry stepping out of his car. "I'm down here," Rick yells to Larry. Larry waves and starts walking toward the boat. When he clears the side of the house, Missy sees him and jumps up from the chaise lounge and runs to him.

"Hi, Mr. Larry."

"Hey, Missy. How are you?" Larry smiles down at her as she runs up beside him.

"Are you going to water ski with Uncle Rick?"

"I sure hope so. Why?"

"Uncle Rick teached me to water ski! Did you know that?"

"No! Wow. That's pretty great."

"Can I water ski with you?" she asks, trying to keep up with his long strides.

"Oh, I don't know about that. We better talk to your mom and Uncle Rick."

"Uncle Rick said he would ask you but I'm asking first."

Larry laughs. "Hey Rick." He reaches out to shake Rick's hand. "How are you? Thanks again for inviting me."

"Are you going to ask him, Uncle Rick?" Missy says, staring at Rick intently.

Rick winks at Larry and says, "Ask him what?"

Missy slams her hands on her hips and looks at him with piercing eyes. "About skiing with him!"

"Whoa, we didn't say anything about skiing *with* him," Rick says.

"Yes, we did!" Missy says angrily.

Rick kneels down and takes her by the shoulders looking into her eyes. "Missy, if you're going to talk like that you won't be riding or skiing today. Now apologize to Mr. Larry for being rude and go on and help your mother."

Missy's eyes fill with tears. Rick glances up at Larry who stands quietly watching.

Missy whispers, "I'm sorry," and turns and runs to the house crying.

"Sorry about that," Rick says to Larry when he stands up.

"Did you really teach her to ski?" Larry asks.

"Yeah and I'm almost sorry I did. She's a natural but she's been driving me crazy since I got here this morning about skiing."

Larry laughs and says, "I don't mind letting her ski a little if you don't."

"It isn't that. She has to learn she can't keep badgering people about it and get mad when she doesn't get her way," Rick says.

"Yeah, I guess you're right. What can I do to help?" Larry asks.

"Come on. Let's go for a ride," and walks over to the boat and starts untying it. He and Larry step in and Larry gives it a shove away from the side of the dock as Rick starts the engine. Slowly, Rick backs the boat out of the slip and when clear, steers it around, facing the open water and shoves the throttle all the way forward. The engine roars and they speed off across the lake.

Larry looks over at him and can see Rick is angry. "What's wrong, buddy?" Larry shouts. "She couldn't have gotten to you that bad, could she?"

Rick slows the boat down to a speed where they don't have to shout to hear each other and says, "Oh, it's not Missy."

"Then what's got your feathers stirred up?" Larry asks.

Rick starts telling him about Nancy and how she started stalking another kid and Becky spotting her following them at the mall. The more he says, the madder he gets. He's throwing in curse words and finally slams his hand against the boat's steering wheel. "We gotta get the—" and he stops talking. Pulling slowly into a quiet cove, he and Larry sit in the gently rocking boat and talk and talk and talk.

* * *

Missy has told her mother that Uncle Rick won't let her ski and wouldn't even ask Mr. Larry like he said he would and ran to her room crying. Carla looked at Becky, shrugged her shoulders, and went back to what she was doing.

* * *

Rick and Larry are gone for about an hour and a half. When Rick has wound down from his anger at all that's been happening with Missy being stalked, they cruise across the lake heading back to the dock. "I just don't know how much more of this Carla can take and she doesn't even know about the last two sightings." Rick says.

"It sounds like Nancy is getting pretty desperate. I wonder why she started stalking the other child?" Larry states.

"I don't know but I think she's stepped into being pretty dangerous now. We have to catch this woman and we have to catch her in the act. A stalking charge is a slap on the wrist. Attempted kidnapping holds a whole lot more weight, as you know," Rick says.

"Yeah, it does but without setting her up, how are you going to catch her in the act? You don't know when she's going to actually try to grab her."

"Becky felt strongly that she was going to nab her at the mall but then Carla suddenly decided to leave. I think if they had stayed a while longer Nancy would have tried to grab her. Oh heck, I can't keep worrying about this. I've got cases coming out my ears to investigate and this thing is driving me nuts. I can't seem to focus on anything else," Rick says as he slowly slides the boat up on the beach.

"That's understandable. She's your niece. Of course it's going to consume you. You'll get her, Rick. She'll try again and you have Becky who will be right there when she does."

"Yeah. You're right." Rick steps out of the boat and continues, "Come on. Let's go to the house. I guess I better see how much damage I did to Missy's ego."

Becky and Carla are sitting on the patio with cold drinks when Rick and Larry walk up. "Did you have a good ride?" Becky asks.

"Yeah, we did. The lake's pretty calm right now. I guess it's too early, there weren't many boats out there this morning," Rick answers then asks Carla, "Where's Missy?"

"She's in her room. What'd you do? She came tearing in here crying and saying something about you wouldn't let her ski," Carla says.

"She got mad and I told her she was being rude and if she continued she wouldn't ride or ski today. She's not going to talk like that to me or my friends," Rick states flatly.

"Oh! Okay. She's been driving everyone nuts with wanting to ski. Even when you're not here she wants me to take her out in the boat. I won't do it," Carla replies.

"I think I need to go talk to her and maybe get some things straight. She can't keep doing this," Rick says.

Carla looks at Larry and says, "Larry, pull up a chair and join the drama." She laughs. "Would you like something to drink?"

"I'll have some ice tea if you have it," Larry says as he sits down at the table.

"I'm going to go talk to Missy. I'll be right back. Make yourself comfortable, Larry," Rick says, pulling open the sliding glass doors.

The two women and Larry sit out by the pool chatting and are laughing when Missy comes tearing out the door wearing her ruffled bikini. "Uncle Rick said I can ski now." She shouts and runs toward the water. Rick steps out a moment later laughing and says, "Give the kid an inch and she'll take a mile."

"Do I need to put my suit on?" Carla asks.

"You have stuff here to do, don't you? I thought if Becky wants to spot then Larry can drive the boat and I'll help Missy." Rick says, watching Missy standing at the water's edge.

"I know how to ski, Rick, if you want to drive I can help Missy." Becky says.

Carla smiles and says, "Why don't we all go. Everything is ready for the grill when we're ready."

"Oh okay," Rick replies and turns to Larry, "Got your ski and trunks?"

Larry stands up and says, "In the car. I'll go get them."

"Come on, Becky, let's change." Carla says and everyone disperses to change.

* * *

Carla is driving the boat with Larry in the seat beside her and Becky acting as spotter. Rick is behind Missy asking her if she remembers what to do as Missy places her feet in the ski cups and Rick holds the ski rope handle.

"Ah huh," Missy answers, concentrating on staying erect. She takes the handle from Rick and leans back a little, getting her "takeoff" position just right. Suddenly she shouts, "Hit it!" and Carla moves the boat forward slowly. Missy pops out of the water and scoots across the glassy surface. Larry is watching and exclaims, "Wow. She is a natural!" Carla has to be very careful not to go too fast even when Missy shouts, "Faster, Mama." Rick stands on the shore watching and the further Missy goes without falling, the more he's amazed. *She really is a natural*, Rick thinks and sits down on the edge of the dock waiting for them to return.

Missy falls and Becky shouts, "She's down," and raises an arm in the air, alerting other boaters that a skier is in the water. Carla makes the turn and glides up beside Missy. The three in the boat are clapping and praising her for going so far without falling.

Carla asks, "Are you ready to come in?"

"No! I wanna go some more! Did you see how far I went?"

"Okay. Put your skis on." Carla replies.

Missy bobs in the water and finally gets her skis back on and takes hold of the rope handle. "Go faster this time, Mama." They all laugh as Carla inches the boat forward.

Missy has skied for almost an hour when she finally admits to being tired and they return to shore where Rick is stretched out in the sun asleep. He wakes up at the sound of the boat motor as they approach the sandy beach. Missy is the first to jump out hollering, "Did you see me, Uncle Rick? Did you see how good I did? I only fell four times."

Rick sits up and says, "You're a born natural, kiddo. You did really good. In no time you'll not be falling at all."

Rick looks at Larry and asks, "You ready to tear up the lake?"

Larry grins and says, "Ready as I'll ever be," and takes his T-shirt off. Carla can't help but notice the slender waist line, dark diamond shaped tuft of chest hair, and dimples as he smiles. Becky is watching her looking at Larry and thinking, *Hmmm. That's interesting,* but says nothing.

* * *

Carla and Missy stay ashore while Rick, Larry, and Becky head out onto the lake. Carla has told Missy she needs to rest and can go again when they get back.

"I can use your help in the kitchen right now," Carla says to Missy as they walk to the house.

"But I wanna ski some more," Missy starts to pout.

Carla stops and kneels down in front of her. "Did Uncle Rick talk to you this morning? Carla asks.

Missy looks down at the ground and whispers, "Yes."

"What did he tell you?"

"He said if I quit asking all the time then I'll get to ski more. That I'm making a nus- nus—"

"Nuisance?"

"Yes, out of myself and it isn't very nice."

Carla tries to keep from grinning and asks, "Do you know what that means?"

"Yes."

"What does it mean?" Carla asks gently.

"A pest!" she answers emphatically.

Carla bursts out laughing and stands up. "Okay and we don't want to be a pest now, do we?"

Missy doesn't answer and runs to open the sliding glass doors.

The day is spent skiing, riding out to a quiet cove, and lounging on the sandy beach in the warm sunshine. Missy has been allowed to ski some more, much to her delight. Carla and Becky have both skied also, but only for a short time. Carla tired quickly and Becky didn't want to be a showoff. Carla drove the boat while

Rick and Larry skied together, cutting back and forth across the wakes and jumping them. Missy insisted on being the spotter so Becky sat next to her holding onto her life jacket strap so she wouldn't fly out of the boat when they bounced across wakes and made turns. In order to pull the two men together, higher speeds were required and the one time Rick fell, Missy was quick to yell, "He's down! Uncle Rick is down!" and would raise her arm to notify other boaters. Becky and Carla would burst out laughing and Becky would stand next to Missy with her arm raised so others could see her.

* * *

Late in the day, the grill is fired up and they all sit at the long patio table by the pool, savoring the fine food and talking and laughing. Missy has curled up on a chaise lounge and is sound asleep.

Larry looks over at her and smiles, "Carla, I think I've fallen in love with your little girl."

Carla laughs, glances at Missy, and says, "It's easy to do." Then she speaks to Rick. "Whatever you said to her this morning, Rick, must have sunk in. She's been really good about not pestering us about skiing today."

Rick smiles, leans back in the chaise lounge, and replies, "Ya, just have to know what to say." They all laugh.

Becky begins cleaning off the table and Rick stands up. "I'll help."

Carla starts to stand and Rick says, "You, sister, stay put! You fixed all this. Becky and I can get it."

Larry looks at Carla and says, "You want to join me down by the water?"

She glances at Missy then says, "Sure."

They walk down to the water's edge and Larry stands looking out over the lake. "It's really nice of Rick to invite me out. I love coming out here. It's beautiful."

Carla looks up at him. "You two have been friends for a long time. He enjoys your company."

"Yeah, we have. It's a darn shame we haven't seen each other but a few times these past few years. I knew when you got married and when Rick became a detective but somehow the time just slipped away and Rick and I kind of lost touch."

Larry sits down on the sand and pats the sand next to him indicating for Carla to join him. She does and they spend the time talking and catching up on the years gone by. Becky and Rick sit on the patio after cleaning up the kitchen and Becky asks, "Do you think they'll become an item?" as she watches them on the beach.

Rick glances at her and replies, "I don't know. I'm not sure Carla's ready to start dating again."

"He seems like a really nice guy and from seeing how he looks at her, he's definitely got a thing for her."

"He had a really big crush on her in high school. He didn't think anyone knew but it was pretty obvious."

"It looks like he still does. He's never married?" Becky asks.

"I don't think so. We lost touch for a few years. I know he's not married now or even dating." Rick says and picks up his glass of tea.

"Well, maybe that will change now," Becky replies while making herself more comfortable on the chaise lounge.

Their conversation turns to police work and when Larry and Carla stroll up they change the subject.

"Listen I better get going," Larry says. "This has been a fantastic day! Thanks, buddy. How many rooms did you say your dad has here?" He laughs, "I may just rent one from him."

Rick laughs and replies, "It's been a lot of fun. We really enjoyed having you. Just give me a call. You're welcome any time."

"Carla, Becky, it's been great fun! Thanks for all the good food. I haven't pigged out like that in a long time."

Both women answer, "Your welcome," at the same time. Everyone says goodbye and Rick walks Larry out to his car. "Oh, darn it! I left my ski in your boat. Let me go run and get it," Larry says.

"Oh just leave it there. You'll be back and you won't have to haul it back and forth," Rick says.

"Are you sure? I mean, I really do love spending time up here but like I said, I don't want to become a nuisance."

"Nah, come on. It's fine. Any time you feel like buzzing around the lake, give me a call. I usually try to have at least Saturday and Sunday off. I enjoy having you." Rick reassures him.

"Hey man, that's great. Thanks. Then I guess I'll see you later." Larry says and gets in his car and starts it. Rick waves bye and walks back around the house.

Chapter 9

Carla and Becky sit talking after Rick has left, Missy is in bed, and Dr. Anderson is still at the hospital. The day has been full with their skiing and then grilling. "It was really a fun day," Becky says.

"Yes, it was. I think we all needed that," Carla replies.

They sit quietly for a few minutes listening to the crickets and night sounds.

"What do you have planned, if anything, for tomorrow?" Becky finally asks.

"I think I want to go to church. If you want to stay here with Missy you can and I'll go alone." Carla glances over at her.

"Is that what you want?" Becky asks.

"Oh, no. I just thought if you didn't feel like going then I could go alone. I just feel like I need to go."

"I'd like to go. Like I said, I don't get to go as often as I'd like to and I really liked that pastor's sermon last time," Becky states.

"Okay. Are you going to be the biker again?" Carla laughs.

Becky smiles. "No. You'll be looking for me if I do that again. Now we can't have that!" she laughs. "Do the same thing as last time. Try to stay near crowds and sit in the center of the row."

"Okay. I think I'm going to head up to bed. I'm pretty tired and you probably are too."

Carla says good night and goes in. Becky sits for a minute then walks out to the pool area. She begins stretching and bending, doing squats, rocks from one heel to the next, and then goes into a karate stance. She practices a lunge punch several times then reverts to more stretches. Carla has forgotten to ask her something and stands at the sliding glass doors watching without opening the door. Becky begins practicing her back thrush kicks, inside and outside arm strikes. She goes through a routine then practices front, side, and back snap kicks. She finishes her practice doing two round kicks that leaves Carla astonished. She spun so fast Carla was taken aback. Becky jogs out into the yard and jogs down to the lake, around the perimeter of the lawn, and ends standing on the patio stretching her arms behind her back. Carla steps out onto the patio and Becky looks up, surprised. "Wow," Carla says.

Becky looks at her and replies, "How long have you been watching?"

"Long enough to know I don't want you coming after me," Carla laughs.

"I thought you went to bed," Becky says, taking a drink of water.

"I was going to ask you how you're getting to the church but then, I don't think you'll tell me." She grins.

"You're right. I'll be there and that's all you need to know." Becky replies with a bit of an edge to her tone.

Carla looks at her for a long moment. "Well, good night." She finally says and reenters the house.

Becky's body is buzzing with energy. She suddenly takes off and runs around the house and races down the street. Carla watches her out her bedroom window. *Lord, help her. I know this has to be stressful for her too. Maybe I should stay home tomorrow.* "Go to church," the Lord whispers.

Carla goes to bed and is fast asleep and never hears Becky return, the soft closing of her bedroom door, or her talking to Rick on her cell phone.

* * *

"Missy, come on. It's time to leave." Carla says, walking past Missy's bedroom door.

"Okay. I'm ready." Missy says and steps out of her bedroom dressed in a pair of pants and a T-shirt with "God loves me" written in pink letters across the front. Carla glances toward Becky's closed door then proceeds downstairs. On the table is a note from Becky, "I've already left. I'll see you in church." A shiver courses down Carla's spine. *Lord, something isn't right. I just have this weird feeling. Something's wrong! Lord, does Becky not want to protect Missy anymore?* She gets no reply, and she and Missy head for the church. She's half expecting to hear the roar of motorcycles even though Becky said she wasn't going in that disguise. Once again, she's had to park further from the entrance than she'd like. Several people are walking from their cars so she quickly joins some women she knows and enters the church. People have already begun filling the seats. Since Carla thinks Nancy hasn't been seen in almost a month, Carla places Missy in the second seat from the aisle and takes the aisle seat about three quarters back from the front when people scoot in to make room.

The music begins and all stand as the choir leads them in the first song. The pastor steps to the podium and says, "Good morning. This is the day the Lord has made and we shall rejoice in it." A few hoots are heard.

Missy is wiggling around, and finally says, "Mama, I have to go to the bathroom."

"Can you hold it for a little while?" Carla whispers.

"No, Mama, I have to go now!"

A woman, sitting directly behind Carla, quietly stands and slips out.

"Missy, try to hold it." Carla whispers.

"I can't! I have to go *now*!"

Carla stands and takes Missy by the hand. "Come on then."

They quietly exit the sanctuary and walk down a short hall toward the bathroom.

Just as Carla starts to push the ladies room door open, Nancy steps out from the end of a large book case. She puts her finger up to her mouth and says, "Shhh. Just give me the kid and there will be no trouble." Carla shoves Missy behind her and stands firm. Before she can say anything, Nancy flicks the blade of a switchblade knife out and holds it out in front of her, pointing it toward Carla. "She's coming with me!" Nancy growls. Suddenly, something comes flying through the air and a foot smashes into the side of Nancy's face, sending her flying through the air and into the far wall. The knife flies out of her hand and lands several feet away. Becky is standing over her with handcuffs swinging. She grabs Nancy by the shirt and jerks her to her feet, spinning her around and quickly snaps the handcuffs on her wrists. Nancy is still dazed as Becky shoves her roughly back down the hall while Carla holds a crying Missy against her.

Rick walks up and asks if Carla is okay. Carla is in shock and doesn't answer immediately. "Sis? Are you alright?"

"Ah yes. I think so." Carla replies stunned.

Rick leans down to Missy. "Hey, honey. It's okay. It's all over now and she's not going to hurt you."

Missy swipes at her tears and hugs her Uncle Rick around the neck. "Who is she, Uncle Rick?"

Rick glances up at Carla whose staring down the hall. "That was Nancy, honey. We got her and she's going to jail. She'll never hurt you now."

"The beach lady?" Missy exclaims. "But she has *red* hair!"

"I know, honey. But believe me that was her. And she's going to jail."

"Mama, can we go home? I don't want to stay for church." Missy suddenly asks.

Carla seems to still be in shock. Rick takes Missy's hand and places his free hand on Carla's shoulder. "Come on, sis, I'll drive you home."

Carla looks at him with a dazed look and replies, "But my car."

"Becky will drive it home."

Carla says nothing more as they slowly walk down the hall toward the entrance. The song words, "There is power, power, wonder working power, in the blood, of the Lamb. There is power, power wonder—" blast through the speakers in the narthex as Rick throws the doors open and they step outside. No one in the sanctuary is aware of what happened in the hallway.

Three police cars are parked by the front entrance with red lights flashing. Rick leads Missy to his black sedan while an officer tells Carla he'll stop by the house for a complete statement. Carla mumbles thank you and looks over at one of the police cars and sees Nancy glaring at her through the backseat window.

After arriving home, Missy is sent to her room and has fallen asleep. Carla, Rick, Becky, and a police officer are in the living room and the policeman is taking Carla's statement. Carla continues to appear in shock and Rick is concerned. "Sis, just tell him exactly what happened then maybe you need to go lay down for a while. Becky and I can tell the rest."

Carla looks at the police officer and says, "Missy had to go to the bathroom and just as we started to enter the ladies room, Nancy suddenly appeared. I'm not sure where she came from." Carla begins to cry.

"Take your time," the officer says.

Becky hands her a tissue and she dries her tears and continues, "I shoved Missy behind me and then Nancy pulled out this huge knife." She begins crying again and everyone waits as she tries to control the tears.

Rick says, "We can tell you the rest. Sis, go lay down."

Carla scoots forward in her chair. "I'm sorry I don't really know what happened after that. The next thing I remember is seeing Nancy glaring at me through the back window of the police car."

Becky gently takes Carla's arm and says, "Come on, let me help you upstairs," and leads her out of the room.

When Becky returns, she and Rick fill in the rest of the information for the officer's report and he leaves. Rick looks at Becky and says, "I need to call dad. He's doing rounds but he needs to know before it hits the news."

"Okay. I'll go check on Carla and Missy," and she leaves while Rick is dialing his cell phone.

"Rick?" Dr. Anderson says when he answers his cell phone.

"Hey, Dad. Sorry to bother you on your rounds."

"Son, what's wrong? Is Carla and Missy okay? Has something happened?" Dr. Anderson asks pointedly.

"We got Nancy. She's in jail."

"Praise God! Is Carla and Missy okay?" he demands.

"Yes, Dad. Carla is pretty shaken and I'm concerned about her and Missy seems to be okay."

"Let me talk to Carla!" Dr. Anderson states.

"She's lying down and Missy is asleep. Dad, they're okay. They weren't hurt," Rick replies.

"What happened?"

"What time are you going to be home? We can talk about all this when you get home. I know you're busy." Rick says, hoping to not have to go through everything on the phone with his father.

"I'll be home in a couple of hours. Are you sure they weren't hurt?"

"Yes, just rattled. I'm going to call Larry and see if he can come over so he can hear it all too," Rick says.

"Good idea. I'll see you when I get home then, son. I'm assuming you're okay?"

"Yeah, I'm fine. I'm really relieved we finally got her. I'll see you at home. Thanks, Dad."

"Okay, son. Bye."

Rick hangs up and redialing his phone, he calls Larry. "Hey, Larry, it's Rick. We got Nancy!"

"That means she tried something. Is Carla and Missy okay?" Larry asks.

"Carla's pretty shook up and Missy seems to be okay," Rick replies.

"So what happened?" Larry asks.

"We're going to have kind of a family gathering when dad gets home to talk about all of this and I thought you might like to be here since you'll be prosecuting Nancy. That way we don't have to go over it a hundred times."

"Sure. Are you sure they're okay?" Larry asks again.

"Missy is asleep and Carla's lying down. They'll be okay. Dad said he'd be home in a couple of hours. Can you be here then?"

"Sure. I'll see you then. I'm going to bring a tape recorder if you don't mind, Rick. That way I can listen to it later too."

"That's fine. I'll see you then," Rick replies and hangs up.

Becky reenters the room and Rick says, "I called Larry and dad. They'll be here in a couple of hours. I need to get to the Marta Station and pick up Berta. I promised I'd pick her up."

"Okay. Carla and Missy are asleep. I'll stay here with them," Becky says.

"Thanks." Rick looks at her intently. "You were great, Becky! I'm still not sure how you knew she would try to grab Missy today, but you were right."

Becky smiles and says, "Well, you just have to trust me!" she laughs. "Go get Berta. We'll be here when you get back."

Rick leaves and on the way home from picking up Berta, he fills her in on all of the mornings events. Tears have filled her eyes as she listens to Rick. "Oh, dear Lord," Berta says as Rick continues to tell her what happened.

"Berta, I'd really appreciate it if you can keep Missy entertained while we sort through all of this," Rick says as he pulls into the driveway and parks next to Carla's car.

"Oh most definitely, that child doesn't need to relive all that!" Berta exclaims.

"Thanks," Rick says and takes a deep breath. "I guess we better get your things inside. Dad and Larry should be here any minute."

"Should I fix some sandwiches or something? Everyone is going to be hungry."

"If you don't mind. I know Carla and Missy haven't eaten. Come to think of it, neither have me or Becky." His stomach growls loudly as a confirmation to his statement.

* * *

Berta is busy preparing sandwiches, Rick is talking on the phone while sitting out on the patio, Becky is in her room doing whatever Becky does in her room, and Carla is sitting on the edge of her bed with her head in her hands trying to decipher all that happened this morning. *Lord, thank you! Thank you for protecting us. Why can't I remember what happened after I saw the knife, Lord? Help me, Father. I can't believe she was really going to kill me to get Missy! Why? Would she have killed Missy too? I don't understand, Lord. Help me to understand.* A gentle knock at her door interrupts her prayer. "Come in," she says and runs her hand through her hair and swipes at the few tears that linger on her cheeks.

Berta steps in and runs to her, throwing her arms around Carla's neck. "Dear God, thank you she's safe." Berta cries. She releases Carla and wipes the tears from her eyes. "Rick told me what happened. I'm so thankful to God that you and my little Missy are okay."

Carla gives her a quick hug and says, "We'll be okay. Is Missy still asleep?"

"Yes. I just peeked in on her. I made some sandwiches and everyone is downstairs."

"Everyone?" Carla asks.

"Rick, Becky, your father, and Larry. They're waiting for you. Come on, honey, and have a sandwich. You must be hungry."

"Why is Larry here? Dad should be at the hospital," Carla replies, confused.

"Come on downstairs. They'll explain everything. You need to eat. Should I wake Missy?" Berta asks.

"No. I'll go wake her and we'll be down in a minute," Carla says and stands.

"Okay, honey."

Berta returns downstairs and Carla brushes her hair and goes in to wake Missy.

* * *

Carla and Missy enter the dining room and when Missy sees her grandfather, she yells, "Pa-pa, you should have been there!" and runs straight to him. Dr. Anderson grabs her up and hugs her tight. "Thank God you're okay." He looks at Carla and standing up, with Missy still in his arms, he rushes around the table to her and places his free arm around her and hugs her. Tears have welled up in his eyes as he kisses her on the cheek. "Praise God you're okay." He releases her and sets Missy down to stand on the floor. They take their seats at the table as Berta brings a large platter of tuna salad sandwiches in and a large bowl filled with potato chips and sets them on the table. "I'll be back with drinks in a second," she says, returning to the kitchen. Dr. Anderson says a blessing over the food and, with tears welling up in his eyes, adds, "Lord, thank you for protecting Carla and Missy and for Becky. I don't want to think about what would have happened if she had not been there. Thank you, Lord. In your holy name. Amen."

Missy immediately starts telling her grandfather how Becky flew through the air so fast she was like superman. "Miss Becky is really a police girl!" Missy states emphatically. The adults let her talk with mere nods of the head and the only interruption was when Carla told her to eat her sandwich and Pa-pa commented on how brave she was. Missy finally winds down, stating, "Uncle

Rick put her in jail and now she can't try to stealed me anymore!" then suddenly asks if she can go swimming. No one corrects her mispronunciation. Berta is leaning near Carla, picking up her dish and whispers, "I'll watch her." Carla looks up at her and says, "Thank you."

Larry has sat quietly the entire meal but has been watching Carla during Missy's exaggerated story of Becky's heroism and the police cars, red flashing lights, getting to ride in Uncle Rick's police car, and descriptions of all the buttons and radio. Missy asks if she can be excused and when told yes she runs upstairs.

Dr. Anderson looks at Rick and says, "I don't know what you told her on the ride home but she sure doesn't seem too traumatized."

Rick smiles and replies, "I was able to convince her that she won't ever be hurt by Nancy and told her that Becky is really a policewoman. It must have made an impact."

"It sure seems to have," Dr. Anderson says.

When the dishes are cleared, the five sit quietly, all in their own thoughts.

Finally, Dr. Anderson says, "Why don't we go to the living room. I want to know what all happened."

They all rise and retire to the living room. Larry walks beside Carla, "I'm glad it's over, Carla. Now we can start getting ready for a trial."

Carla glances at him and says nothing.

* * *

While the adults talk, Berta has convinced Missy she must wait for a little while before going swimming after eating and to keep her from disturbing the adults she's playing a board game with her in Missy's bedroom.

* * *

In the living room, Carla has broken down in tears several times. Larry has started to go sit beside her on the couch several times to comfort her but decides he shouldn't.

"It's over now," Larry gently tells her. "Because she threatened you with the knife, on top of everything else, she'll be in jail for a very long time. Does your neighbor still have the note Nancy taped to the door?"

"Yes. They have it in their safe." She replies while wiping tears on her cheeks.

"I'll need it. Would you ask her to mail it to you? I need the one you found in the mailbox too, Dr. Anderson."

"I have it in my desk. I'll get it for you," Dr. Anderson states.

"Why Missy?" Carla demands. "How did she even know about Missy?"

Rick glances at Becky, then Larry. He takes a deep breath and says, "We found out that her baby was born the same morning as Missy. She was told her baby was stillborn and as you already know, she didn't believe them. Missy was the only other baby born in that hospital that morning and she was convinced she was hers. In time, she found out who you were and Missy's name. She started trying to find you but was so messed up she started stalking other women and getting into all kinds of trouble with the law. She's been in and out of jail and was finally able to locate you in Ivy. She went there with one purpose, to get Missy."

Carla looks at Becky and asks, "But how did you know she was going to be at the church?"

Becky lowers her head, runs her hands across her face, and then looks at Rick, then Carla. "She was parked a few doors down last night when I went running. She stayed there all night waiting. She was still there when I slipped out this morning before dawn."

"But how—"

"Sis, you don't need to know all the details. Becky stopped her and we arrested her. There's no sense driving yourself nuts over all this right now. You've been through enough today."

"I just want to know how you got past her without her seeing you leave the house and how did you get to the church before we did?" Carla forcefully demands.

Becky glances at Rick and he nods, letting her know to go ahead and tell her. "I slipped out the back and ran through the trees and across the neighbor's yard and Rick picked me up about a half mile down the road and we went to the church."

"You sat at the church all that time?" Carla asks incredulously.

"We were there when the pastor arrived," Rick says.

Dr. Anderson and Larry sit quietly through the exchange as Larry tapes the whole conversation.

"So, the pastor knew what was going to happen? But how did you—"

Rick interrupts. "Sis, stop!"

Carla runs her hands through her hair and almost yells, "Rick, I think I'm going crazy! I can't remember anything after I saw the knife and I need to know everything. I *have* to know!"

"Honey, calm down," her father says and goes to sit beside her on the couch.

"Dad, I have to know!"

"Go ahead and tell her son if it will help her," Dr. Anderson says softly holding Carla's hand.

Rick gives in and explains. "Somehow, Becky knew Nancy was going to try to grab Missy this morning. We introduced ourselves to the pastor and told him what was going on. He showed Becky around so she'd be familiar with various places Nancy might try to grab Missy."

Becky interrupts and says, "I saw her sit down right behind you when you and Missy sat down."

"She was right behind me!?"

"Yes. I was in the row directly behind her. When I heard Missy say she had to go to the bathroom the first time, I slipped out the door and ran down the hall to the room right at the end of the bookcase. It was only a minute later Nancy showed up and was hiding in front of that door. I was behind it."

Carla sits transfixed staring at Becky. Dr. Anderson whispers, "Thank God."

"Rick said you knew she was going to grab her this morning. How did you know?" Carla asks pointedly.

Becky looks at her intently and says, "You're not the only one that prays, Carla. The Lord told me last night that I was to be there because Nancy would try to take Missy this morning. He was right."

Carla is silent staring at Becky. Missy suddenly appears. "We're going swimming now, Mama. Do you want to come watch me?"

Carla turns her attention to her daughter and replies, "No, not right now. Berta will watch you swim, honey. I'll be out in a little while."

"Okay." Missy runs to the sliding glass doors as Berta holds them open for her.

Larry leans over and shuts the recorder off. "Carla, you need to rest and try not to think about all this for a while. Rick, if you can get me your files and any information you have on Nancy, I can get started."

Dr. Anderson stands and says, "I'll go get that note for you," and leaves the room.

Carla looks at Becky without moving. "The Lord told you Nancy was going to grab Missy this morning?"

"Yes, Carla. He did. I didn't sleep at all last night. I was too wired because when the Lord speaks to me, I listen, and I believe what He tells me. There was no question in my mind that Nancy would try to grab Missy at church."

Carla jumps up and runs to Becky, throwing her arms around her neck, hugging her so tight Becky can barely breathe. "Thank you." She cries. Tears have filled everyone's eyes as Carla finally releases Becky and steps back.

"Does this mean you'll be leaving now?" Carla asks as she swipes at a tear.

"Yes, I'm afraid so. I'll leave right after dinner if that's okay. I'd like to have one more of Berta's great meals before I go back to eating at Wendy's."

Everyone laughs and the tension has been broken.

Chapter 10

Carla has called April and told her the whole story. She begins by telling her Rick finally told her Nancy had been stalking another child, how she was at the sporting goods store and the mall. Then tells of how Becky knew Nancy would be at church, Missy having to go to the bathroom, the knife, and Becky arresting Nancy. April gasps at various points of the story but doesn't ask questions or interject. When Carla breaks down in tears, April is crying with her. April finally asks, "When are you coming home?"

"I'm in the process of doing laundry and trying to get some things organized now. Dad and Rick want me to stay until after Missy's birthday. It's Saturday after next and Dad wants her to have a little party before we leave, plus I need to take her back to Dr. McDaniel at least once more. I want to make sure she's okay." Carla laughs and adds, "I think I need therapy more than she does!"

"You'll be okay once you get back home and things settle down. When is the court date?" April asks.

"I'm not sure. Larry hasn't said."

"Come home and you can always go back when the time comes. I'm just glad she's caught!" April says.

"What would really be great is if you and Jenny could come to Missy's party. She'd be so thrilled!"

"Oh, that would be great! When did you say it is?" April excitedly asks.

"Not this Saturday but the next at two o'clock. You could come on Thursday or Friday and stay the weekend. We could all drive back to Ivy together."

"Oh that sounds great! I'll ask Alex about it and let you know. That really sounds like fun!"

"Now I'm excited too! I hope you and Jenny can come," Carla says.

"I'll talk to Alex tonight and call you tomorrow."

"Okay. I better go check on Missy."

"Give her a hug for us. Bye," April says and hangs up.

* * *

For the past week, Larry has called checking on Carla to see how she's doing and ask various questions to fill in some areas he's not sure of. Rick has invited him to come skiing on Saturday but Larry has declined due to his caseload. "Maybe next weekend," Larry tells Rick on the phone. They discuss some of the details and information Rick has gathered about Nancy and Larry states, "She's been indicted by the grand jury. We'll be going to court in a few months."

"That's great. Anything I can do to help, you know I will," Rick replies.

"Do you know what Carla's plans are? She mentioned going back to Ivy?" Larry asks.

"Not really. She mentioned the other night to Dad that she would like to leave next week but she has been taking Missy to her psychiatrists to make sure she's okay. I don't know how long that will last. Why?"

"I just need to know where to get a hold of her if something arises or I need statements, signatures, or whatever," Larry says.

He hesitates for a long moment then admits, "Plus I've been thinking about asking her out to dinner but I'm not sure I should since I'm handling her case."

"Larry, you know that creates a conflict of interest! Don't screw up this case because of your feelings for my sister," Rick warns emphatically.

"You're right. I guess I'll just have to wait until this case is finished and put to bed." Larry sighs loudly.

"You'll have time to pursue her *after* this case. Anyhow, long distance relationships are hard. Don't count on anything. She may not be ready yet to start dating. Give her time. There's no rush," Rick states.

Larry agrees and promises not to push it.

* * *

While Larry and Rick were talking on the phone, Carla is in Dr. McDaniel's office talking to the doctor while Missy is drawing a picture at the child's table. "You have been through a lot of traumatic events this past year and a half," Dr. McDaniel tells her. Carla just looks at her and says nothing.

Dr. McDaniel continues, "Carla you lost your husband tragically, you finished school while raising a child alone, you recently moved to a whole new area and are trying to start over. That's a lot to deal with."

"I guess so," Carla says softly.

"You and Missy have been stalked by a woman intent on kidnap, you've come here to protect your child and thought you were safe. Now suddenly, you have a twelve-inch knife blade pointed at you. There's only so much the mind can deal with without shutting down. You'll remember what happened when the mind is ready to reveal what it has protected you from." She reassures Carla and asks, "Why is it so important to you to know what happened after seeing the knife? When everything basically was over?"

"Because I think I'm going crazy! And what if Becky hadn't been there? Would I have been able to protect my baby?"

"Oh Carla. I have no doubt you would have been a mother bear ready to shred anything that threatened to harm your child," Dr. Anderson says reassuringly.

"But if my mind shut down that easy? I was so confused and dazed by what she was doing I just couldn't think. I couldn't believe she'd actually try to kill me! Yet here she is with this huge knife! If that happens again, then what? What if she gets out?" Carla's eyes fills with tears.

"Didn't you say Nancy is in jail? Didn't the prosecutor say she'd be in jail for a very long time? What is the main fear you now have?" Dr. McDaniel asks gently.

Carla begins to sob. Dr. McDaniel waits for her to get control. Carla finally wipes her eyes and blows her nose. "That I won't be able to protect her if this happens again!" She blurts out and begins sobbing.

Dr. McDaniel flips through her rolodex, picks up a small sheet of paper, and writes down a name and phone number on it. She waits for Carla to stop crying and reaches the paper across her desk, handing it to Carla. Carla reaches out, taking it. "That is the name and phone number of a good therapist near Ivy. I think you might want to continue with some sessions with her until you can resolve in your own mind that you can and will protect Missy should the need arise."

Dr. McDaniel walks around her desk. "Let's go see how Missy is doing," she says as she gently leads Carla to the door.

Missy is just finishing her picture and tells Dr. McDaniel that it's a picture of Miss Becky flying through the air and "How Mama and Miss Becky protected me from Nancy."

Dr. McDaniel smiles, "That's wonderful, Missy. So do you think we need to talk more?"

"No, I'm okay. Mama and Miss Becky are heroes!" she states proudly and hugs her mother's waist holding the picture.

"Good! Are you ready to start school?"

"Yes! Mama bought me all new clothes," Missy states happily, letting go of her mother. She looks up at Carla and asks, "Mama, when are we going home? I mean home at the beach?"

Carla smiles and replies, "Soon, honey, real soon."

Dr. McDaniel walks them to the door and upon opening it, Carla turns to her. "Thank you so much for your help. I don't think either of us could have gotten through this without you."

"You're very welcome, Carla. Call the number I gave you and God be with you."

"Bye, Dr. Mac," Missy says and she and Carla leave.

* * *

Rick and their father have convinced Carla to stay until after Missy's birthday so when she and Missy went to church, Missy was allowed to hand an invitation to her friends in her Sunday school class for the following Saturday. Missy is excited and telling everyone, "I'm going to be *six* years old and I'm having a party!" Carla hasn't told Missy that April and Jenny might come for the birthday party and will be staying the weekend.

Rick has been going nuts trying to figure out what to get her for her birthday and Pa-pa refuses to buy her a pony that he has to feed and care for when she lives miles away. "But Pa-pa, I can ride it when I'm here!" Missy begs. "No, honey, I'm not buying you a pony! Now think of something else you'd like," he says.

Carla and Rick are sitting back on lounge chairs next to their father on the patio laughing as they listen to the exchange. "How much do you want to bet he gets her one?" Rick whispers to Carla. "He better not!" Carla laughs.

Dr. Anderson excuses himself and enters the house and Missy jumps in the pool.

"Is it okay if I invite Larry to her party?" Rick asks Carla.

"Sure. The more the merrier."

Rick nods and thinks, *Maybe that will appease Larry for a while.* Rick is quiet for a long moment. He looks at Carla without saying anything.

Carla looks at him and says, "What?"

"Oh, I was just thinking."

"Thinking about what?" Carla asks.

"How do you feel about me bringing a date to Missy's party?"

"I didn't know you were dating anyone. Sure, if you want to bring her," Carla says then continues. "I wouldn't mind checking her out." She laughs. "What's her name?"

"Kay. Kay Wilson."

"So how long have you been dating her?"

"About three months now."

"Three months! You've never mentioned her."

"There really wasn't anything to mention. It's not like it was hot and heavy."

"If you want to bring her then you must want her to meet us," Carla says slyly, grinning.

Rick blushes a little and says, "Yeah, well."

Carla sits staring at him. "Mama, watch me dive," Missy yells and Carla's attention is turned to Missy who is standing on the edge of the pool. Rick decides it's a good time to leave. "I'll see ya later, sis." He says.

"Okay. Oh, don't forget to invite Becky to Missy's party!" Carla reminds him.

* * *

The week is spent planning the party, shopping, trying to organize things for moving back to Ivy, and Larry calling with updates on his information gathering and what his plans are for court. Carla is sitting on the patio watching Missy swim and talking to Larry on the cordless phone. "I want to get as many witnesses as possible that heard her threats. Do you think the man from the variety store will come to testify?"

"I don't know. I can ask him when I get home," Carla replies.

"What about April? Would she come up?"

"Oh, I'm sure April and Alex both will!" Carla exclaims.

"Good! Of course, Rick and Becky will both be there. I may have to subpoena the Sunday school teacher and pastor," Larry states flatly.

Carla wants to focus on the birthday party and "happy things" so she changes the subject quickly. "Did Rick ask you if you could come to Missy's birthday party yet?" she asks.

"Yes. It sounds like fun. She's a sweet kid and I'm glad she'll leave with some fun memories."

"Are you going to be able to make it? I know you're pretty busy," Carla replies.

"Yes. I'll be there. I wouldn't miss it for the world. What kind of gift can I get her?" Larry laughs, then adds, "I haven't been to a kid's birthday party since I went to my own when I was a kid."

Carla laughs and says, "Then you're in for a real treat! She has a pretty good size dollhouse so maybe some furniture or a doll to go with the dollhouse. She plays with that all the time or maybe a board game or something. Anything will be fine."

"Okay, I have a call waiting so I'll see you Saturday. You said two o'clock?"

"Yes. Bring your swim suit. It's a pool party."

"Okay. I'll see you Saturday."

* * *

Carla has been taking calls from mothers saying they'll bring their child and what kinds of toys does Missy like, does she have Barbie dolls, what kind of games, and offers to help. Carla is watching Missy playing in the pool. "Missy, come here for a second, honey. I want to ask you something," Carla hollers. Missy swims to the pool steps and comes bouncing out of the water and runs to her mother sitting at the patio table with a legal pad and pen.

"What do you want to ask me?" Missy says standing dripping water into a puddle around her feet.

"What kind of birthday cake would you like for your party?" Carla asks, smiling.

"I want one with chocolate and white icing! Can we have a picture of me waterskiing on it?"

"I don't know about that but I can try." Carla laughs.

"Oh boy! Are we going to have ice cream, too?"

"Of course."

"And balloons too?" Missy jumps up and down splashing her feet in the puddle at her feet.

"Sure. It's going to be a nice party. You'll have lots of fun."

"And a bunch of presents too!"

Carla laughs and says, "You need to dry off and get dressed so we can go pick out a cake."

"Oh boy!" Missy yells, forgetting to dry off, and runs into the house.

The cordless phone rings just as Carla reaches for her legal pad and pen. "Hello."

"Hi Carla. We're coming! Alex said he thought it was a good idea," April shouts into the phone.

"All right! Oh, I'm so excited now. I can't wait for you to get here!"

"I thought we would come Thursday if that's okay. I can help you get things ready and the girls will have more time to play together. What do you think?"

"Oh, April, that's great! Thursday would be fantastic. Oh I can't wait to see you!" Carla is almost crying she's so happy.

"Are you planning on coming home Sunday?" April asks.

"Yes, I already told Dad we are going to leave early Sunday morning. I'll pack the car Saturday night."

"He's really going to miss you."

"I know and I'll miss him too but I'm more than ready to come home. We've been here most of the summer," Carla replies.

Missy comes barreling out the sliding glass doors, yelling, "I'm ready, Mama."

Carla laughs and says to April, "You probably heard that. We're going to go order Missy's birthday cake."

"Oh, then I better let you go. I'll call you Thursday when we get close to Atlanta."

"Have a safe trip."

Missy grabs Carla's hand pulling her out of the chair. "Come on, Mama. Can I pick out my cake?"

* * *

The baker says he can't put a picture of Missy skiing but he can make waves on the top and add a plastic boat and a skier. He shows them a picture and Missy starts squealing. Carla and the baker burst out laughing. "You can pick it up Friday before five," the baker says to Carla. "That's great. Thank you so much. Come on, honey, we need to do some more shopping." Carla takes Missy's hand and they head to Walmart.

Carla is mumbling to herself as she goes down the aisles and checking off the items on her list as she places each in the basket. A bag of balloons for filling with water, two plastic pails, five foam kickboards, candles, ice cream, Kool-Aid, hot dogs, buns, and the list goes on. She lets Missy help pick out prizes for the winners of the planned games. Missy is asking a number of questions and Carla is trying her best to answer Missy's questions and concentrate on not forgetting anything on her list. Finally, they leave and the car's trunk is filled. "We have one more stop," Carla says as she pulls into a balloon shop. Helium-filled balloons seem to fill every inch of the store. Missy gets to pick out what she wants and Carla places her order and is told she can pick them up Saturday morning after nine. That night at dinner, Missy is talking so fast, telling Pa-pa about all the stuff they bought that he and Carla can't help but laugh. She finally takes a deep, exaggerated breath and exclaims, "I can't wait for Saturday!"

* * *

Thursday afternoon, Carla hears a car pull into the driveway and peeks out the window. She recognizes April's minivan and runs to the front door throwing it open. Missy is upstairs playing in her room. Carla runs out to greet April and Jenny with tears filling her eyes. She grabs April in a hug almost knocking her over as soon as she's stepped out of the car. "I thought you'd never get here!" she says. Carla turns and hugs Jenny and says, "Shhhh. Missy doesn't know you're here and we want to surprise her." They close the van door quietly and walk into the house.

"Missy, would you come here please?" Carla yells, standing at the bottom of the stairs. Jenny and April are in the living room and Jenny begins to giggle.

"I'm coming, Mama," Missy yells.

"Shhh," April says to Jenny.

Missy bounces down the stairs, "What?"

"I need you to help me with something if you will." Carla says, trying hard not to give the secret away.

"With what?" Missy asks.

"Would you go in the living room and get me that pillow off the couch?"

"Okay." Missy runs to the living room and suddenly stops and screams, "Jenny!"

The two girls run into each other's arms and are hugging while April and Carla stand wiping tears off their cheeks watching the girls.

"Come on and I'll show you my room!" Missy says, grabbing Jenny's hand and pulling her toward the stairs. The girls run upstairs and Carla and April stand laughing and sniffing. Berta steps into the room and says, "I have some sandwiches made if you're hungry."

Carla turns to Berta and says, "Berta, this is April, my best friend in the whole world and my neighbor in Ivy." Berta walks over and April reaches out to shake her hand. Berta says, "Oh give me a hug, woman!" and embraces her. They follow Berta into the kitchen. "Would you like to sit outside to eat?" Berta asks. Missy comes tearing into the room, "Mama, can me and Jenny go swimming?"

Carla laughs, "I should have known it wouldn't take long." She turns to Missy and replies, "If April says it's okay for Jenny to swim then yes. But just for a short time. Berta went to all the trouble to fix sandwiches for us."

"I'm not hungry. Can Jenny go swimming, Miss April?" Missy asks.

"If she wants to," April replies.

"Oh boy" Missy yells and runs toward the stairs.

"Missy! Ask Jenny if she's hungry. She's come a long ways to be with you," Carla states.

"Okay." Missy yells and runs upstairs.

Carla and April sit at the patio table eating their sandwiches and discussing what needs to be picked up for the party and when, who will fill the balloons for the balloon toss game, how much of what should be cooked, and in general what is left to be done before Saturday. The girls are splashing in the pool.

"I just can't believe you're really here," Carla says to April.

"We wouldn't have missed this for the world. Jenny has really missed Missy. Those two seem to be closer than sisters," April says, looking over at the two girls giggling and splashing each other.

"I'm glad Dad talked us into staying until after her birthday. I think he was right in wanting her to have happy memories to leave on," Carla says reflectively.

"I'm glad too even though I thought it would never get here! Who's coming to the party?" April asks.

"Well, Missy invited ten kids from her Sunday school class, Rick will be here. He's bringing a date, Larry, Dad, and Becky. You'll be shocked when you see how petite Becky is! And I'm sure some of the moms will stay."

"I definitely want to meet this woman that can take down grown men!" April laughs.

"I can't tell you how much I appreciate her. She's a wonderful person and I really admire her for what she does," Carla says seriously.

"She sounds like quite the woman," April replies.

"Mama, can we have some sandwiches now? We're hungry." Missy yells while hanging onto the edge of the pool and kicking her feet in the water.

"Get out and get dried off. You can eat out here," Carla says.

"I'll go get their sandwiches," April says and goes into the house.

* * *

Friday is spent running errands, stretching a rope across the center of the pool marking where the deep end starts so the children will not venture into deep water, tables and chairs are unfolded and put in place, party favors set out, prizes lined up, the grill cleaned and readied for the hot dogs and hamburgers, and streamers run. By dinnertime, the back patio and lawn look like there's going to be a party. Jenny and Missy have helped and giggles and excitement have been their forte for the day. Berta has been given the weekend off and after hugging Carla and Missy goodbye, she leaves to go stay with friends. Carla and April are more than happy to plop down in the lounge chairs with cold drinks after the girls are in bed.

* * *

Saturday morning is abuzz with getting the last-minute party chores done and running to pick up balloons and forgotten items. Cars start pulling into the driveway at one forty five and Missy and Jenny are already in bathing suits and anxious for the party to begin. A couple of the mothers have worn their bathing suits so they can be in the pool with the children. Rick and Kay have arrived and Rick and Larry have been assigned pool duty to help with the games. Dr. Anderson has been assigned chef duties. "I'm on call today, honey, so I may have to leave in a hurry," he tells Carla as she hands him the bag of charcoal briquettes. "That's fine, Dad. Rick can take over if you have to leave."

By three o'clock the pool is filled with screaming, laughing, and splashing kids. The women are visiting while setting out condiments, chips, and drinks. One mother monitors the "who can hold your breath the longest underwater" game and then Rick and Larry supervise the water-filled balloon toss. Suddenly, all the boys turn and start throwing the balloons at Rick and Larry. The girls scream and huddle together on the pool steps out of danger's way. Splat! One balloon hits Rick in the face and the boys roar with laughter. "Oh, I'll get you for that!" Rick shouts and a water fight starts. The women stop what they're doing to watch. One mother laughs and says, "No matter how old they are, they're still little boys." The women all agree.

When Rick brings the water fight to a halt, the boys sit along the edge of the pool, resting. Carla says, "Let's have a race across the pool for the girls now." The girls line up on one side of the pool and when the whistle blows, they all dogpaddle to the other side. One little girl, with a life jacket on, begins to cry because she doesn't know how to dogpaddle. "You'll be the judge," her mom says. So the little girl sits on the edge of the pool with her mother and when the first child touches the pool wall she screams, "You win, Susie!" When Susie gets out of the pool, the little girl hands her the winner's prize and grins broadly.

Carla leans over to April and says, "They look like they're all pretty tired. Let's get them dried off and eat." Dr. Anderson has hamburgers and hotdogs grilling and a platter full of both ready to be devoured. Carla claps her hands to get the kids' attention. "Who wants hamburgers and hotdogs?" she yells and "I do" echoes across the pool.

It's been a fun afternoon and as everyone finishes their meals, Carla brings the birthday cake out and sets it on one end of the table as another mother brings out the ice cream churn filled with homemade ice cream. Missy sits staring at her cake with eyes wide. She didn't get to see her cake until now. Light blue icing rolls gently across the top creating the appearance of a lake with small swells of waves. One corner of the sheet cake is brown icing in the shape of a small island with six tree-shaped candles. A toy boat is at one end of the cake and an icing rope leads to a toy little girl on a pair of water skis. Missy is ecstatic!

Carla has taken several pictures of the kids in the pool, some of the mothers acting silly, several of Missy, Jenny, and April. Becky let her take one picture of her with Missy. "I'm an undercover cop. I can't have pictures of me floating around," she whispered to Carla. Carla's now snapping several with Missy and her cake. Everyone begins singing Happy Birthday and Missy blows out her candles and they all dive into the cake and ice cream. When the cake and ice cream has disappeared, Missy opens her gifts with squeals. Rick has given her a new life jacket that has flower designs on it to match her water skis. She quickly puts it on and announces, "It's too big, Uncle Rick." "It won't be when you wear it next summer," he replies. Larry gave her a new board game, and Pa-pa managed to find her a pony—a white Barbie doll pony with a pink mane. Rick laughs and says to Carla, when Missy opens the gift and pulls out the pony, "I told you he'd buy her a pony." Becky has given her a doll that's dressed in a karate uniform. "Mama, can I learn karate?" Missy asks. Everyone laughs.

"I'll be right back," Carla says and walks around to the garage. She reappears pushing a pink bicycle, with a big bow attached to the center of the handle bars. Missy runs to her and Carla says, "This is from Pa-pa, Uncle Rick, and me." Missy hugs her and then runs to Pa-pa and Uncle Rick, giving each of them a big hug.

Carla cannot be more pleased with how the party has gone and when all have left, Rick, Kay, Larry, April, and she sit outside having ice tea. Dr. Anderson has left for the hospital to check on some of his patients and Missy and Jenny are in her room playing with some of the new toys she received as gifts.

Larry stands and turns toward Carla, "That was a great party, Carla. I had a lot of fun and I know Missy loved it. I need to get going. Thank you for inviting me."

Carla stands up and says, "I'm glad you could come. It was fun and thank you for Missy's gift. I'm sure she'll have a lot of fun with it."

Larry smiles and replies, "Walk with me to my car." Then adds, "Thanks everyone and it was nice meeting you April, Kay. I'm sure we'll meet again." Everyone says goodbye and Carla walks with him to his car.

"You're leaving in the morning?" Larry asks.

"Yes. As soon as we get everything cleaned up, I'll load the car. April and Jenny are driving back with us in her van," Carla replies.

"That's good. That's a long drive to do alone," Larry says.

An awkward silence lasts for a minute. Carla finally says, "Well, I better get back."

"Would it be okay if I come down to Ivy every once in a while to visit you and Missy?" Larry blurts out.

Carla is surprised and not sure what to say. She looks at him for a long moment and finally replies, "I think Missy would like that. She really likes you."

"And what about you? Would you like for me to visit?"

Carla takes a sudden step back. "Oh! Ah," and says no more.

Larry is disappointed and steps into his car. With the door still open, he looks up at her. "Just think about it for now. I'll call you if I need anything for court. Thanks again for inviting me." He closes the door, starts the engine, and slowly backs out. Carla stands watching him and when he's out of sight she slowly walks back to the patio to join the others.

Rick looks at her and sees the troubled expression on her face. "What's wrong?" He asks concerned. "Oh, ah, oh nothing." She replies. She picks up a paper cup and says, "We need to start cleaning up so I can start loading the car." She quickly moves toward the tables and starts picking up paper plates and cups. Rick remains seated, looking at her intently.

* * *

Kay is about the same size as Carla with the bluest of blue eyes. Her short cropped blonde hair set off her delicate features. A dimple creases each cheek when she smiles and her bubbly personality is infectious. Rick met her when talking to an attorney about an investigation he was doing and was immediately attracted to her. She was introduced as his paralegal. The attraction was apparently mutual for when Rick asked if he could call her sometime she immediately agreed. They've been dating ever since. When Rick introduced her to Carla and Dr. Anderson upon arriving at Missy's party, they immediately liked her.

Rick was alone for a moment before the party began full swing and Carla approached him, "I really like Kay. I think she's a keeper."

Rick looks at her grinning. "Good! Because I think I'm going to ask her to marry me."

"Wow, that's fast!" Carla exclaims.

"Yeah, well," Rick replies and walks away.

Everyone helps clean up the party items and once everything is done, Rick and Kay leave and April and Carla begin hauling suitcases and boxes to the vehicles. "We can carry a lot of this in the van, Carla," April states as she opens the back of her van. The back row of seats is lowered leaving plenty of open space. "That would be great," Carla says as she places a large suitcase into the van. Missy and Jenny carry small items and in no time the cars are loaded. The girls are put to bed and early Sunday morning, after hugging her father goodbye with tears streaming down her face, Carla gets behind the wheel of her car. Missy and Jenny will ride partway with April and then partway with her, giving each of them a break from the constant chatter and giggles.

Chapter 11

Carla and Missy walk through the door at Bill's Variety Store and Missy shouts, "Hi, Mr. Bill. We're back."

Bill walks around the counter laughing hardily and greets Missy. "Boy, have I missed you! Did you have a good time at your Grandpa's?"

"My Uncle Rick teached me how to water ski," she exclaims.

"Missy, it's taught, not teached." Carla laughs.

"Uncle Rick *taught* me how to water ski," Missy corrects.

"I'll bet you're really good at it too," Bill says.

"I am! Uncle Rick said I'm a natural," Missy announces proudly.

"I'll just bet you are!" he says. He turns his attention to Carla. "It's good to see you back, Carla. I hope everything went well there."

Carla glances down at Missy, then back to Bill. "I'll tell you about it later. Missy needs a backpack for school and a few supplies. Do you have any?"

"Oh sure. They're right down there on aisle four, on the left." Bill replies, pointing toward the aisle.

Missy picks out a flowered backpack and they slowly walk the aisles placing pencils, paper, crayons, a couple of T-shirts, and a box of crackers in the basket. They carry their items to the counter and Bill rings them up.

"You look pretty excited, little lady, to be starting school." Bill grins.

Missy is hopping up and down in front the counter. "Can I wear my backpack home, Mama?" she asks.

"Sure, why not," Carla says and shows Missy how to put it on.

Missy skips around in a big circle then stops in front of the candy jars. "Can I have some candy, Mama?"

"Sure, why not." Carla laughs and Missy points to a red lollipop. "That one, please." Carla looks at Bill and says, "I'd like to talk to you later if you have time."

"Sure." He glances down at Missy sucking her lollipop, "You have the phone number or you can come by. I'm always here." He can tell by Carla's expression this isn't something she wants to talk about in front of Missy.

Missy skips down the sidewalk in front of Carla on their walk home. *Lord, I'm not sure Bill needs to testify. He really doesn't know anything. All he heard was Nancy say we would talk. Do I really need to involve him in this?* Carla prays as she walks.

Carla waits until Missy is in her room playing before calling Bill's.

"Bill's Variety Store, can I help you?" Bill says, answering the phone.

Carla can hear voices in the background. "Hi, Bill. It's Carla. It sounds like you're busy."

"I do have customers" Bill replies.

"Maybe I should call at another time. When do you think is a good time to talk? I need to talk to you about Nancy, the woman who was stalking us."

"Oh! Is everything all right?" Bill replies.

"Well, yes, but, well, I'll call you some other time."

"Carla, why don't I give you my home phone number and call me this evening after the store closes. That way we can talk," Bill suggests.

"That would be great. I hate to bother you with this."

"No bother. You and your sweet little Missy have been on my mind all summer. Do you have a paper and pencil?"

Bill gives Carla his home phone number and later that evening when Missy is playing in her room, Carla goes out on the patio and calls him at home. She tells him what happened while at her father's and asks if he'd be willing to testify if need be. "I don't really know what I would be testifying to. I didn't see anything and only heard her say you two would talk." Bill replies.

"I'm not even sure you'll need to but my attorney asked me to ask you," Carla answers.

"Well, sure. I'd have to get someone to watch the store while I'm gone. But if I can help, then I will. Are you and Missy okay? Is that woman still in jail?" Bill asks.

"Yes, she's still in jail and we're both okay. I'm so sorry, Bill. I hate to drag you into this," Carla says sympathetically.

"Now you don't go worrying about that. If need be, I'll be there. I knew something wasn't right with that woman the first time I saw her!"

"Thank you. I'll let you know if I hear any more about this from my attorney," Carla says and they say their goodbyes and Carla leans back on the chaise lounge in thought.

* * *

The next morning, Carla is rushing to get Missy off to school. "Finish your breakfast, honey. We need to get you to school" Carla says, wiping the kitchen counter.

"I'm not going to ride the bus?" Missy asks.

"No, I think I'll take you to school each morning for a while."

"But I can ride the bus. I'm not scared," Missy says with a mouth full of cereal.

"Don't talk with your mouth full. I'll take you for a little while and then maybe you can ride the bus later. But for now, you need to get your backpack and come on."

Carla pulls in front of Ivy Elementary School near the edge of town and kisses Missy goodbye. "Have fun today, honey. I love you so much," Carla says with tears filling her eyes. Teachers are standing along the curb helping the children out of cars and into the building. Missy jumps out of the car and runs a few steps then stops. She turns to look at her mother with a smile that lights up her face, hollers, "Bye, Mama" and waves. Carla blows her a kiss and watches as the teacher takes her into the building.

* * *

Carla's phone is ringing when she returns to the house and she runs to grab it, "Hello."

"Hi, honey. It's Dad."

"Hi, Dad. Is everything alright?"

"Yes. I was just thinking of you and Missy and wondering how it went this morning. Didn't Missy start school this morning?"

Carla laughs. "Yes. I just walked in the door from taking her. She's so excited she couldn't wait to get into the building."

Dr. Anderson laughs. "I thought so. So how are you? I'll bet it's awfully quiet in that house now."

"Oh, I'm fine and yes, it is *real* quiet here." She laughs.

"I remember your mother cried all day when you and Rick started school the first day." He laughs.

"I did that last year so I knew what to expect this year. I'm fine. I'm just glad she likes school so much. So, how are you, Dad?"

"Busy as usual. Rick came by last night. He said he's thinking about asking Kay to marry him and wanted to know what I thought of her." Dr. Anderson says.

"He mentioned that in passing at Missy's birthday party. He just said it and then walked away. What did you tell him?" Carla replies.

"Well, I said I thought he needed to get to know her a little better and that she seemed like a really nice lady. I mean, what can I say? It's his decision and I only met her that one time."

"I really liked her. She has a great personality from what I could tell. She blended in with everyone and from the way they looked at each other, I think they really do love each other." Carla states.

"I just don't want him jumping in too soon. I'd hate to see him hurt again. You know he was pretty hurt when—I can't remember her name, broke their engagement. His line of work makes relationships tough."

"Yeah, I know. Since she's a paralegal she's more aware of the work he does. I would think more so than say, someone else. Rick's a big boy. I don't think he's going to jump into this without any thought. Why else would he come to you about it? He'll be okay." Carla reassures her father.

Dr. Anderson sighs loudly. "You're probably right, just an old man trying to protect his son." He laughs.

"Oh, Dad, you are far from being old! I wouldn't worry about Rick. He was stung once so he'll think this through."

"I'm getting beeped. Give Missy a kiss for me. Bye, honey."

"Bye, Dad."

* * *

Carla and Missy have been back in Ivy for a month and Carla is beginning to get stir crazy now that Missy is in school. *I can only clean house just so much, Lord. What am I supposed to do? I need to get a job. The money isn't going to last forever*, Carla thinks as she vacuums the living room floor. *I haven't worked since I got my degree and now I'm not even sure I can get a job. I don't have any references to amount to a hill of beans!* Carla pushes the vacuum harder and faster as agitation builds. *I just wish this stupid Nancy thing was over! I'm so sick of having that hanging over our heads! I can't do anything-* The phone ringing jars her from her thoughts and shutting off the vacuum, she goes to answer it. "Hello!" she answers.

"Hi, Carla. It's Larry. Are you okay?"

"Oh, hi, Larry. Yes, I'm fine. What can I do for you?" Carla replies sharply while still feeling angry.

"Ah, are you going to bite my head off if I tell you a court date has been set?" Larry asks cautiously.

Carla bursts out laughing. "I'm sorry, Larry. I didn't mean to bite your head off. I'm just feeling very frustrated at the moment."

"I have some time. Would you like to talk about it?" Larry asks.

"Oh, it's just that Missy is in school now and I need to find a job and I guess I'm just getting cabin fever. It doesn't help having this Nancy junk hanging over my head either!" She replies.

"Well, we have set a court date and that's something I do want to talk to you about." Larry says.

"You sound dubious. What's wrong?" Carla asks.

"Before I get into all that, how are you and Missy doing?" Larry asks, hoping to lighten the conversation a little before the explosion he expects from Carla hits.

"We're fine. Missy loves school. I don't have to ask her to get out of bed twice. She can't wait to get back to school."

"That's great. I miss seeing her." He clears his throat, realizing he may have said too much and continues, "The court date has been set for December fifth. I thought—"

Carla interrupts, "That's just before Christmas!"

"Yes, I know. But I'd rather get this in court as soon as possible instead of having to go into next year. The dockets are pretty full and I think we have enough to present in court that will put her away for a long time."

"Well, that's good to hear."

"There is something else, Carla. I already know your answer but I have to present it to you," Larry says.

"Oh, what?" Carla's defenses immediately rise.

"The defense attorney has offered a plea bargain-"

Carla shouts "No! No! No! No!" interrupting Larry.

"Calm down. I already told him you wouldn't go for it, but legally I have to present it to you," Larry says pointedly.

"I don't care what it is! This woman threatened me and my daughter with a knife! No, Larry. Forget it!"

"Carla, *listen* to me! I am fully aware of what Nancy did and how it has affected both of you! I already told him no, but you have to be made aware that a plea bargain was offered and what it is. Will you please just calm down and listen?" Larry is afraid Carla will slam the phone down without letting him do his job.

Carla takes a deep breath and is silent for a moment. "All right, I'm listening."

"Her attorney wants to avoid a trial. He knows Nancy could get life in prison and he's hoping to get a shorter sentence," Larry explains.

Carla says nothing.

"Are you there?" Larry asks since Carla is so quiet.

"Yes, I'm listening. It doesn't change my answer though."

Larry shakes his head and grins. *That's pretty obvious,* he thinks then continues. "He wants us to drop the attempted kidnapping charge and the assault with a deadly weapon charge and she'll plead guilty to stalking and promises to get psychiatric help."

Carla almost drops the phone. Larry holds the phone as far away from his ear as his arm will reach waiting for the explosion. He isn't disappointed.

"What!" Carla screams. "That crazy woman threatened to kill me and my daughter, she has put us through absolute hell. She hunted us down like animals all the way to Atlanta, Missy has been scared out of her wits and had to have therapy because of all this and now they want me to agree to a slap on the wrist? You can tell that attorney, and Nancy, to go to—"

"Whoa, whoa, Carla. Easy. Calm down. Carla, I said *no!*" He can hear Carla breathing hard as though she's hyperventilating and becomes concerned. "Carla, take a slow breath and take it easy. Slow breaths, nice and easy," he says soothingly and waits.

Carla has plopped down on a chair at the kitchen table and places a hand over her eyes while holding the phone. Tears have welled up and she tries to calm herself and do as Larry is saying. The tears turn to sobs. Larry waits.

Carla finally whispers, "I need a tissue," and lays the phone down to go get it. When she returns and picks the phone up, Larry speaks softly, "I'm sorry. I didn't mean to upset you. Are you okay?"

Carla cries softly but is able to tell him, "Yes."

"I had to tell you about their offer. I'm sorry. There's something else I wanted to ask you, while I have you on the phone. I'm speaking at a hotel in Savannah next week. It's just one day but if it's okay with you I'd like to come by. You aren't that far from where I'll be. I plan on staying the weekend since the conference is on Friday. I can use some beach time. Is it okay if I come by and maybe the three of us can spend some time on the beach Saturday?"

Carla is exhausted from her outburst and wants to go lie down so answers flatly, "That's fine. Call me from Savannah."

"Okay. Carla, it's going to be okay. We'll get through this. You just have to hang tough. I'll call you next week. Will you be okay?" Larry is very concerned. He expected an outburst but is now worried this all may be too much for her right now.

"I'll be fine. I need to pick up Missy from school in a little while," she replies in a tired voice.

"Give her a hug for me. Take care," Larry says and gently replaces the phone in its cradle.

Hanging up the phone, Carla sits quietly for a moment then decides to go for a walk. *I need to get out of here for a while.* She shoves the vacuum cleaner into the closet. Grabbing her keys and wallet, she heads down the street toward the beach. "Carla! Wait up." She turns and sees April jogging toward her. April runs up beside her. "Hey. Where you headed, girlfriend?" April asks.

"I thought I'd go walk along the beach. I'm getting cabin fever. Walk with me."

"Sure. I was thinking the same thing. With Jenny in school, I mean how much house cleaning can you do?" April laughs.

"Exactly!"

Walking along the beach, April can see Carla has something on her mind. "So what's up?" she asks Carla.

"Larry just called and they set a court date finally."

"That's great. When is it?" April asks kicking off her sandals and stooping to pick them up.

"December fifth. He said if we don't do it then we can't until next year and he wants to get her in court as soon as possible," Carla says, kicking a small seashell.

"You don't sound very enthused about it."

"That's right before Christmas! I told Dad we'd come home for Thanksgiving and Christmas but what fun is that going to be with a trial going on?" Carla stops walking and turns to April, "I just don't know how much more I can take of this." Her eyes fill with tears.

April embraces her in a gentle hug. "It's going to be okay." She releases Carla and they begin to slowly walk on down the beach. The seagulls squawk above them and some follow behind hoping for a morsel. Carla throws a seashell, "You haven't heard the worst of it yet." She says.

"What worst? They haven't let her out on bond or something, have they?" April asks.

"No. Oh no! But her attorney wants me to agree to a plea deal."

"You're kidding!" April exclaims.

"Nope! I went ballistic when Larry told me. Poor Larry." Carla chuckles. "I was screaming in his ear and then just lost it."

"So what do they want?"

"You *are not* going to believe this!" Carla says and stops walking. "Let's sit down. I'm tired." Carla curls her legs under her and sits in the warm sand letting a fist full of white sand seep through her fingers.

April sits next to her expectantly. "Well, what do they want?"

Carla takes a deep breath, dumps the sand out of her hand, and looks intently at April. "They want to drop the assault with a deadly weapon charge *and* the attempted kidnapping and she'll plead guilty to stalking and will get psychiatric help."

April jumps straight up and slamming her hands on her hips she says loudly, "Are they crazy! I can't believe that! She'd walk with a slap on the wrist! You aren't accepting it, I hope!"

Carla looks up at April placing a hand above her eyes, shading them. "Absolutely not! That's why I went ballistic." She sees a couple looking at them and says, "Sit back down. People think you're going to attack me," pointing to the sand next to her.

April plops down on the sand. "Does Larry want to accept it?" April asks picking up a hand full of sand.

"No! He already told them no but he said he legally has to have me reject it."

"Thank God for that!"

"He's going to be in Savannah next Friday and wants to come spend the day on the beach with us," Carla says.

"What's he doing down here?"

"He's doing some speaking engagement and said he needs some beach time so he's staying for the weekend."

"At your house?" April grins, knowing the answer before she even asks it.

"Noooo, Miss dirty mind." Carla laughs.

April looks over at her with a sly grin on her face. "You know he has the hots for you, don't you?"

"Oh come on, April! We've known each other since high school. He and Rick were buddies. He had a crush on me way back then but that was a long time ago."

"So! I saw how he looks at you Carla. I think it's more than a kid crush."

Carla stands up brushing the sand off her bottom, "Let's go. I need to pick Missy up at school."

"Why don't we ride together and we'll stop at the Dairy Queen on the way home. I'm craving a big fattening banana split!" April says, slapping sand off her legs.

"Only if you get this silly notion out of your head about Larry," Carla replies sternly.

April raises one hand and places the other over her heart dramatically and says, "I cannot tell a lie. I think he is in love with you."

"Oh stop!" Carla demands and begins jogging.

* * *

Saturday morning at ten, Carla's doorbell rings. Opening the door, she sees Larry standing there grinning. "Hi," he says. Larry is dressed in cut-off jeans, a T-shirt, and tennis shoes. His dark hair is trimmed but a curl cascades over one edge of his forehead. Dimples punctuate his cheeks as he stands smiling at her and his dark eyes twinkle. Carla can't help but notice the jeans shorts look *really good* on his slender body. "Hi! Come on in." she says, stepping back from the open door to give him room to pass.

"I'm not too early, am I?" Larry asks, stepping inside.

"No. You said it would be about ten. Would you like some coffee?" Carla asks, leading him into the kitchen.

Larry is looking around and replies, "That would be nice. You have a really nice little place here."

"Thank you. We like it." Carla says, pouring him a cup of coffee and one for herself.

Larry takes a seat at the table and suddenly Missy pops into the room. "Hi, Mr. Larry. Are we going to the beach now?"

"Hi Missy. You look like you've grown since I've seen you," Larry says, ignoring Missy's question. "How's school?"

"It's good. Are we going to the beach now?" she asks expectantly.

"Missy, we'll go in a little while. Why don't you go straighten up your bedroom while Larry and I talk," Carla says.

"But you said we were going to the beach." Missy insists.

"We are, honey, but not right at this moment. Go straighten your room."

"Oh, okay." Missy says and leaves to go clean her room.

Larry chuckles. "She's a good kid," he says.

"Yes, she is." Carla sighs. "She's strong willed for sure." She laughs.

"How is she doing since you've been back?" Larry asks and takes a sip of his coffee.

"She's done great. It's almost like nothing ever happened. She's amazing," Carla replies.

"How about you? How are you doing?" Larry looks at her intently.

Carla takes a drink of her coffee stalling. "I'm not doing as well as she is, that's for sure."

"I don't mean to be nosy but Rick said you were getting some counseling. Is that helping? It's been pretty rough for you." Larry states.

"Missy's counselor gave me the name of a therapist down here and I saw her a couple of times. It went well and I'm okay now. I just want to put all of this behind us and move on. It's like a black cloud hanging over our heads."

"I understand. That's why I wanted to get a court date as soon as possible but I have to have time to get as much evidence as I can before we go to court," Larry says sympathetically.

"Have you gotten anything else besides what we already know?" Carla asks.

Larry takes a deep breath, sips his coffee, and replies, "Yes. I'm going to subpoena her parents and maybe one of the people she lived with for a while."

"Her parents? Why them?"

"They can testify as to her actions before they threw her out," Larry replies.

"You mean because of the Ouija board?"

"Yes." He hesitates then adds, "Among other things. Hey, let's head to the beach before it gets too hot. I brought some drinks in an ice chest and it's out in the car." Larry stands up and looks at her. "Let's not ruin the day with all this," he says and goes to the car.

Carla has a picnic basket filled with fruit, sandwiches, cookies, and chips. She walks to Missy's bedroom door and Missy is sitting on the edge of her bed in her new bikini she got for her birthday. "Are you ready to go to the beach?" Carla asks, grinning.

"Oh boy, are we going now?" Missy jumps up off the bed.

"Yes. I need to put my suit on. Larry is getting a cooler out of his car. Maybe you can help him," Carla says as she turns to go to her room.

"Okay," Missy yells and tears down the hall to go help Larry.

* * *

The day is spent playing in the waves, talking, and relaxing. Carla and Larry are stretched out on the blanket talking and watching Missy playing in the shallow water, when Missy screams. Carla jumps up and runs to the water's edge. Missy is crying and Carla sees that a jellyfish has come close to shore and stung Missy. Larry stands beside her as Carla looks at Missy's leg. "I think we may need to get her to the ER. Those things can be poisonous. I'll go get the car while you get the blankets and stuff," Larry says and bolts across the sand running to get his car.

Missy is treated at the emergency room and the doctor assures Carla and Larry that she'll be fine. "Take her home and let her rest for a while. That medicine I gave her has a mild sedative in it so she'll probably sleep."

"Thank you," Carla says and they take Missy home.

* * *

Missy is asleep and Carla and Larry sit in the living room talking. "I'm glad she's okay," Larry says.

"I didn't realize jellyfish would come that close to shore. She was in pretty shallow water," Carla replies.

"That was just a small one and they'll get washed close in if the tide has been up."

"We did have some wind last night so maybe that's how it got washed in."

"Probably," Larry says, looking at her. Carla looks at him and sees something in his eyes she's not sure she wants to see. Suddenly, Larry says, "Can I ask you something?"

Carla hesitates. "Sure." She finally replies.

Larry looks down at his hands then up to gaze at Carla before asking. "When the trial is over, would you be willing to go out with me? You know, dinner, movie, that sort of thing."

Carla looks out the window, then at the TV, then the floor, and says nothing.

"I don't mean to push you but—"

Carla interrupts. "Ah, I don't—"

Larry suddenly says, "Carla, I know you lost your husband and maybe you're not ready but when you are I'd like to see more of you. We didn't really know each other in high school very well." He blushes.

Carla sits quietly looking at him. She then starts telling him about her marriage and that she knew he had a crush on her in high school and she has no plans of moving back to Gainesville and things are just too messed up right now to think about dating anyone. They spend a couple of hours talking when she hears Missy calling her. "I'll be right back," she says as she goes to tend to Missy. Larry gets up and strolls around the room looking at pictures and thinking, *Well, she didn't say no. At least that's a good sign. Oh, is Rick going to kill me if he finds out! To heck with Rick! This is between me and Carla. At least she didn't say no.* Carla rejoins him. "Missy is hungry and I'm getting hungry too. Would you like to stay for dinner?" Carla asks.

"Do you think she's up to going out? Why don't I take you two out for dinner? I hear that fish place in town is good," Larry says.

"Are you talking about The Happy Oyster?" Carla asks.

Missy strolls into the room yawning and has heard. "Are we going to The Happy Oyster, Mama?" she asks.

Larry walks over to her and squats down in front of her. "How are you feeling?"

Missy rubs her eyes and replies, "I'm better. It doesn't hurt now."

"Good! Would you like to go to The Happy Oyster?" Larry stands up.

"Yes. I like the shrimp," Missy states and sits down on the couch.

"What do you think?" He asks Carla.

"That's awfully nice of you. I think that's a great idea. Missy, how about you put on some long pants? That way you won't bump your sting." Carla says and Missy goes to change clothes.

"I have slacks and a shirt in the car. I'll go get them." Larry says and goes to his car.

* * *

Missy is quiet at dinner as Carla and Larry talk. "Has Rick said anything to you about marrying Kay?" Carla asks as she takes a bite of her baked tilapia?"

"He's mentioned it. I know Kay from having worked with the attorney she works with. She's a great person. I think they'll make a nice couple." Larry replies.

"Mama, are you and Mr. Larry going to get married?" Missy blurts out.

Carla chokes on her food and sits coughing. Larry blushes a bright red and jumps up to pat Carla on the back as she tries to stop coughing. She takes a sip of water.

"Are you okay?" Larry asks concerned but quite embarrassed.

Carla pats her mouth with her napkin, takes another sip of water, and looks at Missy. "We're just friends, Missy."

Larry sits back down and is sucking down ice tea like he's been stranded in a desert for a month.

Missy starts giggling. "I think you should," Missy says through her giggles.

"That's enough!" Carla says sternly.

Larry places his empty glass on the table, clears his throat, and asks, "Are you going to get dessert, Missy?"

"Yes! I want some chocolate cake and ice cream."

The rest of the meal is spent quietly and upon returning to the house, Larry thanks Carla for the wonderful day and she reciprocates. "I'm so glad you were here when Missy got stung. I couldn't have handled it all by myself. Thank you for dinner too," she says as they stand beside his car.

"I'm glad I was here too and that she's fine. I better get going. I'm heading back to Atlanta instead of spending the night. I have a lot of work to do," Larry says, stepping to his car door. He stands looking down at Carla. *I want to kiss you so bad I can't stand it,* he thinks, then grabs the door handle and flings open the door. "I'll talk to you later. Tell Missy I said bye." Larry says and gets into his car.

"Drive safe and thanks again," Carla says and Larry backs out of the driveway..

* * *

Carla has made arrangements with Missy's school for her to be out over the Thanksgiving break and through the trial December fifth. Carla and Kay are helping Berta in the kitchen with the Thanksgiving dinner preparations. The table is set with Carla's and Rick's mother's best china. Crystal wine glasses sparkle at each setting and a large cornucopia is sitting filled with fruit in the center of the long dining room table. A tall, white candle stands in a silver base near it. The candle has been a tradition their mother began many years earlier. "It represents God's presence and His light," she had explained. Dr. Anderson and his children have carried on the tradition.

Dr. Anderson is playing chess with Rick and Missy and Larry are sitting on the floor coloring at the large coffee table in the living room. Carla invited Larry to dinner when she learned he was going to spend Thanksgiving alone in his apartment doing briefs. Laughter rises up from the kitchen as Rick and his father study the chess board intently.

"You know you can't win, son. I've got your king cornered. Give it up." He laughs.

"Just once I'd like to be able to whip you at this game!" Rick says and shoves his chair back. "I give up!" he laughs and walks into the kitchen where the women are setting hot food on the counter to bring to the table. He sneaks up behind Kay and suddenly wraps his arms around her waist from behind and nuzzles her neck. "You look cute with flour on your nose," he whispers.

Carla turns, "Okay, you two." She laughs.

Berta chimes in, "Love is grand but the turkey needs to be on the table."

Rick releases Kay and Berta hands him the large turkey on a platter. "Please take this to the table." She grins.

"Oh, that smells good," Rick says, carrying it into the dining room and setting it at the end of the table where his father will do the carving.

A large baked ham with slides of pineapple, hot buttery rolls, tossed green salad, stuffing, fresh green beans, homemade cranberry sauce; potatoes au gratin, and sweet potato casserole are all carried into the dining room. Dr. Anderson takes Berta's hand in one hand and Rick's in the other as they join hands around the table and he says the blessing. Love and laughter fill the room and when everyone is holding their stomachs and exclaiming how good the food was Rick looks at his father, then at each person sitting at the table. *This is perfect. My whole family is here*, he thinks.

He stands up looking down at Kay with love in his eyes and says, "This is the most perfect moment, with all my family here, my best friend, and you looking so beautiful."

The room falls silent. Rick lowers himself onto one knee beside her chair as she looks down at him. "Kay Wilson, would you do me the great honor of being my wife?" He's holding a small velvet box in his hand with the lid open revealing a three-quarter carat brilliant round diamond ring.

Tears have sprung up in everyone's eyes, except Missy's. She starts giggling. Berta and Carla are holding their breath as their eyes flood with tears. Larry is watching but then turns his eyes on Carla. She has her hand over her mouth waiting expectantly. "Yes!" Kay shouts and jumps out of her chair knocking Rick backwards. He's sprawled in a sitting position with his legs outstretched. She lands on his lap and throwing her arms around his neck she kisses him passionately.

Shouts and applause break out and as Rick places the ring on her finger, everyone begins laughing. Missy has suddenly hopped off her chair and joined Kay and Rick in a pile on the floor. "Can I be in the wedding?" Missy asks. Rick and Kay are laughing and Rick suddenly leans back against the wall grabbing Missy around the waist and pulling her on top of him tickling her. "Of course you can." He laughs as Missy wiggles and squirms laughing hysterically.

* * *

The next few days are spent decorating the house for Christmas. April and Carla have agreed April, Alex, and Jenny will come the Saturday after Thanksgiving and stay with Carla and Missy at her father's house. "We have more than enough room for all of you," Carla tells April.

"That would be great. The girls can play and we can help you do whatever it is that you need to do," April replies.

"Then it's settled. We can go shopping too." Carla says. April knows that Carla is putting on a brave front. Carla has already told her she's scared to death about going to court. "I don't know what I'll do when I see Nancy," she said. "You'll be fine," April assured her.

* * *

Early Saturday evening, Missy is playing in her room with Jenny when Rick and Kay arrive with a large Christmas tree tied in the back of Rick's truck. Missy comes running out the front door, Jenny right behind her. They're both excited about being able to put up the Christmas tree.

"Are we going to decorate it right now?" Missy asks Rick as he tugs the big tree out of the truck bed.

"I don't know. That's up to your mother. Honey, can you grab that end?" he asks Kay. They haul the tree into the living room and stand it in its stand. The tree reaches almost to the twelve foot ceiling and Missy stands gaping at it with her mouth hanging open. "Wow!" she finally exclaims.

"Holy cow!" Jenny exclaims.

Rick looks at the girls and teases, "I don't know, Missy. It may be too small." Rick winks at Kay. "Maybe we better go find another one."

"No! I like this one." Missy states, walking to it and running her hand over one of the branches.

"Oh. Okay. I guess this one it is." Rick laughs and walks to Carla and gives her a hug. "Hi, sis. What do you think?"

"It's beautiful," She says.

Suddenly the living room is filled with people—Alex, Rick, Kay, Missy, Carla, April, Berta, and Jenny. Dr. Anderson enters through the kitchen. He sets his briefcase on the table. "Where is everyone?" he asks loudly.

"We're in here, Pa-pa," Missy yells. "Come see our Christmas tree!"

Dr. Anderson walks into the living room and stops suddenly gaping at the large tree. "Wow! That's a big one."

"Can we decorate it now?" Missy runs to Pa-pa and stands looking up at him expectantly.

Pa-pa picks her up and holding her in his arms he looks to the tree and then to her. He suddenly plants a kiss on her cheek making a loud smacking sound and says, "You need to ask your Mama."

Missy giggles as Dr. Anderson stands her down on the floor. "Mama, can we decorate it now?"

"We will after dinner."

"Are you and Miss Kay going to help, Uncle Rick?" Missy asks.

"We sure are unless you run us out of here." He laughs.

"Oh, goody. I'm going to go get some decorations!" Missy says and runs out of the room.

That evening, everyone is gathered in the living room and Christmas music is playing, boxes of decorations are scattered across the floor and laughter and chatter fills the room. Pictures are being taken with Missy holding Christmas balls in each hand and silver tinsel draped across her head, Missy and Jenny standing side by side with Christmas lights wrapped around their bodies, Carla and her father hanging Christmas stockings on the fireplace, Kay and Rick kissing under the mistletoe, Alex holding April up in the air as she hangs a decoration on one of the higher branches. When the boxes are empty and after Dr. Anderson stands on a ladder placing the Christmas angel in her renowned position at the top of the tree, gasps are given as he flips the light switch and the room is bathed in white light.

Kay begins singing, "Oh Christmas tree, oh Christmas tree" and everyone joins in. Jingle Bells, Rudolph the Red-nosed Reindeer, and several more songs are sung. Carla glances over at Missy. She's sound asleep lying on the couch with her head resting in Rick's lap. Tears fill Carla's eyes. She glances at April. April has her arms draped across Jenny's legs. Jenny is stretched across Alex's lap with her legs across April's. Carla smiles and whispers to April, "I think we finally wore them out!"

Chapter 12

The newly renovated and modernized Hall County Courthouse is now an impressive sight in downtown Gainesville, Georgia. The original courthouse was built in 1883 and served the people well until a tornado came through in 1936, destroying the courthouse and many businesses and homes. It was rebuilt around 1938 and renovated again some sixty-five years later.

To sit on a bench in the courtyard or stroll down the sidewalks past the crape myrtles lining the square, there's a sense of peace. Carla does not sense the peace of an afternoon stroll through the town square. Her nerves are on edge as she and Larry walk briskly into the courthouse and pass through the security checkpoint. He leads her to courtroom number 3. A smaller courtroom is being used since this is not a highly publicized case and there will be no large numbers of reporters with cameras and notepads.

The American and Georgia flags are displayed in one corner of the room. The judge's bench sits prominently in the front of the room, positioned higher than the rest of the chairs, with the defense and prosecution tables across the aisle from each other. The Georgia state emblem with "In God We Trust" is prominently displayed on the wall behind the judge's bench. A jury box sits empty with twelve chairs stair cased on one side of the room near the front. In this courtroom, there are no windows, nothing to distract from the procurement of justice. Carla sits quietly beside Larry at the prosecutor's table as he lays papers onto the table in neat stacks and places bags of evidence in a line in the order that he will present them.

Carla's hands are shaking. Larry glances down at her and she quickly hides her hands beneath the table. "It's going to be okay," Larry says, placing his hand on her shoulder. Carla nods her head and gives a weak smile. The defense attorney walks quickly down the aisle and turns to Larry before taking his seat at the defense table. He nods at Carla and reaches out to shake Larry's hand. "Sure you don't want that plea deal?" he grins and gives a quick glance at Carla. Carla sucks in her breath and opens her mouth to speak but Larry quickly lays a hand on her shoulder to silence her and says to the defense attorney, "We've made our decision." "Okay," the attorney states and walks across the aisle and sits down at his table.

Carla leans toward Larry and whispers, "Where's Rick? I thought he would be here." "He will be but he's a witness so he'll be called later," Larry responds. Just as Carla is about to ask Larry another question, a door at the side of the room opens and Nancy is escorted in. Carla begins shaking all over and Nancy stops at the edge of the defense table looking at Carla as the deputy removes handcuffs from around her wrists. The two women are silently staring at each other for a moment. Nancy's attorney suddenly stands and tells her to sit down and to say nothing! Nancy balks but does as he says, never taking her eyes off Carla. Larry grabs Carla's hand and squeezes tightly. "It's okay. Don't look at her. She wants you to be afraid," Larry whispers. Carla turns her focus on a legal pad and pencil in front of her on the table. Nancy's attorney leans toward Nancy and whispers, "Take the necklace off. It won't help you." Nancy glares at him and states flatly, "No!" People have filed into the courtroom and taken seats. Most are retirees that enjoy observing courtroom proceedings, some are waiting for their own hearings and step in to kill time, and there is one reporter for the local newspaper that got wind of the case.

A Hall County sheriff's deputy steps forward. "All rise. The honorable Judge Norman B. Willows presiding." The rustle from his long black robe can be heard as Judge Willows quickly walks to his bench and sits down. "Be seated," the deputy commands and takes his place near the wall on the defense's side of the room.

When the people are seated, Judge Willows says, "This court is now in session. Bring in the jury," and twelve Hall County citizens file in and take their seats in the jury box.

Seven women and five men from various backgrounds sit quietly waiting. Their ages appear to be from about forty to seventy. The oldest is a seventy-year-old white-haired man with half glasses resting on the top of his head. He's holding a legal pad and pencil ready for the proceedings to begin. When Larry questioned him during the jury selection, he very proudly stated he had ten children, fourteen grandchildren, and two great, great grandchildren.

"Do you want me to name them?" he asked.

Larry laughed and replied, "I don't think that will be necessary but I bet you could."

Larry and Mr. Orge stand to introduce themselves to the judge. "Larry Dunn for the prosecution, your Honor," Larry announces, facing the judge.

"Wilford Orge for the defense, your Honor," Mr. Orge states and they sit back down.

"Mr. Orge," the judge says and Mr. Orge approaches the jury for his opening statement. "Good morning," Mr. Orge smiles politely to the jury then continues. "What you hear this morning may be quite shocking to some of you. My client sadly fell into the influence of a group of people at a time in her life that is very susceptible to all kinds of influences, both good and bad. Because she believed what she was hearing, she became more deeply involved in those beliefs to the point that she didn't know right from wrong. Her beliefs and actions led her on a destructive path. It is that path that has led us to be here today. I ask you to listen closely and in doing so you will see a woman that has lost touch with reality. I don't condone what she has done but we will show she did not, and still does not, realize her actions were wrong. Wrong in society's eyes and wrong in the eyes of the law. I ask that you give her the psychological help that she needs. She needs psychiatric counseling, not jail. Thank you."

Mr. Orge returns to his seat. "I ain't crazy!" Nancy sneers when Mr. Orge sits down next to her. He has deliberately not mentioned the plea of "guilty by reason of insanity" because Nancy goes ballistic upon hearing those words and he hopes to prevent any violent outbursts during the trial. She finally agreed to that plea when Mr. Orge convinced her that's her only chance of staying out of prison for the rest of her life. Nancy has been glaring at him the whole time during his opening statement and he sighs with relief that she kept quiet.

"Mr. Dunn," the judge says. Larry stands, adjusts his suit jacket, and walks slowly, stopping in front of the jury members. He rubs his chin thoughtfully then looks at each jury member before speaking. "It's always someone else's fault!" he begins forcefully. "A group of kids I got tangled up with eventually caused me to believe it is okay to stalk a small child, to threaten a mother and her child with a switchblade knife, to terrorize a five-year-old little girl and try to kidnap her, to forcefully try to steal her away from her mother. Is that what the defense is trying to get you to believe? It's not her fault. She didn't know it was wrong! Ladies and gentlemen, what happened to taking responsibility for our own actions? What happened to recognizing evil when it stares us in the face?"

Larry paces slowly back and forth in front of the jurors, and stops. "You will see evidence that will prove that this woman knew *exactly* what she was doing and took very calculated steps to try to accomplish her goals. She's accused of stalking, attempted kidnapping, and assault with a deadly weapon. We will prove beyond a shadow of a doubt that she bought the knife she used. We will prove that for five long years, she intentionally and with forethought searched and planned to kidnap a child. She hunted down her victim, a five-year-old child and her mother! When my client and her daughter fled for their safety, she hunted them down again. Oh, she knew what she was doing! Let there be no doubt in your minds and the evidence will prove it. Thank you." Larry returns to his seat. Carla takes a deep breath and looks at him, saying nothing.

"Mr. Orge, you may call your first witness," the judge says.

* * *

Mr. Orge is a short man of stocky build in his early fifties. His dark brown hair reminds one of a cartoon character that has plugged his finger into a live socket. Thick bifocal glasses keep sliding down his nose. His dark brown suit and striped tie look to have been dug up from the attic.

* * *

"I call Carol McPhee," he states, facing the judge. Nancy stands up and glaring at Carla, she walks to the witness box beside the judge's bench and plops down on the chair. She has been allowed to wear street clothes rather than the jail-required jumpsuit. Her brown curly hair has grown, leaving black roots crawling across the top of her head. She's wearing a plain blue dress but what catches Carla's eye is a long heavy chain necklace with a skull and cross bones with the numbers 666 embossed in silver across the front dangling at the end of it. A crease in her dress partially covers the ornament but Carla has seen it as well as Larry. Carla shivers.

"Miss McPhee," the attorney begins.

Nancy butts in, "I go by Nancy!" she snarls.

"But your real name is Carol McPhee, is it not?" Her attorney counters. His frustration with his client is evident.

"If you say so," Nancy responds.

"Let's start with, did you have a child when you were seventeen years old?"

"Yes." She glares at Carla.

"Was it a boy or a girl?"

"A girl."

"How do you know that?" her attorney asks.

"Duh, I gave birth to her!" Carla responds sarcastically.

"But in fact you weren't told what the sex of your baby was nor were you allowed to see it, is that true?"

"I saw her in the nursery. But *they* wouldn't let me hold her!"

"Who is 'they'?" her attorney asks.

Carla leans over to Larry and whispers, "He sounds like he's the prosecutor."

"He's filed an insanity plea," Larry whispers.

"*They* are the stupid nurses!" Nancy snaps.

"Carol, ah, Miss McPhee, have you ever seen your baby since then?" Mr. Orge gently asks.

"I told you my name is Nancy and yeah after *they* gave her away!"

Mr. Orge turns to the judge, "Your Honor, with your permission, may I address my client as Nancy to hopefully lessen my client's hostility?"

"Mr. Dunn, do you have any objections?" the judge asks Larry. Larry quickly stands, says, "No, your Honor," and sits back down.

"You may do so, but," the judge replies then looks at the jurors and continues, "may I remind the jury of the defendant's true name, Carol McPhee." He looks back to Mr. Orge and says, "You may continue."

"Now Nancy, where were we?"

Nancy quickly answers, "We were talking about my baby being *stolen* from me!"

"Were there any other babies in the nursery when you first saw this child?"

"No. Just her."

"And you are positive this was your child?"

"Yes! They gave her to *that* woman!" Nancy points to Carla as she spits out the words.

"Let the record show Miss McPhee, Nancy, is referring to Mrs. Bloom," Mr. Orge states.

"Where did you see your child when you saw her again?" Mr. Orge addresses Nancy, once again shoving his glasses higher on his nose.

"In Ivy."

"That's Ivy, Georgia?"

"I don't know of any other Ivy," Nancy states flatly.

"How long had it been since you'd seen her the first time? When you saw her in the hospital nursery?"

"Five long years." Nancy tears up.

"That's a long time. How did you know she was in Ivy?" Mr. Orge asks.

"I tracked her down!"

"You tracked her down," he repeats.

"Yeah! She's mine and I'm going to get her back!" Nancy glares at Carla and fingers the skull and cross bones hanging on the chain.

"How did you know she was in Ivy?"

"My god told me."

"Your god? How does he talk to you?" Mr. Orge pointedly asks.

Larry leans over to Carla and whispers, "This is where it gets good."

Carla looks at him with a puzzled expression and says nothing.

"What do you mean?" Nancy asks.

"Just what I said. How does your god talk to you? How does he communicate to you?"

"Through the Ouija board." She hesitates for a second then adds, "And other ways."

A gasp is heard from the jury box and the old man is writing frantically on his pad.

"Who is your god, Nancy?" Mr. Orge gently asks.

Nancy sits up straight, throwing her shoulders back, which exposes the skull and cross bones hanging at her breast, raises her chin, and proudly pronounces, "Satan!"

A shiver runs down more spines than just Carla's. Four women in the jury box suddenly cover their mouth with a hand as they gasp. A loud groan is heard near the back of the room from one of the spectators. Whispers fill the room.

"Order!" Judge Willows demands, slamming the heavy gavel down.

Mr. Orge continues, "So, is Satan the one that told you the baby in the nursery was yours?"

"Yes."

"Is Satan the one who told you that your baby was in Ivy?"

"He helped."

"Satan helped you track down the child in Ivy. Is that what you want this jury to believe?" Mr. Orge asks incredulously.

Nancy jumps up and screams, "My god Satan knows all! He knew where to find her and he told me to look in the records and that's how I found her!"

A bailiff, standing at the end of the jury box, moves away from the wall and walks closer to the witness stand. Judge Willows commands, "Sit down, Miss McPhee!" Nancy glares at him and plops down onto the chair.

"I have just a couple more questions, Nancy." He looks at her sternly, looks at the jury members, walks closer to the witness box and states, "Isn't it a fact that your child was stillborn? The child you had that died at birth, was in fact *not* a girl, but a boy! Isn't it a fact, Miss McPhee, that you never knew the sex of your child? Isn't that true, Miss McPhee?"

Carla gasps loudly and begins sobbing. *Dear God, her baby was a boy! We went through this and it wasn't even a girl! Oh my God.* Larry places his hand on her shoulder.

Nancy flies up out of the chair and screams, "You're a liar! My baby did not die! That's a stinkin' lie! The Ouija board told me they were lying. Satan *never* lies. That woman has my kid and I'm going to get her back!"

"Miss McPhee, sit down! Sit down right now or I'll have you removed from this courtroom. Sit down!" Judge Willows is shouting at Nancy and pounding the gavel down trying to get order. The deputy has quickly walked to the witness stand and takes hold of Nancy's arm. She jerks away from him and with one hand, she grabs the skull and cross bones, raising it to her mouth and kisses it. "You're a stinkin' liar just like the rest of them!" she screams and plops down on the chair.

"Your Honor, I have no more questions," Mr. Orge states and turns to return to his chair at the defense table. His glasses have fallen, dangling from his ears and rest across his mouth. Grabbing his glasses and repositioning them, he sits down heavily at his table. Nancy continues to scream, "She's my kid and I'll get her back. You're a liar!"

"Bailiff, remove the defendant!" Judge Willows orders. As the bailiff takes hold of Nancy's arm and walks her across the room in front of the counselor's tables, Nancy screams at Carla, "You'll see this isn't over yet!" and spits at her. The bailiff jerks her toward the door and shoves her through it. Carla is sobbing when the judge announces, "We'll take a one-hour lunch break. Be back here at one o'clock to resume. Mr. Dunn, you may cross examine when we return. The jury may be excused." Judge Willows waits as the jury files out of the room. He rises and stalks out of the room.

Carla sits sobbing and Larry touches her arm, lets her cry, picks up the items on the table and places them in his briefcase, and gently says, "Come on. Let's get some lunch." Larry reaches for her arm to help her up. One woman who has been watching the proceedings approaches Carla with tears in her eyes. "Mrs. Bloom. I'm so sorry. This has to be awful for you and I just want you to know me and my friends are praying for you." Carla wipes a tear, says thank you, and Larry guides her to the elevators.

* * *

Larry's secretary has brought in Chic-fil-A sandwiches, French fries, tossed green salad in containers for each, and cold drinks and has them on the conference table in Larry's office. The coffee pot is brewing on the counter when Larry and Carla walk into the room. Carla plops down on one of the chairs and sobbing uncontrollably, lowers her head onto her folded arms on the table. Rick walks into the room and says something to Larry. Carla hears his voice and shoots out of the chair into Rick's arms, sobbing. He holds her tight and lets her cry. Once she is able to slow her tears, he gently releases her and guides her to the table. "Sit down, sis, and have some lunch," he says softly.

"I'm not hungry." She replies wiping her tears.

"Then have something to drink. You want some coffee?"

"Okay."

Rick pours her a cup of coffee and takes the seat next to her.

Carla's hands are shaking so badly that she slops some of the hot coffee out of the cup onto her hands. Rick grabs the cup and says, "Maybe you better have a cold drink."

Carla looks at him, smiles weakly, and states, "Very funny."

Larry takes a bite of his salad and says nothing.

Carla looks at Larry. "I can't do this. This is just more than I can deal with. Give her the plea deal and let's go home."

Rick immediately grabs her arm, "No! You can do this! If you let her get away with this, sis, she'll hunt you for the rest of your life! You aren't the only one she's stalked!"

Larry nods, puts his fork down, calmly states, "Rick's right."

"Her attorney is right! She's insane. Didn't you see her kiss that thing on her chain? She needs to be locked up in an institution."

"Giving in to their offer won't do that, Carla," Larry replies.

"Sis, listen to us. If she gets off with a slap on the wrist, like she wants, she will not get help. Remember that was part of her probation before and she skipped. You're stronger than you think. You can do this. Think of Missy. Do you want her to be stalked for years to come? There's no telling what Nancy will do if she doesn't get locked up for a very long time."

"They'll just let her out on probation in a couple of years anyway so what difference does it make?" Carla replies reaching for a French fry.

"That's not going to happen," Larry replies.

"And why not? Murderers get out in a few years!" Carla says stubbornly.

"Georgia law says that anyone who attempts to kidnap a child under the age of twelve, the sentence is twenty-five years to life. The judge can add no parole," Larry states as a matter of fact then takes a bite of his sandwich.

Carla sits thinking and slowly reaches for her sandwich. Larry and Rick remain quiet.

"Where is April and Alex, and the other witnesses? I thought they'd be in the courtroom." Carla asks and takes a small bite of her sandwich.

"I have them separated in different rooms. I don't want the defense to say they got their stories together. Each will come in when they're called. After they testify, they can stay in the courtroom if they want," Larry explains. His cell phone rings, he listens for a couple of minutes, says, "thanks" and hangs up.

"I want to call home and see how Missy is," Carla suddenly states.

Rick pulls out his cell phone and dials. He hands the phone to Carla as it's ringing. Carla talks to Berta for a minute while Missy comes to the phone and talks to Missy for a couple of minutes, reassuring her that everything is okay and they'll be home later in the evening. When she hangs up, Rick asks, "Is she okay?"

"Yes, Berta said they've been playing outside."

"They didn't take the boat out, I hope!" Rick exclaims, causing Carla to burst out laughing and she punches him on the shoulder.

"It's time to get back in there," Larry states, standing and stretching.

Rick hugs Carla as they stand at Larry's office door. "Hang in there, sis. I know this is rough on you but you're doing what has to be done. You're keeping Missy safe and that's what all of this is about."

Tears well up in Carla's eyes and she nods.

I'm keeping Missy safe, she thinks as they walk back into the courtroom and take their seats at the prosecutor's table.

Chapter 13

"All rise. The Honorable Judge Norman B. Willows presiding," the bailiff announces. Judge Willows strides into the courtroom and, once seated, announces, "This court is now in session. Bring in the jury." Nancy is sitting quietly next her attorney. Larry leans near Carla and whispers, "Be strong. This might get brutal." Carla looks at him, squeezes the tissue she has wadded in her hands, and nods.

"Mr. Dunn, do you wish to cross examine?" Judge Willows asks.

"Yes, your Honor," Larry replies.

The judge looks at Nancy and says, "Miss McPhee, you are still under oath, please take the stand."

Nancy walks slowly to the stand and takes her seat. She's wearing a black dress, black lipstick, and black nail polish. The skull and cross bones necklace rests against her chest. She looks at Carla then down at her hands.

"Miss McPhee, Nancy," Larry begins. "Are you on any medications?"

"One," Nancy responds.

"What is that medication?"

"It's a tranquilizer. I don't know the name of it." Nancy appears to be drunk.

"How long have you been on this tranquilizer?" Larry asks.

Mr. Orge stands. "Your Honor, what has this to do with anything?"

Larry quickly answers, "That will become evident in just a moment, your Honor."

"Overruled," the judge replies and looks at Nancy. "You may answer the question."

"Ah, what was the question?" Nancy asks, slurring her speech.

"How long have you been on this particular medication?"

"I just started it."

"When did you start it? Last week, yesterday, or maybe an hour ago?" Larry states.

Nancy's head bobs and she jerks her head up. "Ah, an hour ago." Her head bobs back down.

"Your Honor. I think it's obvious that this witness is unable to be cross-examined at this time. I would like to excuse her with the right to call her at a later time when she's more able to testify."

Mr. Orge stands, "No objections, your Honor."

"The witness may be excused," the judge states.

Nancy is helped from the stand and the bailiff assists her back to her seat. She plops down onto the chair and lays her head on her crossed arms on the table.

"Your Honor, may we approach the bench?" Larry asks.

Judge Willows nods yes and Larry and Mr. Orge walk to the bench facing Judge Willows. "Your Honor, it looks to me like this defendant has been deliberately drugged so I cannot cross examine her effectively!" Larry angrily says.

"That's not true!" Mr. Orge demands.

"It's pretty obvious she's drugged!" Larry states.

"Mr. Orge, your client has obviously been given something that is about to lay her out! Do you have any explanation for that?" Judge Willows says skeptically raising one eye brow.

"She was combative when she left the courtroom for lunch and began fighting with other inmates. The guards had to restrain her and she was given a shot. I was not made aware of this until after the fact, your Honor."

Larry looks at him incredulously and exclaims, "You really think we're going to believe that?" He looks to the judge. "Your Honor, she was in a *holding cell! Alone!*"

Judge Willows holds up his hand indicating Larry to stop and turns a stern look to Mr. Orge. "If I learn this is some underhanded ploy, Mr. Orge, to sway this jury or prevent testimony from your client, I will personally see to it that you will be selling hot dogs on Peachtree Street and never practice law in this state again! Do you understand me?"

Mr. Orge shoves his glasses up higher onto his nose and nods yes.

"I didn't hear you!" the judge demands.

"Yes, your Honor. I understand." Mr. Orge replies, embarrassed that he was called on the carpet.

"Let's proceed," Judge Willows states. The two attorneys return to their tables.

"Call your next witness," Judge Willows says to Mr. Orge. Mr. Orge stands, clears his throat, swipes at his glasses, and replies, "I call Dr. John Mulberry."

Dr. Mulberry is a short man wearing round glasses. His bald head glistens in the overhead lights and he walks quickly and with purpose to the stand. He's sworn in and sits stooped in the witness chair.

"Dr. Mulberry, have you had an occasion to examine my client, Carol McPhee?" Mr. Orge asks.

"Yes."

"And what were your findings?"

"She's heavily into worshipping Satan and as I told her, 'I do not deal in spiritual matters.'"

"Thank you. Your witness." He says to Larry.

"How many times did you see her, Doctor?" Larry asks.

"Once."

"And how much time did you spend with her?"

"Thirty minutes."

"In your professional opinion, does she know right from wrong?" Larry asks.

"In my opinion, she knows exactly what she wants and how to get it!"

"Thank you. That's all the questions I have." Larry leans back in his chair.

"Call your next witness," the judge says.

Mr. Orge calls Dr. Mark Mathews to the stand. Dr. Mathews recites his credentials.

"What conclusion have you come to after examining my client, Dr. Mathews?" Mr. Orge asks.

Dr. Mathews scowls, glances at Nancy, then states flatly, "I found her to be quite angry and heavily into the occult."

"In your professional opinion, Doctor, has this affected her sense of right and wrong?"

"I found that to be inconclusive."

"Inconclusive?" Mr. Orge asks, surprised.

"Yes. Who am I to tell someone who their god should be?" Dr. Mathews exclaims.

Mr. Orge has a surprised look on his face when he says, "Thank you, Doctor."

Larry whispers to Carla, "He wasn't expecting that."

"Do you wish to cross examine, Mr. Dunn?" the Judge asks.

"I have no questions of this witness, your Honor," Larry replies quickly.

"Call your next witness, Mr. Orge," the judge orders.

"I have no further witnesses, your Honor. The defense rests," he replies.

"Mr. Dunn, you may call your first witness."

Larry stands. "I call Mrs. Melba McPhee."

The courtroom doors are opened and a short woman with gray hair pulled into a bun at the nape of her neck slowly starts down the aisle. Carla turns to look at her and sucks in a breath. She and Nancy could almost be twins, excluding their age difference. The woman's sunken pale cheeks cause Carla to wonder if she is ill. The woman's dress hangs loosely on a frail body. There is no gleam in her eye as she passes the defense table walking toward the seat next to the judge's bench. She's sworn in and the bailiff helps her to step up to the chair and sit down.

"Good afternoon," Larry states.

"Hello," she replies softly.

"Am I correct in that you are Carol McPhee's mother?" Larry asks.

"Yes," Mrs. McPhee whispers.

"Please speak up, Mrs. McPhee. I know this is difficult for you."

She clears her throat and speaks louder. "Yes, I'm Carol's mother."

"When was the last time you saw your daughter?"

Tears well up in her eyes. "When she gave birth. Six years ago."

"You haven't seen her since then?"

"No."

"That's quite a while. Why is that?" Larry asks.

"She moved out. We've not had a good relationship for some time." Mrs. McPhee is twisting a hanky in her hands as she answers.

"How old was she when she moved out?"

"Fifteen, I think. Fifteen or sixteen," she replies, straightening the hanky out and twisting it again.

"That's pretty young to be on your own. Where'd she go?" Larry asks.

Carla is listening intently.

Mrs. McPhee glances at her daughter at the defense table. "With friends," she replies softly.

"Did you know these friends?" Larry asks.

"I didn't know them personally."

"Did you ever have any of them in your home?" Larry presses.

"A few of them," she whispers.

"Speak up, Mrs. McPhee. The jury needs to hear you."

"There were a few of them that came to the house." Mrs. McPhee angrily answers louder.

"You didn't want them there, did you?"

Mr. Orge jumps up, "Leading the witness."

"I'll rephrase," Larry says. "Did you want these friends in your home?"

Tears stream down her face. "No!"

"Isn't it natural for your child to have friends over? Why didn't you want her friends in your house, Mrs. McPhee?"

Mrs. McPhee begins crying. Larry waits. She dabs her eyes and suddenly shouts, "Because they're evil!"

Gasps rise from the spectators section and Judge Willows pounds his gavel. "Order!" he demands.

Larry walks to the stand and places his hands on the rail. Softly, he asks, "Did something happen that made you think they were evil?"

The courtroom is totally silent as several spectators lean forward listening intently for her answer. Carla is holding her breath.

"Please answer the question." Larry instructs.

Mrs. McPhee takes a deep shivering breath, glances at her daughter, and then lowers her head while twisting the hanky. "I walked into her room one day and they had painted a pentagram on her carpet. They had candles lit in the center of it and they were sitting around it chanting something." She begins sobbing.

Judge Willows leans toward her and asks, "Do you need to take a break?" She nods yes as she sobs.

Judge Willows announces, "We'll take a thirty-minute break. Court dismissed." He leaves the room and Larry assists Mrs. McPhee off the stand.

* * *

"That poor woman," Carla says to Larry as they sit in a lawyer's lounge sipping coffee.

Larry just looks at her and flips through a file laying in front of him.

"Larry? Do you think Nancy's attorney really drugged her to keep her from testifying?" Carla asks thoughtfully.

Larry closes the file and looks at her. "Yes. He knows what he's up against with all the evidence and witnesses. If he can make the jury think she's so sick she has to be drugged, then maybe she'll get placed in an institution instead of jail. I do believe he resorted to drugging her."

"Can you prove it?" Carla asks.

Larry sighs and leans back in his chair. "That's not really my priority right now."

Carla removes her cell phone from her purse and stands. "I'm going to call Missy."

"Okay." Larry returns to his file. Carla walks to the other end of the room and speaks to Missy.

* * *

"This court is now in session" Judge Willows announces. Looking out over the room, he notices there are fewer empty seats and there's now four journalists seated near the back.

Mrs. McPhee is sitting quietly on the stand as Larry sorts through a few papers on the table.

"Mr. Dunn?" The Judge says.

Larry turns to Mrs. McPhee and begins. "Are you feeling better now?"

"Yes. Thank you," she replies softly.

"Before the break, you told us you had walked into your daughter's room and saw a pentagram painted on the floor. That's a satanic symbol, is it not?" he asks.

"Yes."

"What else did you see in the room, if anything?"

"Two boys were playing an Ouija board."

"What, if anything, did you do? Please speak up so everyone can hear you."

"I told them all to get out! I was screaming to get out."

"Did they?" Larry asks.

"Carol was screaming and cussing at me, but yes, they all left except her."

"What happened after that?"

"Her father pulled up the rug and we burned it in the backyard." She begins crying.

"Did you do anything else?" Larry asks.

"I grabbed the Ouija board and was going to burn it too but Carol grabbed it out of my hands and ran into the bathroom and locked the door."

"Is this when Carol moved out of the house?" Larry asks.

"No."

"Did she continue to play with it?"

"Yes. We tried to stop her but she was obsessed with it."

Nancy sits looking at her mother with a blank stare. Carla has tears in her eyes.

"When did she move out and was there something that precipitated that move?" Larry asks.

A shudder courses through Mrs. McPhee. She takes a deep breath while looking at her daughter.

"Please answer the question, Mrs. McPhee, and be specific," Larry instructs.

Mrs. McPhee lowers her head and twists the hanky. Looking up at Larry, she takes a deep breath, sits up a little straighter in the chair, and then pronounces, "It was about a month later. We were asleep. Her father and I. We heard something and when her father opened his eyes, Carol was standing beside the bed with a butcher knife raised above him."

Gasps and whispers fly around the room. Nancy suddenly sneers, "I should have killed you both!" she whispers.

"Order! Order in this court!" Judge Willows demands pounding the gavel down several times.

When the room is quiet, Larry asks, "What happened then?"

"We were afraid to move. She just stood there with the knife raised in the air. Then she lowered the knife to her side and turned and walked out." Tears stream down her face and she sits crying and dabbing at her eyes.

"Did you call the police?" Larry asks when she's able to stop crying.

"No."

"Why not?"

"Because she's our *daughter!* We love her and didn't want her to go to jail."

"So what did you do?" Larry asks.

"We locked our bedroom door and the next morning, we told her she had to move out or we'd call the police and she'd go to jail. She wanted to move in with her friends. She moved out."

"When did you see her next?"

"She was seventeen and had gotten pregnant. She called and said she was scared and asked if I'd be with her when the baby was born."

"Were you? Were you there when she delivered the baby?"

"Yes. I spoke to the doctor when she was being prepped and he said the baby was dead. It would be a still birth and asked what I wanted to do."

"What did you tell him?"

"I told him not to let Carol see the baby and I wanted it cremated immediately."

"Did he agree?"

"Yes. He said he thought that was a wise decision."

Nancy's attorney is gripping Nancy's arm and whispering frantically in her ear.

"Did *you* see the baby when it was born?" Larry asks gently.

"Yes, he was a beautiful little boy," she replies through tears.

Nancy shouts, “You’re a liar!” Her attorney grabs her arm and whispers frantically to be quiet.

“Please control your client, Mr. Orge,” the judge orders.

“To the best of your knowledge,” Larry continues, “was Carol ever told the sex of her baby?”

“She told me she didn’t want to know and had told the nurses and everyone not to tell her. She wanted it to be a surprise.”

“When did she tell you this?”

“When she called asking me to be there and again at the hospital. I didn’t know she was pregnant until then.”

“Thank you.” Larry walks to his table and picks up three papers. He hands a copy of each to the defense attorney then hands the documents to the judge. “Exhibit A and B and C, your Honor.” The judge looks at them and hands them back. Larry walks to stand in front of Mrs. McPhee and continues, “Would you look at this document and tell me what it is?” he says, handing it to her.

Mrs. McPhee looks at it and states, “It’s a birth certificate.”

“What is the name on it?”

Tears stream down her face as she answers, “Baby McPhee.”

“And who is shown as the mother?” Larry asks.

“Carol McPhee.” Mrs. McPhee sobs.

“What is the sex of the child shown?”

“A boy.” She sobs.

Larry waits. When she’s finally able to control her crying, he hands her the other document. “Can you identify this document?” he asks, handing it to her.

She dabs at her eyes and says, “It’s the death certificate.”

“What is the name on it?”

“Baby McPhee.”

“What is the sex shown?”

“Male.”

“Please look at this one. What is this document?” Larry asks, handing her the third document.

“It’s a certificate of cremation,” she replies.

"What is the name on it?"

"Baby McPhee."

"Thank you." Larry retrieves the documents, turns to return them to his desk and suddenly stops. He turns, hesitates, and then asks, "Where is your husband now, Mrs. McPhee?"

"He died two months ago."

Nancy glares at her mother and states, "Good!" Mr. Orge reprimands her and apologizes to the judge.

"I'm sorry, and you? How is your health?" Larry gently asks.

Mrs. McPhee looks down at her hands in her lap and softly says, "I have cancer. I'm dying."

"I'm very sorry to hear that." Larry says sympathetically then states flatly, "I have no further questions for this witness," and returns to his table.

Judge Willows glances at his watch and says, "Its five o'clock and I think this is a good place to stop for the day. We'll reconvene at nine o'clock tomorrow morning." Turning to the jury, he continues, "You are not to discuss this case with anyone. Report back here at nine o'clock sharp tomorrow morning. You may be excused." The jury files out. "This court is adjourned." He slams the gavel down, everyone stands, and he strides out of the room.

* * *

Rick is waiting outside the courtroom doors when Larry and Carla exit. Larry turns to Carla, "I'm going back to the office. I still have work to do. I'll see you in the morning. Try to get some rest." He turns to Rick and says, "Make her rest," grins, and walks away.

Rick looks at Carla and says, "Why don't I take you home."

"I have my car and besides, April and Alex rode with me. I'll be fine but thanks."

"Okay but only if you promise to rest. This has been a tough day for you."

"Yeah, it has. I just can't believe she did all this and her baby wasn't even a girl!" Carla exclaims.

"Here come April and Alex. I'll see you in the morning." He leaves heading toward the front doors of the courthouse.

* * *

Carla, April, and Alex are quiet for a short time on the ride home. April wants to question her but Alex has said to let her be for the moment. Finally, Carla says, "I feel so sorry for Nancy's mother. This has to be absolutely horrible for her. Did you know she has cancer?" she asks no one in particular.

April replies, "Yes. Rick mentioned it."

"I just wanted to jump up and hug her when she left the stand," Carla says.

"That's that old soft heart of yours," Alex states.

"I can't imagine having my child turn out like Nancy has. Rick said they were Christians and they took her to church. So how does she turn out like this?"

"They start out innocent enough. The Ouija board is advertised as just another kid game and it looks fun. So they try it. So many of the books for kids are witches, magical powers, and the like and parents don't realize its witchcraft or occult messages. They even have this stuff in school libraries!" April exclaims.

"You're kidding! They can't have Bibles but they can have witchcraft and that stuff?" Carla exclaims.

"Yep!" Alex states. "All that kind of stuff. The atheist organizations will sue in a heartbeat if a kid prays but it's fine to be taught about the occult! It's disgusting!"

April continues, "The more that kind of stuff is available, the more interest a kid will have and pretty soon the child gets hooked up with some group that worships Satan or get into witchcraft. They don't realize what they've gotten into. Before they realize it, they're watching movies depicting unrealistic powers, magic spells, and what have you and will probably start reading about reincarnation, going to séances or fortune tellers thinking it is all fun and games and no harm in doing it. The further into it they go, the tighter the grasp the enemy has on them. Before they know it, the devil has control over their minds and it goes from there."

"It's sad but true." Alex agrees.

Carla shivers and pulls the car into her father's driveway.

* * *

Day two of the trial is not quite as harrowing as the first. Larry calls Carla to the stand.

"Good morning," Larry greets Carla as she adjusts her skirt when sitting down.

"Good morning," Carla replies, taking a deep breath. *I'm keeping Missy safe.*

"When did you meet Miss McPhee?" Larry begins.

"On the beach one day at the beginning of summer. I don't remember the exact date."

"Had you ever seen her before that?"

"No."

"How soon after that did you see her again?" Larry asks.

"That same day. We stopped in the variety store and she was there."

"Please tell us on what other occasions she appeared."

"Objection to 'appeared,'" Mr. Orge states.

"I'll rephrase. On what other occasions, if any, did you see Miss McPhee?"

Carla begins telling about Nancy showing up at her house, at the Publix, the variety store, and post office. "She showed up at church and tried to take Missy from her Sunday school class," Carla says, tearing up.

"What happened? How was she stopped?"

Carla looks down at her shaking hands, wipes a tear, and then states, "I'm not proud of it but I attacked her."

Larry hides a smile, remembering Carla telling him about the incident. "You attacked her? Tell us what happened."

Carla tells about finding Nancy holding Missy by the arm and trying to drag her out of the room, the teacher yelling, the fight, and the pastor breaking it up. "That's when we decided to leave Ivy and come here," Carla says.

"Refresh my memory, how old is your daughter?" Larry asks loudly.

"She was five. She's six now."

"Thank you," Larry states, shaking his head and repeats, just loud enough for the jury to hear it again, "Five years old!" then continues, "What, if any, effect did this have on you and your daughter?"

"Missy has been in counseling because she was scared to death Nancy would come and take her. She wouldn't leave the house, she slept with me, she had nightmares, and wouldn't even play outside unless I was right beside her." Carla begins crying.

Larry looks to the jurors as he waits for Carla to stop crying and sees two women have tears in their eyes. The oldest man, with half glasses resting on the tip of his nose, is writing frantically on his legal pad.

"And you?" Larry asks when she's regained her composure. "What effect has it had on you?"

"I wasn't sleeping, I was afraid to open my door because she might be standing there, I feared for my child's safety all the time!" Carla says, tearing up again.

"Have you had any counseling because of this?" Larry asks softly.

"Yes."

"And because of your fear and wanting to protect your five-year-old daughter, what did you do?" Larry asks.

"We came here to stay with my father."

"Did you feel safe then?"

"Yes, for a short time," Carla says, wiping her tears.

"Why a short time?"

"Nancy left a note in my father's mailbox-"

"Objection, your Honor. Hearsay." Mr. Orge interrupts.

"Sustained," the judge replies.

"Were you made aware that Ms. McPhee found you at your father's?"

"Yes."

"What action, if any, was taken to protect you and your daughter?" Larry asks emphatically.

"An undercover policewoman was assigned to us. She lived in my father's house with us and went everywhere with us."

"Was there an occasion when Ms. McPhee tried to take Missy again?"

Carla breaks down sobbing. Larry waits.

Judge Willows leans toward Carla and asks if she needs a break. Carla replies, "No, thank you. I'm okay."

Larry repeats the question.

"Yes! She threatened me and my daughter with a knife at church! That's when she was caught and arrested," Carla states loudly, glancing at Nancy.

"Thank you. That's all the questions I have for this witness, your Honor," Larry says.

"Do you wish to cross examine?" the judge asks Mr. Orge.

"No, your Honor."

Larry assists Carla back to the table and he calls his next witness. By the end of the day, Alex, April, Becky in disguise, Rick, Pastor Greely, the Sunday school teacher, and Dr. Anderson have all testified. The knife is shown with the testimony of the clerk where Nancy bought it, the note Alex found with Nancy's fingerprints on it, the note Dr. Anderson found in the mailbox with her fingerprints, and billing statements from therapy are produced. Larry has laid out a case that he feels cannot be refuted as to the guilt of Nancy and that she knew what she was doing.

Larry chose not to recall Nancy after observing her head bobbing on occasion, her blank stares, and occasional outbursts. After the attorneys give their summations, the judge instructs the jury and they leave the courtroom for their deliberations. Rick and Becky leave to return to their duties. Dr. Anderson gives Carla a kiss on the forehead and apologizes for not being able to stay and returns to the hospital. Pastor Greely and the Sunday school teacher has left to return to Ivy, leaving Carla, Alex, April, and Larry to wait for a verdict. At five o'clock, the judge announces that the jury may be excused and dismisses them to resume their deliberations in the morning.

Larry turns to Alex and April and thanks them for being there and tells them it isn't necessary for them to return. "There's no way we'll stay away!" April replies emphatically. Larry smiles and says, "I didn't think so," and walks to his office. Carla, Alex, and April go back to her father's house.

* * *

The next morning, the jury returns for deliberations and Carla, Alex, April, and Larry wait in his office across the street. Larry is working at his desk and the women and Alex sit chatting in the conference room. Larry pokes his head in the door and states, "Jury's back." They all rush back to the courthouse.

"This court is now in session," Judge Willows announces. "Bring in the jury." Nancy is once again dressed in all black. The light from overhead reflects off the skull and cross bones, giving it an eerie appearance. Carla shivers when she sees it.

Judge Willows goes through the list of charges asking, after each charge, the jury's verdict. Nancy has been found guilty on all accounts. They have found her not guilty by reason of insanity.

Carla bursts into tears of relief and Nancy angrily plops down onto her chair. Before dismissing the jury, Judge Willows looks at his calendar and states, "I will pass sentencing December twentieth at nine a.m. sharp. Thank you for your service," he tells the jurors. Slamming his gavel down, he exclaims, "Court is adjourned!"

Carla has called Berta and told her the news and said they'd be home soon. Upon entering the kitchen, Carla is grabbed into a tight hug from Berta with tears streaming down her face. "I am so happy they found her guilty," Berta cries. Carla is exhausted but knows she needs to talk to Missy, explaining the verdict and reassuring her that she's safe and will never see Nancy again. Alex and April go to find Jenny and Carla goes to talk to Missy. When they all return downstairs, Berta declares a celebration is warranted. A cake sits on the table with "Praise God" written in blue icing on top. Glasses, forks, saucers, and drinks accompany it.

"We get to eat it now?" Missy exclaims.

"Just a little piece since we haven't had dinner yet." Carla laughs.

Suddenly, the door opens and Rick and Kay enter. "A celebration! We're just in time," Rick shouts and everyone laughs. They all sit down around the table and the cake is sliced and served.

The next morning, Berta has laid the newspaper on the kitchen table. "Satan Worshipper Found Guilty" in bold black letters lay across the top. Carla sees it, shivers, and slides it to the other end of the table.

Friday afternoon, Carla is on the phone with Missy's teacher while April, Alex, and Jenny are packing to leave. "Since it's so close to the Christmas break, why don't you stay there and enjoy Christmas with your family? Missy has kept up with her homework and another week isn't going to make much difference," Missy's teacher suggests.

"That's very thoughtful of you. I think we will stay. It's a long drive to go back and forth. Thank you for understanding and I hope you have a very Merry Christmas," Carla replies.

"You too. I'll see Missy after the first of the year then. Have her keep doing the homework I send."

"I will. Thank you again. Bye."

* * *

"Well, we're all loaded," April says, walking into the kitchen.

"I'm going to miss you so much," Carla says and hugs April.

"So you've decided to stay until after Christmas?" April asks.

"Yes. I can't see going home and turning around and coming right back. Missy's teacher even suggested we stay."

"That was nice of her."

"Yes, it was."

April and Carla hear Alex calling to come on. "We need to hit the road before the work traffic."

The two women walk outside and Jenny is sitting in the van. Missy is standing beside the open car door telling her goodbye.

Carla hugs Alex, then Jenny, and finally April. "You got our Christmas presents?" Carla asks her.

Alex replies before April can, "Yes, they're all in the back." Carla can see suitcases, an ice chest, and a box filled with gifts in the back of April's van.

Another round of hugs and Alex pulls out of the driveway with Missy yelling, "Bye, Jenny," and Carla waving with tear-filled eyes.

Chapter 14

Larry, Dr. Anderson, and Rick are watching a ball game on TV while Carla and Kay sit talking in the kitchen. "Have you set a date for your wedding yet?" Carla asks Kay.

"Yes. August first. We're not going to have a big wedding."

"Why not? I thought everyone wants a big wedding," Carla replies.

"I already had that. Been there, done that, and don't want to go through that again." Kay laughs.

"I didn't know you had been married before." Carla says.

"Yes. I got married at eighteen. My mother insisted on the big wedding. You know, the whole shebang. He was abusive and after three years I got a divorce."

"I'm sorry to hear that."

"Thank you, but it was definitely for the best," Kay says.

"So what kind of wedding do you want?" Carla asks.

"Just a small one. Rick wants to have a preacher marry us on the pontoon boat." She laughs.

"You're kidding! Surely you aren't agreeing to that, are you?"

Kay laughs and replies, "No. But I thought it would be nice to have an outside wedding here if your father will let us."

"Oh, that sounds great! I'm sure Dad will be thrilled." Carla excitedly replies.

"Would you help me plan it if your Dad agrees?" Kay asks.

"I'll be in Ivy. But I'll do what I can."

Kay looks down at her hands then to Carla. "Rick and your dad really want you to come home, Carla. They're worried sick about you."

"Why? Nancy is locked up and I love it there." Carla suddenly feels a little agitated.

"I shouldn't have said anything. I'm sorry." Kay apologizes.

"What have they said? Obviously they've said more." Carla presses.

"Maybe you should talk to them. I've said too much."

"Please, you can tell me. What have they said?" Carla replies a little too forcefully.

"Rick knows you left to get away and think after your husband went to be with the Lord. He just feels like your future is here. That's all."

Carla sits thinking and says nothing. Just as she's about to speak, Larry walks into the kitchen, "Can I bother you for more chips?" Larry grins broadly.

Carla jumps up, "Sure!" and gets a fresh bag of chips from the pantry and hands them to him.

"Thanks. Why don't you two join us? It's a good game," Larry says, taking the chips.

"I need to see if Missy has awakened from her nap," Carla says, walking out of the room.

Larry watches her with furled brows then turns to Kay. "Did I say something wrong?"

"No, but I think I did," Kay says quietly.

The two walk into the living room and Kay sits down beside Rick and Larry returns to his seat. Kay leans over to Rick and whispers, "I need to talk to you." Rick looks at her and sees she has a troubled expression on her face. "Okay. Now?" he asks.

"When the game is over," Kay replies and they watch the rest of the game. After the game is over, Dr. Anderson excuses himself and goes to his office. Kay pulls Rick into the kitchen on the pretense of him helping her with something in order to talk to him in private. She tells Rick what she said to Carla and how Carla reacted and feels bad that Carla got upset. "I shouldn't have said anything," Kay says to Rick.

"She'll be okay. Don't worry about it," Rick tells her and gives her a quick hug. "Hey, we're going to dinner, why don't we invite Larry and Carla?" Rick suddenly suggests.

Kay smiles broadly, "Are you now playing match maker?"

"Not really but Larry does want to start dating her now that the trial is over."

"Do you think she'll go? What about Missy? She'll need a sitter," Kay replies.

"Berta usually does that and as to whether Carla will go, all we can do is ask her."

Larry, Missy, and Carla are playing a board game in the living room.

Rick picks up a glass of water and he and Kay join the others. "Hey, guys, Kay and I are going out to dinner later. Carla, Larry, why don't you join us?" Rick asks.

"What about me, Uncle Rick?" Missy asks.

"I think tonight is going to be big people night. You can go some other time," Rick says.

Larry looks at Carla and lays his game piece down. "Would you like to go, Carla?" he asks hopefully.

Before Carla can refuse, Rick quickly adds, "Come on, it'll be fun. A night out on the town will do you a world of good."

Kay adds, "Yeah, it will be fun. Come with us."

Carla looks at Larry, then each of the others and sighs. "Oh, all right. Maybe it will do all of us some good. That is if Berta will watch Missy!"

"But I want to come too," Missy says.

"Not tonight, honey. We'll go shopping tomorrow and have fun then," Carla replies.

* * *

The evening is spent having dinner in downtown Atlanta. With laughter and kidding around, they deliberately avoid any mention of the trial. Rick knows of a nice hotel with a live band and dancing and they all agree that sounds like fun. The four have danced to every song and at two in the morning, Larry is standing on the front porch with Carla. He leans down and kisses her ever so softly. Much to Carla's surprise, she leans into him, deepening the kiss then suddenly jerks back. Larry smiles and gently pulls her to him and wraps his arms around her, holding her. "That was nice," he whispers in her ear. He slowly releases her and holding her at arm's length looks into her eyes. "I had a great time tonight." Carla looks down at the ground then raises her head with tears in her eyes. Larry gently wipes a tear off her cheek and asks, "What's wrong?"

Carla unlocks the front door and quickly punches the alarm system buttons, "Come in for a minute."

Larry follows her into the living room and they sit down on the couch.

"Larry," Carla begins, taking a deep breath. "I like you but I feel like I'm betraying Mike if I go out with you, or anyone for that matter."

Larry scoots close to her and replies. "I guess I can understand that, but let me ask you this? Do you think Mike would want you to be alone for the rest of your life?"

Carla swipes at a tear and looks down at her hands in her lap. "I'm just confused right now. I don't know."

"I didn't know Mike, Carla, but I'd be willing to bet that he would not want you to have to raise Missy alone or be an old maid."

Carla chuckles, "An old maid?"

"Well, alone. You know, a gray-haired old lady living all by herself." He reaches over and places his index finger under her chin and gently raises her head so he can look into her eyes. "I'd like to spend more time with you, with you and Missy, but I'm not going to push you. If you need time, then I'll wait. I'm not going anywhere." He says seriously. When she makes no reply, he asks gently, "Can I call you tomorrow?"

Carla looks at him and nods yes. They stand and she walks him to the door. Larry turns and kisses his fingers then places them on her mouth. "Good night, pretty lady." He smiles and walks to his car. Carla gently closes the door, resets the alarm, and slowly climbs the stairs to her room.

* * *

The next two weeks, Missy and Carla have shopped, played board games, shopped some more, and it's as though the trial is far behind them. Larry has called several times and they've spent time talking on the phone. They've gone to dinner twice since their double date with Rick and Kay. Carla finally approaches her father and talks to him about her feelings about dating Larry.

"I know you loved Mike with all your heart, honey, but you have to move on. I don't think Mike would want you spending your life alone," he says sympathetically.

"I just feel like I'm betraying him," Carla says earnestly.

"After your mother died, I felt the same way. I wanted to ask a very nice lady out to dinner but I didn't because I felt I was betraying your mother."

"But *you* haven't dated since mom died." Carla responds.

"Sure I have but no one has been able to live up to your mother. Carly, no one will ever take Mike's place in your heart. But you can love again. It's a different kind of love because it's a different person. We love each person for who they are. Mike was a wonderful man. He loved you and Missy. I think Larry is a wonderful guy and if you should fall in love with him you won't be betraying Mike or what the two of you had together. There's room in your heart for more than one love."

Carla sighs loudly. "I'm just confused."

"Understandably so. Honey, you've gone through hell these past months. Give it time. There's no harm in going out with Larry. Have some fun and just see where it goes."

"I suppose you're right." Carla suddenly yawns and stands. "I'm tired I think I'm going to call it a night." She gives her dad a hug. "Good night, Dad. Thanks."

"Good night. Sleep well."

* * *

The next day, Carla is busy wrapping Missy's gifts in her room when there's a gentle knock on her door. "Telephone, Carla," Berta says and walks away. Carla picks up the cordless phone in her room, "Hello."

"Hi Carla. How are you?" Larry asks.

"I'm good. How are you?"

"I'm feeling *real* good right now." Larry chuckles.

Carla hesitates a bit confused at his exuberance.

"Don't you want to know why?" Larry playfully asks.

"Ah. Okay. Why?" Carla asks.

"Have you forgotten what today is?"

"Larry, what are you getting at?" Carla asks exasperated.

"The sentencing hearing!"

"Oh my gosh! I was thinking it was tomorrow. What happened?"

"The judge sentenced her to twenty-five years to life with no possibility of parole for the first twenty-five years. After that it's lifetime parole." Larry exclaims.

"What does that mean, lifetime parole?" Carla asks cautiously.

"It means that if she's paroled after serving twenty-five years, then she's on parole for the rest of her life. She has to check in with a parole officer all the time."

"But she can still get out." Carla exclaims.

"Carla, you'll never see her again. She'll be an old woman!" Larry states emphatically.

Carla sighs loudly. "Well, at least she's behind bars for a long time but I was hoping for the rest of her life!" Carla exclaims angrily.

Larry hesitates before answering. "Vengeance is Mine sayeth the Lord."

Carla says nothing.

"I need to go. I have another hearing in twenty minutes. How about we take Missy to a movie Friday night? There's a Disney movie. I don't remember the name of it," Larry says.

"Okay. I'll see you then."

"We'll stop for dinner so I'll pick you up about six?" He asks.

"That's fine."

"Okay. I'll talk to you later," Larry says and hangs up.

Carla plops down on the edge of her bed laying the phone down on the bed beside her.

The word *forgive* flicks through her mind. "I can't, Lord. I just can't forgive that woman for what she did!" Carla says out loud and picks up the phone to call April to tell her the news.

"Hi, April, I can't talk but a minute but I wanted to let you know the judge sentenced Nancy to twenty-five years to life with the possibility of parole after twenty-five years."

"That's great!" April responds.

"He should have given her life after what she did!" Carla replies angrily.

April is silent for a long moment. "Twenty-five years is a long time."

"It isn't life in prison! She can get out and come after Missy again!"

"Carla, I can understand how you feel but you are going to have to find a way to forgive her and move on. She'll be in prison for a long time. There's nothing saying she'll be paroled." April replies gently.

Carla grips the phone tighter then replies, "Yeah, well." She hesitates. "Listen, I better go. I promised Missy we'd go shopping today. Take care. Bye." Carla hangs up. *I don't think so!* Carla thinks and stomps downstairs.

* * *

Carla has invited Larry for Christmas dinner after he said his parents were on an around-the-world cruise and didn't know when they'd be back. Of course, Rick and Kay will be there, and she's looking forward to a wonderful family Christmas.

Two days before Christmas, Carla is helping Berta with preparations for Christmas dinner. They have Christmas music playing and Missy is busy using the cookie cutter to make tree-shaped cookies, Santa heads, and stars.

"Can I put sprinkles on them?" she asks.

"Sure. Just be careful not to get them all over the counter and floor." Carla laughs.

Berta smiles while listening to the exchange.

Missy suddenly asks, "Mama, are we going home after Santa comes?"

Carla suddenly stops what she's doing and looks at her. "Yes. We can't stay here forever."

"I wish we could live with Pa-pa forever," Missy says thoughtfully.

"But, honey, we have a home in Ivy. I thought you liked the beach." Carla replies.

"I do but I like it here too. I can't ski in the ocean. Are you going to marry Mr. Larry?"

Berta stops midstride on her way to the oven waiting to hear Carla's answer.

"Missy, Larry and I are just friends. We're going home after Christmas. You have to go back to school and that's where you go to school," Carla says firmly.

"I wish you'd marry Mr. Larry. I like him! I can go to school here!" Missy states firmly.

"That's enough, young lady! Now finish cutting the cookies so we can get them in the oven. I don't want to hear any more about this. Is that understood?"

"Yes, ma'am," Missy says and continues to cut cookies.

Berta resumes what she was doing, whispering, "Lordy, Lordy, Lordy."

* * *

Christmas morning is filled with excitement. Gift wrapping, empty boxes, and bows are scattered across the living room floor. Missy is buried in a pile of toys, books, and clothes and Dr. Anderson has his new sweater on. Everyone is laughing as Rick struts around the room modeling the Captain's hat that Carla bought him for when he's piloting the boat. Kay fingers her new pair of earrings Carla gave her, telling Carla, "They are really pretty. I like them. Thank you." A small diamond pendant that Rick gave her sparkles at her neckline.

Berta is sitting next to the fireplace holding the round trip ticket to Europe to visit her sister that she hasn't seen in ten years that Dr. Anderson presented to her. Tears stream down her face as she hugs the ticket to her chest watching the others enjoy their gifts. Carla finally stands, "I guess we should clean up this mess," she says to no one in particular. "I'll help," Kay says and begins picking up the empty boxes and wrapping. Berta goes into the kitchen after hugging Dr. Anderson for the fourth time and thanking him again. The doorbell rings and Larry strides in loaded down with an armful of gifts. The excitement rekindles and Kay says, "Oh, what the heck," and drops an armload of crushed Christmas paper in the middle of the floor.

* * *

A feast is set before them—roast duck, turkey, baked ham, sweet potatoes, brown rice, three different kinds of vegetables, croissants, rolls, salad. There's barely room for the plates with all the food spread across the long dining room table. Everyone is enjoying the food and conversation and laughter fills the room.

"Are you serious?" Dr. Anderson asks Rick. "You really want to get married on the pontoon boat?"

Rick is laughing at the expression on Kay's face. "Sure but this sweet thing doesn't like that idea," he replies, leaning over and nudging Kay.

Kay rolls her eyes and addresses Dr. Anderson. "What I would like is to be able to have the wedding in your backyard with the lake in the background."

"I think that's a wonderful idea!" Dr. Anderson states.

Rick continues to tease them. "Borrrring," he replies, laughing.

"I think Kay's right. Landside would be much more appropriate." Dr. Anderson laughs.

Missy chimes in. "They should get married on the boat. Then they can go swimming." She giggles.

Rick immediately agrees saying, "Yeah. We can wear bathing suits and not fool with suits, ties, and wedding dresses. We'll just say 'I do' and jump in the water!"

Missy bursts out in hysterical laughter. The rest of the meal is spent in silly conversation with everyone adding even more ridiculous ideas until everyone is laughing and wiping tears from their eyes.

Larry thanks everyone for a wonderful Christmas dinner and Carla walks with him to his car. "So when are you leaving to go back to Ivy?" Larry asks Carla.

"I'm going to spend the next two days gathering things together and we'll leave the next day."

"I'm sure going to miss you. Are you sure you don't want to move back here?" Larry says taking her hands in his.

Carla removes her hands from his and looks up at him. "My home is in Ivy. I wish everyone would stop pressuring me about moving back here!"

Larry draws her to him and gently says, "That's because we all love you."

"I know but I love living in Ivy," Carla whispers.

Larry releases her and looking down at her, "There's a couple of long weekends coming up. If I can get away, is it okay if I drive down and visit my favorite two girls?" he smiles.

"Let me know ahead of time and I can reserve a room at the Hyatt for you," Carla replies.

"Ouch!" Larry bursts out laughing.

Carla turns bright red.

Larry continues to laugh as he steps into his car. He motions with his index finger through the window for her to come close. She leans down and he takes her face in both of his hands and kisses her. "I'll call you tomorrow." He releases her and begins laughing again. Carla can still hear him laughing as he backs out of the driveway.

Chapter 15

The months have passed. Larry has come to Ivy twice and he and Carla talk on the phone everyday. Missy will be out of school for the Easter break soon so Carla tells her father they plan to visit for the week-long break. "I was hoping you would say that," Dr. Anderson tells Carla while talking on the phone. "We miss you," he says.

"I miss you too. We'll be there in a couple of days," Carla replies.

"Okay, honey. I need to run. Be careful driving."

"I will. Bye."

Larry is ecstatic that Carla and Missy are coming. Rick is sitting in Larry's office. He's come for some information about a case they're working on but Larry decides to change the subject. "Carla and Missy will be here Saturday. If I pay to fill up the boat with gas and the weather is nice, how about we take your boat out. We can work the winter kinks out." He laughs.

Rick looks at him suspiciously. "Why do I get the feeling there's more to this than working the kinks out, as you put it?"

Larry laughs and hedges.

"Come on. What's behind this? You know the lake will still be freezing cold," Rick persists.

"Nothing is behind it! I just thought we could all go buzzing around the lake for a little while," Larry replies.

"Okay. I get it. You're not going to tell me so, yeah, if the weather is nice we can go out on the lake. No need for you to pay for the gas though." Rick concedes.

Larry's intercom buzzes and his secretary says, "Mr. Dole is on line one."

Rick picks up his file. "I'll see you Saturday," and walks out of the office.

* * *

Carla wants to get on the road before sunrise, hoping to be at her father's by noon. The day is warm and beautiful and pulling into her father's driveway, she parks next to Rick's truck. Missy hollers, "Uncle Rick is here!" Carla told Larry last night on the phone what time she planned to be at her father's. She hardly steps out of the car when he pulls up behind her. "Mr. Larry is here too!" Missy yells and runs to his car. "Hi, Mr. Larry." She grabs him around the waist giving him a hug. He picks her up and hugs her. Carla stands beside her car waiting and watching. He sets Missy down, and grinning, walks slowly to Carla. "Hi," he says and pulls her to him, giving her a passionate kiss hello. Missy giggles.

"Your timing is perfect," Carla says, smiling.

"I took a calculated risk that you were here already or would be right behind me," Larry says as they walk around to the patio.

Rick and Kay are sitting at the patio table as Carla, Missy, and Larry round the corner of the house. They stand to greet them. Missy runs straight for Rick, yelling, "Hi, Uncle Rick. We're here." "So you are," Rick says, hugging her. Everyone hugs everyone and Carla says, "We need to get the suitcases out of the car." Larry and Rick immediately offer to do that for her and the women and Missy go into the house.

Rick looks at Larry as Larry pulls a suitcase from the trunk. "What'd you do, follow her from Ivy?" Rick halfway teases.

"Nah. She said she'd be here at noon so I just took a chance," Larry replies.

Rick reaches out, placing his hand on Larry's arm. Larry stops and sets the suitcase on the ground. Rick is looking at him with a very serious expression on his face. Larry says nothing, waiting for Rick to say something.

Rick clears his throat. "Okay, buddy, I want to know what's going on. You're messing with my sister and that concerns me," Rick says seriously.

Larry glances down at the ground then faces Rick. "I'm not *'messing'* with Carla, Rick. I love her. I have since high school. I think you already know that."

Rick studies him for a long moment before saying, "What's all this urgency about taking the boat out?"

Larry laughs, "Come on, Rick! What? You think I'm going to tie a block to her foot and throw her overboard or something?"

"You didn't answer my question," Rick states.

"Hey, if you don't want to take the boat out, that's fine. No big deal. I just thought it would be fun." Larry throws his hands in the air then turns and picks up the suitcase and begins to walk away.

"Larry!" Rick walks to him. "Hey man, I'm sorry. I know you love Carla. I guess I've just been a detective too long," he says.

Larry slaps him on the back. "It's okay. You love her too."

* * *

Dr. Anderson is at the hospital and Berta has gone shopping. Rick and Kay are sitting on the edge of the pool dangling their feet in the water watching Missy splash around. Larry and Carla sit at the patio table sipping ice tea.

Rick suddenly stands up and hollers, "Hey, Missy. You wanna go for a boat ride?" He glances back at Larry and winks.

It takes Missy a split second to shoot out of the water, jumping up and down shouting, "Oh boy."

Larry looks at Carla and says, "I hope the water isn't like ice. I'd like to do a little skiing."

"Are you nuts? That water is still freezing!"

"Oh it shouldn't be too bad. I need to work the kinks out of this old body. I'll be right back," and he walks off to his car.

"Can you believe him?" Carla asks Rick and Kay. "He wants to ski!"

Rick shrugs. "If that's what he wants to do then it's okay by me but I'm not getting in that water."

"Can I ski, Mama?" Missy asks jumping up and down.

"That water is so cold you'll freeze just putting your skis on."

"No I won't. Please." Missy begs.

"Come on. Let's walk down to the water and see how cold it is." Carla replies grabbing Missy's towel.

"I'll come too." Kay says and the three walk to the water.

"Okay, Missy. Wade out there up to your chest and see how cold it is." Carla says. Missy begins wading out into the water and when it hits her bare stomach she lets out a scream and runs back to shore shivering. Carla and Kay stand laughing. "Do you still think it's not too cold?" Carla asks Missy as she wraps the towel around her. Missy's teeth are chattering so she just nods.

Larry has changed into a pair of jean shorts, T-shirt, and flip-flops. Rick looks at him and just shakes his head and steps into the boat. He reaches into a compartment and pulls out his captain's hat Carla gave him for Christmas, puts it on, and hollers, "All aboard that's coming aboard." Everyone laughs and take their positions in the boat.

Rick watches Larry as he takes a seat placing his ski at his feet. *He's either crazy as heck or he's up to something!* Rick thinks and slowly backs the boat out of the slip. They speed around the lake for a short time when Larry tells Rick to stop, he wants to ski.

"Man, that water is like ice! Are you sure you want to do this?" Rick asks him upon stopping the boat and bobbing in the water.

"Oh, it isn't going to be that bad," Larry replies and prepares to jump in. He drops his ski over the edge, Carla tosses the rope out and suddenly Larry takes a deep breath and jumps. When his head returns to the surface he lets out an agonizing yell. Missy and everyone burst out laughing. Kay just shakes her head and says, "He's got to be crazy!"

Larry's teeth are chattering so badly he can hardly speak, "Tighten the rope." Rick pulls the boat forward very slowly stretching the rope and when Larry hollers to hit it, Rick shoves the throttle forward and they speed off with Larry flying behind.

Larry signals Rick to make a wide turn when they're out in open water. As Rick makes the turn, Larry maneuvers himself so he can ski close to the boat. He reaches behind his back with one hand and unties a string. Suddenly an eight foot banner releases behind him. He skis as close as he safely can to the boat and everyone starts screaming. Carla's hands fly to her mouth as she reads the banner. "Carla, will you marry me?" Suddenly, Larry falls and Rick spins the boat around to pick him up. Larry grabs hold of the side of the boat, handing his ski in and his lips are blue from the cold. His teeth are chattering when Carla leans over the edge. "Yes! You crazy man." She laughs. She leans over the edge even farther to kiss him and Larry jerks her over the edge. With a big splash, she hits the water screaming. As soon as her head reappears, Larry grabs her and kisses her passionately.

Missy is laughing hysterically, Rick is grinning from ear to ear, and Kay is crying. Larry finally releases Carla and hoists her up to get back in the boat. She sits huddled on the seat shaking violently. Missy hands her a towel and Carla tries to put it around her shoulders but is shaking too badly. "Here," Kay says and wraps the towel around her. Larry hoists himself into the boat with the banner hanging behind him in the water. He's shaking violently and struggles to put his hand in his shorts pocket. He pulls out an engagement ring but drops it on the boat floor. His hands are shaking so badly that he can't pick the ring up so he looks to Kay and whispers, "Help." Kay laughs and picks up the ring, handing it to him. Carla is still shaking uncontrollably. Rick is turned in the captain's seat watching the fiasco and laughing until tears come to his eyes. With shaking hands, Larry reaches out to take Carla's hand and after four tries, he is finally able to slip the ring on her shaking finger and says through chattering teeth, "I lo- lo- love you." Kay pulls the rope and the banner in. "Hold on," Rick yells and they speed back to shore.

The boat bumps the dock and Carla jumps out immediately and races toward the house. Rick tells Larry, laughing, "Hit the shower in my room." Larry hops off the boat and races to the house. Rick, Missy, and Kay are left to dock the boat, pick up, and cover it.

"Uncle Rick, does this mean Mama and Mr. Larry are getting married?" Missy asks.

"It sure does." Rick laughs.

Kay and Missy begin laughing about Larry pulling Carla into the cold water and all three are laughing as they each help to store the boat.

* * *

Carla appears downstairs and Kay hands her a cup of hot chocolate. Larry appears a few minutes later clad in Rick's old bathrobe. When he enters the kitchen, everyone bursts out laughing. Embarrassed, Larry's face turns bright red and he meekly says, "I'll get my dry clothes from the car," and hurries out the door. Carla holds her hand out, gazing at the one carat marquis diamond. On each side of the diamond are three smaller diamonds lined along the band. "It's beautiful!" She says and tears well in her eyes. Kay walks over and takes her hand, looking at the ring. "I'm so happy for you. Hey, we could have a double wedding!" She says then hugs Carla.

"Let me see." Missy exclaims. Carla shows her the ring on her finger.

Missy grins from ear to ear and exclaims, "I'm glad someone around here listens to me!" Rick roars with laughter as the women hug again.

Berta has gasped, cried, and hugged Carla three times when Carla flashes her engagement ring under her nose. They all enjoy a good laugh as Carla retells the whole event. "Oh, honey, I am so happy for you," Berta says, wiping tears off her cheeks.

That evening, after Larry, Rick, and Kay leave, Carla grabs the phone and when April answers, Carla yells, "I'm getting married! Larry proposed."

April screams. "Tell me, tell me all about it. How? When?"

Carla tells her all about taking the boat out, Larry skiing and freezing to death, how everyone thought he was crazy, and continues telling her every detail. The two women talk for an hour on the phone laughing and sharing.

"So when are you getting married?" April finally asks when they've calmed down.

"We haven't set a date but I've been thinking about something Kay said," Carla replies.

"What's that?"

"When she was looking at my ring, once I thawed out," she laughs, and continues, "Kay said we could have a double wedding. Her and Rick are getting married August first and we're planning a garden wedding here at Dad's for them."

"I like that idea! That would be so cool," April replies.

"Yeah, I kind of think so too. I'm going to ask Kay if she was serious. The more I think about it, the more I like the idea," Carla says thoughtfully.

"Well, let me know! Of course I'll be there."

"Oh you'll be here! I want you to be my maid of honor," Carla exclaims.

April gasps. "Oh, Carla, I would feel so honored." April squeals then shouts, "Carla's getting married and I'm going to be her maid of honor!" The two women laugh and continue their conversation.

After hanging up, Carla walks down stairs when her father enters laying his briefcase down. Carla grins from ear to ear and hides her left hand behind her back. "Hi, Dad."

"Hi, honey. Where is everyone?" he asks.

"Missy is asleep and Larry, Rick, and Kay left a couple of hours ago."

Dr. Anderson looks at her, grinning, "What are you hiding behind your back?"

"Oh nothing." Carla laughs.

"I recognize that twinkle in your eyes. You did the same thing as a kid. What are you hiding?"

Carla laughs and pops her hand out from behind her back shoving her ring up close so he can see it."

"Oh, honey," he says, taking her hand in his.

"Larry proposed today and I said yes." Carla laughs.

"That's wonderful. Come on in the office with me and tell me about it. I need to get off my feet. I had a ten-hour surgery today and I'm pooped."

Carla and her father go to his office and Carla begins telling him every detail and events of the day.

Dr. Anderson finally asks, "So does this mean you'll be moving back here?"

Carla looks down at her hands in her lap, "I don't know, Dad. We haven't talked about that."

He studies her for a long moment, looks at his watch, then replies, "Well, it's something you two will have to work out. It's almost midnight and I have a surgery at eight. I need to get some rest. I'm happy for you, honey."

"Thanks." Carla walks to him and hugs him, "I love you. Good night."

"I love you too."

* * *

The next morning, Carla, Larry, and Missy go to the Easter worship service at the church where Nancy was arrested. Carla shivers as she passes the hallway where Nancy had drawn the knife on them. Larry has deliberately engaged Missy in animated conversation as they pass the hallway. After the service, they go to a local restaurant for lunch. During the conversation Carla decides to tell Larry about the idea of having a double wedding with Rick and Kay.

"Have you asked Kay if she was serious?" Larry asks.

"Not yet. I thought I'd call her tonight. We've been kind of making plans for their wedding. I wanted to see how you feel about it before saying anything to her," Carla explains.

"I think it's a great idea! If that's what you want, then I'm all for it."

"Can I be in the wedding too, Mama?" Missy asks.

Carla and Larry grin. "Of course! You can be my flower girl."

"What's a flower girl?" Missy asks while taking a bite of her fish.

"The flower girl throws flower petals down in front of the bride as she walks down the aisle." Carla explains.

"But she'll walk on them!"

Carla laughs. "That's what she's supposed to do."

"Oh."

Larry looks across the table at Carla. "We do have some things we need to talk about."

Carla knows where this is headed and nods her head yes. "I know but later."

As though Missy knows what they mean, she suddenly asks, "Are we going to live here?"

Carla and Larry look at each other. Larry replies, "Do you want to live here?"

"Yes!" Missy states emphatically.

"That's something Larry and I have to talk about. Finish your lunch and we'll get ice cream on the way home." Carla says, hoping to change the subject.

* * *

That evening, Carla calls Kay. "Were you serious when you mentioned we could have a double wedding?" Carla asks her.

"Yes! I think it would be fun. Neither one of us wants a big wedding and your dad said we could have it there."

"Then let's do it." Carla laughs.

They begin talking about how they can coordinate things since she lives in Ivy and Kay finally asks, "Carla, have you and Larry talked about where you'll live?"

Carla sighs. "No, but I'm just about convinced I'll have to move back here. He can't very well quit his job to move to Ivy."

"That's true," Kay says softly.

"He's coming to dinner tomorrow night and we're going to have to talk about all this. If I'm going to move back here, I need to start making some decisions about the house in Ivy." She sighs loudly.

"It's a lot to think about. I know you two will work out whatever is best. When are you leaving to go home?" Kay asks.

"The day after tomorrow. Missy goes back to school Friday. I have a lot to do when I get home."

"Well, if I don't see you before then, I'll talk to you later in the week. Oh this is exciting! I can't wait to tell Rick."

"Do you think he'll object?" Carla asks.

"Oh heavens, no! I had even mentioned it to him before Larry purposed." She laughs.

"You knew he was going to purpose!?" Carla asks incredulously.

"No. It was just that it was so obvious Larry loves you and I had told Rick that if the two of you decided to get married then we could have a double wedding."

"Oh! It was that obvious?" Carla says, surprised.

"Yeah. To everyone but you." Kay laughs.

"I guess we just see what we want to see. I better let you go. You have to go to work in the morning and I need to start getting things ready for us to leave."

"Okay. Listen, I'll call you the end of the week. Have a safe drive home," Kay says.

"Thanks. Bye."

* * *

Larry and Carla sit together on the couch in the living room after dinner, talking about their future.

"I can quit my job here and open my own practice down there or we can live here," Larry says.

"I can't ask you to do that. I'll go where you want to live," Carla replies.

"Ivy is a small town, honey. It takes quite a while to build a practice even in big towns. I know you love Ivy but realistically we'll do better here."

Larry wraps his arm around her shoulders and pulls her to him. Carla nuzzles up against his chest. "You're right." She sighs.

Larry kisses the top of her head. "We could keep the house in Ivy for a summer house." Larry suggests.

Carla raises up and turns to look at him. "I hadn't thought about that! I thought we'd just sell it."

"Well, we can do that if you'd rather. But we all love the beach. We could keep it for a while and if we decide later to sell it, we can always sell it."

"Let's do that. Keep it for a summer house for now." Carla exclaims.

"When does Missy get out of school?"

"The end of May sometime."

"I can start looking around for a house if you want and when she's out of school then we can move you."

"Can we afford one on the lake? I'd really like to have one with a dock and have our own boat." Carla grins.

"Now you're talking!" Larry laughs.

Carla suddenly yawns. "Oh, excuse me. It's late and the car is loaded. I want to leave before work traffic in the morning. That way, Missy will sleep most of the way and I won't have to stop every five miles."

"I'm going to be in court all day but call and leave word with Sara that you're home when you get there." Larry pulls her to him. Looking deep into her eyes he slowly lowers his face to hers and their lips touch softly. Larry groans and draws her into a deep passionate kiss. Carla melts into his arms. Finally, Larry releases her and clearing his throat he says, "I better get out of here." Carla chuckles, gives him a quick kiss and Larry leaves.

Chapter 16

Carla arrives back in Ivy and as she and Missy take suitcases out of the trunk, April and Jenny see them. April comes running down the street with a handful of Carla's mail she's been picking up for her while they were gone.

Jenny yells, "Hi, Missy," as she tries to keep up with April.

Missy drops the small box she's holding and runs to greet Jenny. "Mama and Mr. Larry are getting married!" Missy excitedly tells Jenny.

April runs up to Carla, "Let me see, let me see." She laughs excitedly.

Carla holds out her hand showing April her engagement ring. "Oh, it's beautiful!" April exclaims. She grabs Carla and hugs her. "I'm so happy for you that I could spit." April laughs.

Carla grabs the handle of a suitcase and tiredly says, "Thanks. Come on in."

"I brought your mail," April says as they enter the house.

"Just throw it on the table. I'll go through it later. It's probably all junk mail," Carla states.

Missy and Jenny run to Missy's bedroom. Carla and April can hear the girls giggling.

"Would you like some coffee?" Carla asks, walking to the cabinet.

"Sure. I'll bet you are beat after that drive."

"Yeah, I'm pretty tired," Carla replies, filling the coffee pot with water.

"So did you talk to Kay about a double wedding?" April asks while taking a seat at the table.

"Oh yes! We're going to do it. I'm really excited about it." Carla sits down in a chair across from April at the table while the coffee brews.

"When did you say it is?"

"August first. Oh, and Larry and I talked and I am going to move back home."

"I figured you would. Dog gone it, Carla, I'm going to miss you so much." April makes a pouting expression.

"Oh, but we're not going to sell this house right now! We've decided to keep it as a summer house."

"That's great! You'll get to spend the summers here. That's a great idea!" April exclaims.

Carla gets up and pours them each a cup of coffee and sits back down. She reaches over and fans through the mail and stops suddenly with her hand on a letter.

"Carla? Did you hear what I said?" April says when Carla hasn't answered. She notices Carla looking at the letter and that her face has gone pale.

"Carla? What's wrong!?" April asks concerned.

Carla picks up the letter and looks more closely. The return address is from a prison and Carla throws it down as though it burned her fingers. Her hands are shaking.

April slowly reaches across the table and picks up the letter. "Oh my gosh!" she exclaims.

Carla is shaking. "It has to be from Nancy!" she whispers glancing toward the hallway that leads to Missy's room.

"Don't open it! Call Larry and tell him. He'll know what to do." April says and drops the letter onto the table.

"I can't believe she has the nerve to write to me!" Carla whispers angrily.

"Call Larry!"

"He's in court all day today. Oh shoot. I need to call and let him know I got home okay. He said to leave word with his secretary. I better call right now before I forget." Carla reaches for the cordless phone while tears well up in her eyes. "I'll just be a minute," she says to April, dialing Larry's office number.

"I'll go check on the girls," April replies.

Carla tells Larry's secretary to tell Larry she got home okay and to please have Larry call her as soon as possible.

"You sound upset. Are you okay, Carla?" Sara asks.

"Yes. No. Just have Larry call me the minute he can. Thanks." She hangs up and swipes at a tear.

April returns and sits back down. "The girls are playing."

Carla begins to cry. "I can't believe this. Will we never be rid of this crazy woman?"

April walks around to her and embraces her. "Maybe the prison can stop her from sending you mail. Larry will know what to do." She soothes Carla.

"Mama, we're hungry!" Missy announces running into the room. She skids to a stop, "Why are you crying?" she asks Carla.

April releases her and Carla coughs, quickly shoves the letter under the other mail hiding it, swipes at her tears, and says "I'm okay, honey. I'm just tired."

"Can me and Jenny have a sandwich?"

Before Carla can answer, April says, "We need to go home, honey. She can have a sandwich at home. Jenny come on, we need to leave." April shouts. April can see Carla is really upset so suggests Missy come play at their house for a little while and she'll feed the girls. Carla agrees and walking outside, April turns to her, commanding her not to open the letter until she talks to

Larry. Carla promises and walks to the car to haul more stuff into the house while April, Jenny, and Missy walk down the sidewalk to April's house.

* * *

That evening, Carla is drying Missy off from her bath when the phone rings. "Go ahead and put your PJs on," Carla says, reaching for the cordless phone.

"But it's too early to go to bed." Missy says.

"You don't have to go to bed right now. Hello," she quickly says into the phone.

"Hi, honey. Are you okay?" Larry asks.

"I just got Missy out of the tub and was drying her off." She turns to Missy, "Missy, go put your PJs on!"

"It sounds like a bad time. Do you want me to call you back in a little while?" Larry chuckles.

"Ah. No," she answers, walking down the hall.

"Sara said you sounded really upset when you called. What's going on?" Larry asks concerned.

Carla glances down the hall to see if Missy is in her room then sits down on the couch. "I got a letter from Nancy! It was in the mail April brought over. What do I do?" Carla's voice begins to sound frantic.

Larry swears under his breath. "What did she say?"

"I haven't opened it. I don't care what she said! Should I just burn it?" she exclaims.

"No. Put it in an envelope and send it to me. Carla, don't read it. I'm sure it will just upset you," Larry states.

"Larry, why is she writing to me? Why is she doing this?" Carla begins to sob.

"Honey, calm down. Carla. Honey. Take it easy. Mail it to me and I'll take care of it. Do you have a pencil and paper? I'll give you the office address. Honey?"

Carla dries her tears and goes to the kitchen table. "Okay. What's the address?" she sniffles. With a shaking hand, she writes down the address and blurts out, "I wish we could move right now!"

"I know, honey. It will be okay. I'll put a stop to the letters and that will end it," he reassures her. Carla calms down and they talk about other things.

* * *

Carla finally crawls into her bed late that night. She's put Nancy's letter in an envelope and has it ready to mail to Larry. She's had to resist opening it even though a large part of her doesn't want to know what she wrote. She finally won the tug of war of her will and shoved it into an envelope and sealed it. Her mind seems to be on a fast track of its own so it takes her a while to finally fall asleep. Her sleep is fitful and in the middle of the night she screams. Her eyes fly open and she's sitting straight up in her bed grasping the blankets like a lifeline. Once she is able to calm down, she thinks about the dream. *It's the same dream I had before Nancy stalked us. The wave is about to overtake us.* She shivers and lays back down. *That scripture on the wall is in Revelations. What in the world does it mean? Lord, help me to understand if this is something you are showing me.* Carla is finally able to go back to sleep but her sleep is troubled and when she awakens in the morning, she feels like she's been in a battle and lost.

* * *

Friday morning is back to the routine of getting Missy to school. Sitting in the long line of parents dropping off their kids in front of the school, waiting to pull up to the entrance, someone knocks on her car window. She turns and Pastor Greely is smiling at her. Carla quickly lowers her window. "Good morning," Pastor Greely says.

"Good morning," Carla replies.

"I thought I recognized you. Hi, little lady." He adds, addressing Missy.

"I didn't know you have children going here," Carla says.

"Yes. I have three. First through third grade. They missed the bus this morning so I told my wife I'd drop them off on my way to the church."

Carla nods.

"How are you doing?" Pastor Greely asks.

"We're doing pretty well. We've been at my Dad's over the Easter break and just got back." Carla replies.

Pastor Greely glances down at the ground then back at Carla. "I hope everything has worked out with that situation." He glances at Missy.

Carla knows what he's talking about and replies. "I'd like to come talk to you about something if that's okay."

"Sure. I have an hour or so later this morning if you'd like to come by."

"What time?"

Pastor looks at his watch, "How about ten o'clock? Will that work?" he asks.

"Yes. Thank you." A horn beeps behind her.

Pastor Greely steps back and says, "I'll see you then."

Carla pulls forward, kisses Missy bye, and Missy jumps out of the car and runs to the school doors.

Carla returns home and places the breakfast dishes in the dishwasher. Her phone rings and Larry says, "Good morning, my sweet thing."

Carla laughs and says, "Good morning to you."

"I only have a minute but I wanted to see how you are this morning," Larry states.

"I didn't have a good night, if that's what you mean," Carla replies.

"I'm sorry. Are you okay?" Larry asks concerned.

"I had that dream again."

"The one with the waves?"

"Yes. I don't understand it. It's like the Lord is telling me something but I don't know what," Carla says, taking a sip of coffee.

"Maybe the pastor can help you. Have you thought about talking to him?"

"As a matter of fact, I have an appointment with him this morning. He saw me dropping Missy off this morning and we talked for a minute."

"That's good. Listen, honey, I need to run. I'm due in court in ten minutes. I'll call you tonight. Love you."

"I love you too. Fry'em!" Carla laughs.

Larry laughs and hangs up.

* * *

Carla knocks gently on Pastor Greely's open door. He looks up, smiles. "Carla, come in," he says, laying a pen down on his desk.

Carla steps in and takes a seat across from him. "Thank you for seeing me," she says, setting her purse on the floor next to her.

"I've been meaning to call you and see how things have been going since the trial. I apologize for having to leave so quickly after I testified but I had a funeral to perform the next morning and needed to get back."

"I understand completely. I'm grateful you came."

They talk about the trial, the verdict that was passed down, Carla becoming engaged this past week, her plans to move back home, and finally she looks down and remains silent for a long moment. Pastor Greely looks at her. "Is there something else you wanted to talk to me about?" he gently asks.

Carla takes a deep breath. "Yes. I've been having a dream and I don't understand it. I don't know if the Lord is telling me something and I thought maybe you could help me."

"I'll try. Let's pray first."

They pray, asking the Lord to reveal any insights or revelations and to bar the enemy from interfering. When done, Carla begins telling him about the dream. "It started before Nancy started stalking us," she begins. "Then, just as the wave is about to overtake me, I always wake up scared to death!" she finishes.

Pastor Greely reaches for his Bible and is flipping through the pages.

"That scripture written on the wall, in the dream, what does that mean? Is that what the Lord is showing me? I don't understand," Carla says.

"Here it is. That's Revelation 12:16." He reads the scripture out loud then begins to explain. "This is where Satan is waiting for Jesus to be born and God takes Mary to a safe place. The dragon, Satan, wants to destroy her and the child." He begins reading the scripture. "'So the serpent spewed water out of his mouth like a flood after the woman that he might cause her to be carried away by the flood.'" He closes his Bible and looks at Carla.

"But what has that to do with me?" Carla asks, confused.

Pastor Greely leans back in his chair gazing at Carla intently. "I think your dream is a warning," he finally says.

"A warning?"

"Yes. Not just to you but to all of us. Scripture shows, in these passages, that Satan is wanting to destroy the Savior of the world. If he can do that, he destroys all that Jesus will do. That wipes out Jesus dying on the cross and our eternal salvation. Of course, he didn't succeed, praise be to God! I think the waves in your dream represent the waves of evil that Satan sends out. There's more than one wave so I think that represents his demons. The waves are furious. The waves are all consuming and will destroy all that is in their path. That's what Satan and his demons try to do. They rob, steal, and kill. The people running—men, women, and children—represents both Christians and nonbelievers. You said you asked the Lord to help you in your dream."

"Yes."

Pastor Greely continues, "You asking for God's help represent the Christians crying out to God. The woman bumping into you, cussing, and almost knocking you down could be the Lord's way of representing nonbelievers. For you personally, I think the Lord was warning you about Nancy. But He was also showing you that He will protect you and Missy. 'The earth swallowed up the flood' that you saw written on the wall shows God's protection of His child. He protected your child from Nancy, who was/is being influenced by the dark forces."

Pastor Greely leans forward, placing his elbows on his desk. "Carla, since Adam and Eve, man has been given a choice as to whom they will follow. Satan is not happy about that because many will follow Christ. Satan's whole purpose is to sway people, trick them, influence them, and get them to follow him rather than Jesus. He'll use any means he can to accomplish that. He uses the internet, TV, books, video games, movies, and even other people to hook people in. If he can influence even the smallest child he will do so because usually what we are taught as children is what we will believe later in life. That's why it's so important that we teach our children about the Lord and monitor what they watch, who they hang out with, and what they do. Nancy is a perfect example of that. Dark influences are all around us."

Carla has tears in her eyes. "You gave a sermon on that," Carla whispers.

"Yes, I did."

"I remember that so clearly because that's when I think the Lord showed me that's what Nancy was up to. She was going to try to kidnap Missy." Carla begins to cry.

Pastor Greely walks around to her and stands with his hand on her shoulder. "The Lord protected you and your daughter."

Carla whispers, "Thank you, Jesus."

Pastor Greely hands Carla a tissue and softly asks, "Have you been able to forgive her?"

Carla shakes her head no as she blows her nose.

"Then we need to do that," he replies, leaning against his desk.

"I don't know that I can," Carla says, stuffing the tissue down into the top of her purse.

"Forgiving someone can be very difficult at times. I don't think the Lord ever says, 'I don't think I can forgive Carla right now.'"

Carla looks up at him, wiping tears from her eyes.

"Carla, God forgives us! He doesn't wait until it feels right. He doesn't let anger or hurt get in His way. He also says that not forgiving is a sin and that if we do not forgive others He will not forgive us."

"But she threatened us with a knife!" Carla exclaims.

"I understand that, all the more reason to forgive her. It isn't for her, Carla. It's for you. You will not be free of the anger and the bitterness toward her until you release it through forgiveness. Give it to God, let Him deal with it."

Carla sits quietly for several minutes. Pastor Greely returns to his seat behind his desk and sits praying quietly.

Carla finally looks up at him, "Okay."

Pastor Greely returns to Carla's side and kneels down next to her chair. "Would you like me to lead you in the prayer?" he asks gently.

"Please," Carla whispers.

"Then let's pray." Pastor Greely leads her in praying forgiveness for all that Nancy has done, naming everything specifically. He then leads her in asking the Lord to forgive her for any part she knowingly or unknowingly played in the situation and asking God to release her from the anger and bitterness she has toward Nancy. "Set her free, Lord Jesus. In your Holy Name. Amen."

Carla ends the prayer sobbing uncontrollably.

Chapter 17

In the next two months, Carla is very busy sorting through, throwing out, and giving away items the Lord is showing her she no longer needs. Clothes that are too small for Missy are neatly folded and placed in one box, clothes that she no longer wears goes in another. Books, CDs, old dishes, and toys that Missy no longer plays with are all placed in bags or boxes and are set in the corner to donate to the Salvation Army. She's been cleaning closets and cabinets, tossing things out of the garage. She and Kay have been on the phone making plans for their wedding and Larry has contacted a realtor and looking at houses.

Carla is scooting a heavy box across the floor when her phone rings.

"Hello." She says out of breath.

"Hi, honey. You sound out of breath," Larry greets her.

"I am. I'm trying to move a heavy box and ended up having to shove it across the floor."

"So how's the packing going?" he asks.

"It's going. I didn't realize I have accumulated so much stuff in such a short time. But I'm getting there. It helps with Missy being in school."

Larry laughs. "Yeah, I would imagine she wouldn't be that big of a help."

"She can help with some things but it just makes it easier this way. So how are you?"

"Busy. I just won another case. Praise God."

"That's good."

"What I called about is I think I found our house."

"Really? Tell me." Carla plops down at the table.

"I really think you'll like it but I want you to see it before I put an offer on it. Can you come up for a couple of days? Maybe April can take care of Missy."

"You mean now?" Carla asks incredulously.

"Yes. The house is on Lanier, honey, and has been reduced in price like you wouldn't believe. I need to get a contract on it pronto before someone else snatches it up. I don't have time to go into the details right now but I'm almost positive this is what we want."

"Okay. I need to call April. When do you want me to come?"

"Tomorrow. I'll call the realtor and let her know you'll be here. What time do you think you can come?"

"Wow, this is awfully sudden."

"I know. I'm sorry but we have to act fast if this is what we want."

"You're sure this is it?"

"I'm pretty sure you're going to love it. I gotta go. I'll call you later this afternoon. Can you know by then?"

"Yes. I'll call April right now. I hope she's home. Larry, I can only stay overnight. I just have too much to do here."

"We'll talk about it later. Love you, bye."

Carla whispers bye and gently lays the phone down deep in thought. *Lord?* "Go for two nights," the Lord whispers. Carla picks up the phone and dials April's number. April answers on the first ring. "Wow, you must have been sitting on the phone," Carla says.

"I just hung up with a friend and had barely put the phone down. How are you?" April asks.

"Stressed out like a stretched rubber band about to break." Carla sighs.

"What's going on? I know you're sorting through stuff."

"Larry just called and wants me to come see a house he thinks is what we want. He said I need to come tomorrow so he can put a contract on it."

"He sounds like he's pretty sure then," April replies.

"He is but I'm over my head with things to do here and I'll need to be there two nights. That's why I've called."

"Say no more." April laughs. "Of course Missy can stay with us. She and Jenny will have a great time and I can handle getting them off to school."

"Oh, April, I don't know what I'll do without you," Carla says, relieved.

"What time do you want to bring her?" April asks.

"I thought I could get her off to school in the morning and leave from there but now I'm not so sure."

"Why don't you bring her over tonight and then you can get some rest tonight and leave early like you have been doing?" April suggests.

"Are you sure? That would really help."

"Of course! One more night isn't going to make any difference."

"You are a Godsend. Thank you. I'll get her a bag packed with school clothes and bring her over about seven. Is that okay?"

"That's fine. The girls can take a bath and I'll have them in bed by eight." April says.

"Okay. I'll see you then. Thanks again."

As soon as Carla hangs up, she heads to Missy's room and begins putting Missy's things together that she'll need. *Lord, help me here. I'm feeling overwhelmed and I just have so much to do.* "You'll be fine. I'm with you," the Lord reassures her.

* * *

Missy is in a mood and fussing about wanting to go with Carla. Tears are flowing and Carla is stressed and not wanting to argue with her.

"Missy, you can't go this time. I'll only be looking at houses and I'll be back in two days. You have school. Now stop crying and help me get your things in the suitcase."

"But I want to go!" Missy cries.

Carla throws Missy's suitcase on the bed and walks out of the room. *Lord I need your strength!*

The phone rings and Carla grabs it. "Hello!"

"Oh that didn't sound good," Larry states.

"I'm stressed, I'm tired, Missy is in a mood and I still have to pack my stuff for tomorrow. I just don't know if I can do this by myself!" Carla exclaims exasperated.

"I'm sorry, honey. What can I do to help?" Larry says sympathetically.

Carla plops down on the couch. "Oh nothing. It's just been one of those days."

"Do you think it will help if I talk to Missy?" he suggests.

"You can try. Hold on. Missy, come here, honey. Larry wants to talk to you," she hollers.

Larry talks to Missy for a short time while Carla places Missy's clothes, toothbrush, hairbrush, and pajamas in her suitcase. She hears Missy giggling. Missy walks in with a smile and hands the phone to Carla. Carla walks back into the living room and sits down. "Wow, what did you tell her?" Carla asks.

"I told her about the house and told her it's a secret and she could come and pick out her room when school is out. She liked that idea." He laughs.

"You told her about the house and I don't even know about the house." Carla laughs.

"You'll see it tomorrow. Honey, I just know you're going to love it!"

"Okay. I need to go. I'm leaving before dawn again so I hope to be at dad's before noon."

"Okay. Drive safe. I'll see you tomorrow. Call me before you get to your dad's and I'll meet you there. I took tomorrow off. Carla? I love you! Bye."

Carla walks back to her room and hauls out a suitcase. Missy comes in smiling and giggling. "Mr. Larry told me a secret and I can't tell you." Missy giggles.

"He did? I guess I better not ask you what it is if it's a secret," Carla says, relieved Missy is in a better mood now.

"Can we go to the beach?" Missy asks.

"No, honey. I have to pack my things and we're going to go get pizza for supper in a little bit. Do you have your things ready to take to Jenny's?"

"Yes. Can Jenny go with us?"

"Not tonight," Carla replies, placing slacks in the suitcase.

Carla continues to pack and Missy goes to play with her dolls.

By bedtime, Carla is exhausted and when the alarm goes off at four she feels as though she's only slept a few minutes. She's called Larry so isn't surprised to see him sitting in his car in her father's driveway when she pulls in four and a half hours after leaving her house in Ivy. He hugs her tight, kisses her, and says, "You look exhausted!"

"I am."

"The realtor is going to meet us at the house in an hour."

"That sounds good. Come on. Maybe Berta has the coffee on," Carla says, taking his hand and walking to the back patio.

They spend the time talking and drinking coffee and Larry refuses to tell her about the house except that it's on the lake. "It's a surprise." He laughs when she presses him for details.

* * *

They pull into a long driveway that leads to a two-story house. The realtor is waiting and steps out of her car when they pull up. Larry introduces Carla to her. "Susan, this is my fiancée, Carla."

"Hi, Carla. It's nice to meet you. Are you ready to see what might be your new home?" she smiles.

"Yes." Carla says looking at the beautifully cared-for front yard. A large bird bath stands in the center of a flower garden. Red azaleas are in full bloom along the front of the house with a full-length porch. Potted plants in decorative pots are scattered amongst wicker chairs and love seats.

Entering the front door, Carla gasps. Larry grins from ear to ear. She enters a great room with huge windows taking up almost a whole back wall. The cathedral ceilings stretch throughout the open floor plan. Carla says little as they walk through the house with Susan, pointing out various amenities, upgrades, and special features.

Larry follows behind Carla, grinning and saying nothing. He laughs each time she gasps or says, "Oh, it's beautiful!" The house has four bedrooms, three full baths, a large den with a stone fireplace. Walking from the formal dining room into the kitchen, Susan states, "This is a chef's kitchen with all the latest appliances and upgrades." Carla runs her hand across the smooth granite countertops and stainless steel appliances. Upstairs, she walks into a bonus room and looks around. The room is empty and she looks at Susan with a questioning look. "It's a bonus room," Susan explains. "Mr. Dunn said you have a six-year-old daughter. This would make a wonderful playroom for her."

Susan is finding it rather odd that Carla and Larry are saying nothing. Most clients ask several questions or make comments. What she doesn't know is that Larry wanted Carla to walk through the house once and say nothing until after she's seen the whole house. Carla steps into the master suite and can't help but exclaim, "Oh my gosh! It's gorgeous!" Large French doors open onto a balcony. Carla steps out onto the balcony and gazes out over Lake Lanier. Tears come to her eyes and she turns to Larry. "I can't believe this. It's absolutely beautiful!" Larry laughs and says, "Come on. You ain't seen nothing yet," and takes her hand, guiding her into the master bath. A four-person spa takes up one corner with a large decorative frosted window above. The shower is big enough for three people and marble counters hold two large sinks. Carla can't believe her eyes. Larry takes her hand and guides her back downstairs and they enter the full size finished basement.

Carla looks at him and grins. "Can I talk now?" she asks, laughing. Susan grins.

"Yes." Larry laughs and grabs her in a hug then releases her.

Carla screams, "I love it! I can't believe how beautiful it is! Oh, my gosh, honey, I can't believe this." Larry and Susan stand laughing as she runs through an office area, a bedroom, a full bath, and living room with a fireplace. She exits through the outside door from the small kitchen and stands gaping at a beautiful backyard with a manicured lawn, a brick fireplace at one end of a swimming pool, and a large ground level deck. She turns and runs up the stairs leading up to a large wooden deck and plopping down on a patio chair, she stares out over the swimming pool and at the lake. A ski boat sits gently rocking in a covered slip at the end of the yard. Larry and Susan are talking quietly as they climb the stairs and Larry walks over to Carla. Looking down at her, he raises one eyebrow and asks, "Well?" *As though I even need to ask,* he thinks. Carla jumps up and tells Susan, "You just sold yourself the most beautiful house in the whole world!"

Susan grins and asks, "You don't want to see the other two we have picked out?"

"No!" Carla states flatly and turns to Larry. "I absolutely love this one! Let's go look again," and she enters the house through the patio doors off the kitchen. This time, her tour of the house is not in silence. When all of her questions have been answered and she's gone through every room at least three times, Larry takes her back to her father's to rest, stating he'll be there for dinner since she's invited him. He and Susan meet at her office to take care of the paperwork.

* * *

After checking with Berta, Carla decides to call Kay and invite her and Rick to dinner. Since she's in town, she thinks it's a good time for them to talk about some of the wedding plans including Rick and Larry for their input. At dinner, Carla is telling everyone about the house and Larry expounds on the great deal he was able to negotiate on it. "The owner's wife passed away and he said he just couldn't stand being there anymore and was anxious to sell," he says.

Carla interrupts, saying, "We'll leave you three to chat and we're going to the kitchen." She runs her hand across Larry's back when she passes behind him going toward the kitchen.

"So where's it at?" Rick asks when they've left.

"About a mile from here." Larry replies.

"That's great! We'll have to ride by it and see it," Dr. Anderson says.

"What's really great is the owner is going ahead and moving out. We'll close before Missy gets out of school so Carla can move in as soon as Missy is finished."

"And you?" Rick grins with a mischievous glint in his eye.

"Me? I'll be in my apartment until we get married."

Rick bursts out laughing. "Yeah, right!"

Dr. Anderson looks at the two of them, clears his throat, and says, "I think any temptations can be resolved quite easily by Carla and Missy staying here until the wedding."

Rick roars with laughter and Larry turns red.

The two women are in the kitchen talking wedding plans and hear Rick laughing.

"I wonder what all that's about," Carla says.

"There's no telling. Now, what are we going to do about a cake? What do you like?" Kay asks.

"It really doesn't matter to me. If we're only going to have fewer than a hundred people then I would think a three tier would be more than big enough. What do you think?"

"I think that should be plenty. We're not going to have a reception dinner kind of thing so let's just plan on cake and drinks. How's that sound?" Kay states, writing on her list.

The women continue to plan until Carla begins yawning. "You're exhausted. We need to leave so you can get some rest. What time are you leaving Wednesday?" Kay asks, shoving her notepad and pencil in her bag.

"Probably about nine. I'll miss the work traffic and hopefully be home before Missy gets out of school," Carla replies, trying to smother another yawn.

Rick and Kay leave, Dr. Anderson heads for the hospital, and Carla and Larry are saying their goodbyes beside his car. Larry hugs her tight.

"I can't wait until you get moved back here," he states, holding her.

"Yeah, me too. I can't believe how beautiful that house is," she says, looking up at him.

Larry grins. "I knew the minute I saw it you'd love it." He releases her.

"We're going to have to buy some furniture. Even if I bring all of mine and what you have, it still won't be enough."

"We can buy new stuff to fill in what we don't have. Plus you want to leave some in the Ivy house, don't you, for when we go there?" Larry asks, leaning against the car fender.

Carla yawns, covering her mouth, she shakes her head. "I don't know. Let's talk about it later. I need to go to bed."

Larry draws her to him and kisses her lightly. "Call me when you get home. I love you so much." He kisses her again, more passionately.

"I love you too," Carla says and Larry leaves.

* * *

Missy sees Carla leaning against her car in front of the school and screams, "Mama," racing to greet her mother. Carla grabs her up hugging her. April is standing beside her car a few car lengths behind Carla's and laughs. She walks to Carla, "I think she's one happy little girl right now."

Carla lowers Missy and hugs April. "Come over after a while. Boy, have I got a lot to tell you! The house is beautiful!" she states.

"Okay. Let's get the kids settled and I'll be over in about an hour. I'll bring Missy's things with me," April replies then tells Jenny to get in the car so they can leave.

* * *

Carla tells April, in great detail, all about the house while the two sit together having coffee. "It sounds absolutely beautiful," April finally says then continues, "I have something I want to run by you. You and Larry can talk about it and see what you think."

"Would you like more coffee?" Carla asks pouring herself another cup full.

"No, thanks. I think I've had enough. I talked to Alex's mother this morning. They live in Michigan. They're thinking about moving down here. The cold weather is starting to really bother them."

"It does get cold there!" Carla replies.

"Well, I was telling her about you getting married, keeping the house here, and all that and she asked if you might be interested in renting it."

"Oh, wow. I don't know."

"I told her I would ask you about it. I know you said you were going to use it for a vacation home but I wouldn't think you would be coming down this summer with just getting married, honeymoon, and getting settled there. Maybe they could rent it for the summer until you decide what to do," April suggests.

"That's an idea and you're right. We'll be moving as soon as school's out and with wedding plans and all that. Let me talk to Larry. How soon do they need to know? Oh, will they bring their own furniture? We may take some for the new house."

"They have all their own furniture! They plan to move, not just stay for the summer," April states.

"Okay. I'll talk to Larry tonight and let you know. That may be the best thing for right now."

"Well, listen, I know you're tired so we need to go. I can't wait to see your new house." April hugs Carla.

"I wish I had taken some pictures. I was just so tired I forgot. Thank you so much for taking care of Missy. I hope she wasn't a bother," Carla replies.

"Lord, no. She was great. You know those two. They're perfectly happy being together. Jenny, come on, honey, we need to go," April hollers.

"Mama, can Jenny spend the night with me now?" Missy asks when the two girls enter the room.

Carla and April burst out laughing. "Haven't you two spent enough time together already?" Carla asks Missy.

The girls giggle and Missy says, "No."

Carla looks at April, "I don't think so. I've had a long drive and I'm tired. We need to use tonight to rest."

"Okay. But tomorrow night?"

"Let's wait and see." Carla laughs walking the three to the door.

* * *

Carla is busy packing. She and Larry decided to allow Alex's parents to rent the house so she has lined up movers, notified the various services that need to be changed, and is busy with those things that are required with any major move. She and Kay have been back and forth in phone conversations about the wedding plans and Carla is feeling more and more overwhelmed with the moving date getting closer and closer. Missy will be out of school in another week and April has had her playing at her house a good bit of the time trying to help Carla while she handles the last minute moving preparations. Carla's phone rings. She drops a stack of books onto the cluttered couch and grabs the phone. "Hello."

"Collect call from—"

Carla clicks the phone off and throws it onto the couch. She knows its Nancy calling. This is the third time in the past two weeks that she has called. Carla shoves items on the couch aside, making room, and plops down in the vacant spot. Her hands are shaking. *Something has to be done, Lord. Make her stop calling here!* The loud ring of the phone startles her, causing her to jump. She ignores it, letting it continue to ring. It finally stops. *I thought Larry put a stop to this!* She thinks and takes the phone and places it back in its cradle. A moment later, the phone rings again and angrily she grabs it and shouts, "Stop calling here!"

"Carla? Carla, it's me." Larry shouts into the phone.

Carla bursts out crying.

"Talk to me, honey. What's going on?"

"She called again!" Carla sobs. "I can't take any more, Larry! I thought you put a stop to Nancy calling."

"When did she call!?" Larry demands.

"Just now! I don't need this!" she cries.

"Calm down, honey. I'll call the prison again. I'll take care of it!" Larry states emphatically. "How's the packing coming?" He asks more gently.

Carla wipes her tears, takes a deep breath and replies, "I'm down to just the beds. We're using paper plates because I've packed all the dishes."

"I wish I could have been there to help you with everything," Larry says softly.

"I know. I'm sorry. I feel like I'm about to have a nervous breakdown. I'll be so glad to get this move over with."

"The moving van is coming Saturday. It won't be long now. Should I come down there this weekend? I can help when they get there."

"Can you take the time? You said you had a big trial coming up," Carla asks, hoping he can take the time.

"I'll make the time. Honey, I know this has been so hard on you. I'll tell you what. I'm going to take Friday off. How about I come Thursday after I get out of court? That way I'll be there Friday and Saturday when they get there. Will that help?"

Carla bursts out crying tears of relief. "Oh gosh, yes. Thank you!"

"Okay. I'll call you when I leave and, honey, I'll take care of the phone calls. Check your caller ID before answering," he instructs.

"I always do but I've been so busy I just end up grabbing the phone."

"I love you. I'll see you in a few days," Larry says.

"I love you too. I can't wait for you to get here. Bye."

* * *

Missy is playing with Jenny at April's while Larry helps direct the movers. Carla is vacuuming the rooms as they're emptied out. Finally the house is empty and Carla stands in the middle of the living room. *I love this little house. In a way, I hate to leave it but in another way I don't. Thank you, Lord, for the good times we've had here and for bringing me here to heal. It would have been better if that woman hadn't spoiled everything but you protected us. Thank you, Father.* A loving and gentle voice replies, "This is a new chapter in your journey, My child. Go in My peace."

Missy is in the car waiting. "Are you ready?" Larry asks, wrapping his arms around Carla's waist from behind. Carla turns in his arms, smiles, and replies, "Yes." Larry kisses her gently and they walk out to the cars. April, Alex, and Jenny stand together to see them off. Carla hugs each with tears in her eyes. "I'm going to miss you," she says to April.

"I'm going to miss you too. Call me as soon as you can," April replies with fresh tears forming.

The moving truck engine roars and slowly pulls away from the curb. Carla gives April another quick hug and runs to her car. The cars pull out following the moving van and April, Jenny, Alex, Carla, and Missy are all shouting goodbye and waving when they disappear around the corner.

Chapter 18

Carla has been busy unpacking. Larry is involved with a big publicized case so has left the decisions for furniture choices to Carla. He has had little time to be of much help but helps as much as possible in the little time he has away from court and hearing preparations. Missy is ecstatic about getting to pick out the curtains for her room and helps Carla unpack her clothes and placing her toys, dolls, and dollhouse in the bonus room that is to be her play room. While furniture shopping, Missy sees a four poster bed with a sheer canopy. She runs to it and flops down on the edge. "Mama, please, please, please can I have this bed?" She begs.

Carla laughs. "You already have a bed."

"But not like this one! Please, Mama, can I have this one?"

Carla looks at the sales lady and asks the price. The saleslady gives her the price, adding, "We can give you a small discount on it since you're buying several items if you want the bed."

"Pleeease, Mama."

"Okay." Carla laughs and the saleslady writes down the information, adding it to the lamps, rugs, bedroom suite, couch, recliner, and bookcases.

* * *

Carla decided to stay with her father until the wedding. She and Missy go to their new home during the day to do the necessary things but Carla told Larry she didn't want to stay there, feeling they should all move in as a family after the wedding. He agreed and Dr. Anderson was delighted, stating, when Carla told him, "Human nature being what it is, I think that's a wonderful idea." Carla and Berta burst out laughing and Carla hugs her father.

* * *

Rick is busy packing and moving furniture and boxes to Kay's home. He sits with Larry in a fast food restaurant. "So how is your moving coming?" Larry asks, taking a bite of his hamburger.

"It's coming. My partner came Saturday and we got the truck loaded with some furniture. The place really looks bare." Rick laughs.

"Are you moving in with Kay before the wedding?" Larry asks grinning.

"Nah. I thought I'd move in with you." Rick laughs hardily. "We could make your apartment a bachelor pad for a few weeks."

"My apartment! Shoot, I'm down to paper plates, a bed, and my desk." Larry laughs.

"Maybe we should have had separate weddings. I think it would have been easier."

"Don't say that to the women if you want to live long!" Larry laughs.

"Yeah. They're pretty excited. So where have you two decided to go for a honeymoon?" Rick asks, grabbing a French fry.

"Carla said she'd like to go to Acapulco. I really don't care. I haven't had time to think about anything but this trial. Where are you going?"

"We decided on the Bahamas. Are your parents going to be able to come to the wedding?" Rick asks.

"Yeah. They'll fly in a few days ahead of time. I made reservations for them at the Hilton. They said they'll be leaving the next day for Europe."

"Wow, they sure like to travel. Kay's sister and parents are coming in from Arizona. They'll stay with her and from what I understand will leave while we're in the Bahamas."

"Well, old buddy, we aren't going to be footloose and fancy free for very much longer. A couple of the lawyers said they want to give me a bachelor party," Larry states but doesn't seem too thrilled about it.

"Yeah, some of the guys at the precinct are planning one for me." Rick laughs and adds, "That's going to be one wild party, I can tell you. Get a bunch of cops together and only the Lord knows what will happen!"

Larry laughs and says, "I'll go to yours and you come to mine."

They both laugh, finish their meal, and each leaves to go back to work.

* * *

Carla and Kay have made reservations at a nice restaurant in Atlanta for two days before the wedding for dinner. Larry's parents, Kay's parents and sister, April, Alex, Dr. Anderson, Berta, and the brides and grooms will gather for a pre-wedding meal and as an opportunity for everyone to meet and get acquainted. Berta feels especially thrilled to be included in the gathering. At first, she declined the invitation, stating, "Honey, I'm just the housekeeper."

Carla looks at her incredulously, "You are like a mother to Rick and I! Don't give me that 'I'm just the housekeeper.' You have been, and are a part of this family, and I won't take no for an answer!"

Berta tears up and hugs Carla tightly. "I love you two as though you were my own. Thank you."

"Then you're coming?" Carla asks.

"It doesn't sound like I have a choice now, does it?" Berta laughs. "I would love to."

* * *

The wedding party and parents are gathered at a long table in the banquet room of the restaurant. Everyone is enjoying their meals and getting acquainted. Larry's parents tell about their world cruise and where they plan to go in Europe after the wedding, Kay's parents talk about the mission trip they took, Rick and Larry deliberately avoid the topic of their bachelor parties, and Missy and Jenny giggle together about being flower girls. By the end of the evening, everyone is acquainted and excited about the upcoming wedding.

* * *

The morning of the wedding, and although the wedding isn't until seven thirty that night, Carla steps into the kitchen very early and looking toward the center island, her hand flies to her mouth as she gasps. Berta is putting the last touch to the wedding cake she has created for them. "Oh, my gosh! It's beautiful!" Carla exclaims.

Berta turns, grinning from ear to ear. "It has turned out nice."

Carla gazes at the three-tier butter cream cake. It's sixteen inches at the bottom with each white frosted layer a bit smaller than the next. Elegant pastel yellow and cream-colored banners float down and around from the top. Three daisy bouquets of flowers enhance each layer. A large matching bouquet sits atop.

"I can't believe you made this!" Carla says, standing before it. "I can't wait for Kay to see it." She grabs Berta into a hug with tears of joy and gratitude in her eyes.

"I'm so glad you like it." Berta says, stepping back to admire her work.

Carla is just flabbergasted at its beauty. "It is just so beautiful! How did you ever learn to do this?"

Before Berta can answer, Kay steps into the kitchen still wearing her night gown and robe. "Oh, my gosh!" She exclaims and runs to gaze at the cake. "Berta, it's beautiful!" She quickly turns to Berta and grabs her in a hug.

Berta is laughing, "I should do this more often. I get lots of hugs," she says.

Carla and Kay stand looking at the cake. Berta is so pleased they like it. She's caught up in more hugs when April enters asking if the coffee is hot.

The doorbell rings and opening the door, a man tells Berta, "We have your chairs and stuff. Where do you want us to set them up?" Berta tells them and in no time one hundred white chairs are being set up in the backyard facing the lake. The wedding arch is decorated with white satin gracefully flowing to the ground and has a floral bouquet at the center top and one on each side. Large pastel-colored balloons in yellow, rose, and white float above one end of each row of chairs. A long white runner is placed on the manicured lawn leading the happy brides to their future husbands.

The large covered patio now has a portable bar, stereo system, and a long table has a white linen cloth and pastel yellow flower petals scattered on it. Plates, napkins, and utensils are already in place. The huge patio surrounding the pool is lit by paper rose streamers with soft lights. The patio plants and flora are decorated. Kay, Carla, and April stand looking at all that has been done. "It's beautiful," Kay says.

"I love the arch," April adds.

"Yeah, me too," Carla replies, turning to Kay. "I can't believe we're really getting married today. Are you nervous?"

"Are you kidding? I didn't sleep at all last night! Are you?" Kay responds.

"Yes! I didn't sleep much either. Kay, thank you." Carla doesn't mention she dreamed Nancy was chasing Missy and woke up shaking and gasping for air.

"For what?" Kay asks.

"For everything you've done, for agreeing to have a double wedding. For—"

Kay interrupts, "That was my idea."

"I know but with moving and everything I haven't been much help."

Kay hugs her and replies, "You have had your hands full and even with that, you helped a lot. We did it!" She bursts out laughing, raises her arms, and dances in a little circle.

Carla and April laugh, "Group hug!" April states and the women hug and return inside.

* * *

Upstairs is bustling with activity as all the women are dressing and helping each other with their hair. Berta is helping dress Jenny and Missy in their dresses. The girls insisted on dressing alike. Each is adorned in white knee-length yoke-style dresses. Each has a satin bodice. Coral flowers are scattered about the full tool mesh skirt. Their white satin shoes with a small coral bow match. Missy giggles as she watches Berta place a halo headband with coral and white silk flowers and bows on Jenny's head. Coral and white ribbons cascade down intermingling with Jenny's long hair. "Your turn," Berta says, holding the same designed headband for Missy.

Kay's sister is wearing a soft yellow dress with a scalloped-edge neckline and spaghetti straps. The skirt is chiffon balloon style, tea length. She's wearing the small diamond heart necklace that Kay gave her as her bride's maid gift. Tears fill her eyes as she gazes at Kay. "You look so beautiful."

"Thank you," Kay responds, patting her hair.

April's pastel green dress enhances her dark tan. Her dress is also tea length but strapless with intricate lace and a scalloped hemline. The A-style flows down her slender body. A teardrop green emerald necklace sparkles on her chest.

"How did you know that was my birthstone?" April exclaimed when opening her gift. "Alex told me." Carla grinned.

"It's beautiful, I love it!" April replied and quickly put it on.

Kay's mother is dressed in a taupe elegant lace and sequin dress. Cap sleeves and a tiered skirt accentuate her slender body. Her dark, short-cropped hair enhances her oval-shaped face and dark eyes.

Larry's mother is wearing a sleeveless, very elegant, plum two-piece ensemble of over lace, sheath dress with a sheer caplet overlay. Her gold slingback sandals complete the ensemble. Each mother has a corsage of white alstromeria, green hypericum, and Italian ruscus.

Berta enters the room where the women are gathered and tells Carla, "The girls are dressed and staying in Missy's room until time to go. How can I help you now?"

"Oh, Berta, what a dear you are! Thank you." Carla glances at the clock and continues, "The guests will be arriving in about thirty minutes. Why don't you hurry and get dressed. April can help me put my gown on."

Berta hugs her quickly. "Okay. I'll be back in a minute," and rushes out of the room.

"Here, let me help you with that." April laughs as Carla tries to latch the fine chain of her necklace with shaking hands. She's wearing pearl and rhinestone drop earrings that were her mother's and a single pearl necklace. A tendril of curl hangs loosely on each side of her face with her hair pulled back in soft waves cascading down her back.

In the meantime, all the men are at Kay's house dressing. Larry and Rick are dressed in light brown slacks, white long sleeve shirts, and light brown vests with a yellow tie. Larry's father is his best man and dressed in a dark blue suit with a green mini cymbidium orchid boutonniere. Rick's partner is his best man and is dressed similarly to Rick in tan slacks, white shirt, and vest with a yellow pinstripe tie.

Dr. Anderson has a dark blue suit on with a small white carnation boutonniere and is helping Rick tie his tie. Rick is shaking all over and looks pathetically at his father. "What if she changes her mind at the last minute?" he asks nervously.

"Now, son, she's not going to do that. She loves you very much," Dr. Anderson says while concentrating on the tie.

"But what if she does? What will I do?"

"Rick! She isn't going to leave you standing at the altar alone! Now get a grip, son," Dr. Anderson replies, finishing the tie knot.

Rick turns and begins pacing. He's walking funny and when Larry steps into the room, he watches him for a second then says, "Why are you walking funny?"

"These darn new shoes hurt!" Rick states and continues to pace.

Larry looks down at Rick's feet and bursts out laughing. He laughs so hard he can't speak and plops down on the edge of the bed.

Rick glares at him. "What the heck is so funny?"

Larry holds his ribs then points to Rick's shoes. "You have them on the wrong feet!" He howls with laughter. All the men stand looking at Rick's feet laughing.

"Damn!" Rick groans and kicks them off.

* * *

Becky steps into Carla's room, smiling brightly. "You look so beautiful," she says, giving Carla a hug.

"Thank you. I wasn't sure you were going to be able to come." Carla replies.

"I wouldn't have missed this for the world. Here, I have a little pin you can wear. Something borrowed something blue." She smiles, handing Carla a very small blue flower stick pin.

Carla hands it back to her, "Help me put it on. My hands are shaking so bad I can't manage to even comb my own hair." She laughs.

Becky pins it on her. "I'll see you downstairs. Oh, Berta said they're ready for you."

* * *

Carla, Kay, Kay's sister, April, Missy and Jenny gather at the sliding glass doors going out to the patio. The music begins playing loudly over the speakers and April and Kay's sister step out and begin walking toward the gathering in the yard. Several of Larry's lawyer friends stand with their wife beside them, police officers are dressed in uniform with wives or girlfriends, and several detectives have joined in the celebration. Dr. Anderson's secretary and receptionist as well as a few of the nurses that know Carla are in the group of guests. Kay's boss and a few coworkers and friends stand smiling as they watch the two maids of honor stand at the end of the runner. Missy and Jenny are guided through the door carrying their white lacy basket with pink rose petals and walk to stand behind April and Kay's sister.

Two pastors stand under the wedding arch smiling. Larry and Carla wanted her pastor to marry them and Kay and Rick wanted Kay's pastor to marry them so the pastors agreed to coordinate the ceremonies for them. Rick stands to one side and Larry stands across from him on the other side, waiting and watching for their brides. April and Kay's sister begin their slow walk toward the altar when someone bursts out laughing. Everyone suddenly turns to see what is so funny as more join in the laughter. Two squirrels have decided this is an opportune time to chase one another across the lawn, scamper up one side of the archway, across the top and down the other side, racing off toward the trees at the far side of the property. April and Kay's sister have stopped and are laughing with everyone else. Slowly, the laughter dies down and they resume their walk. Missy and Jenny are laughing hysterically until Berta gives them a stern look and motions for them to begin walking and tossing the rose petals. The wedding march music begins as the two girls giggle all the way to the front.

Carla and her father walk slowly across the lawn. Her ivory chiffon sheath halter dress, with a beaded applique at the center of the waist and ruching at the bodice flatters her slender figure. The sweeping train flows behind her. A slight breeze ruffles the one-tier chapel-length ivory veil. Her father leans over and kisses her on the cheek. "I love you, Carly. Be happy." Tears well up in her eyes and she whispers, "I love you too." Oohs and aahs are whispered, tears fill some of the women's eyes, and Larry's eyes are transfixed on her. He quickly pats his vest pocket for the tenth time to make sure the ring is still there.

Kay is waiting until Carla is handed to Larry by her father. As soon as Carla is standing beside Larry, she and her father slowly begin walking toward the front. His silk blue suit shines in the sunlight. Rick looks at her with tears in his eyes and smiles. Her off-white sheath dress with a V neckline plunges into a cross-ruched bodice with a beaded motif. The V back releases into an elegant train. Her 1950s' style five-tier shoulder-length veil isn't pestered by the breeze.

Halfway to her future husband, a small Yorkshire dog with a bright pink bow holding a tuft of hair above its bright black eyes comes scampering up beside her, wagging its tail frantically. Its owner stands near the end of the house, calling it in a whispered voice but the little dog pays no heed. The guests once again burst into laughter and Kay tries to shoo the dog away with one hand at her side while continuing to walk. The dog refuses to leave and walks beside her right up to where Rick is standing laughing. Kay's father places her hand in Rick's and steps to the side, trying to gently push the dog away with his foot. Missy and Jenny are giggling standing next to April. The two brides and two grooms step to the center facing the pastors and the dog darts between the two couples and sits quietly, looking up at the pastors. The owner has run to the edge of the wedding party and stands quietly red-faced and saying nothing. The dog obviously is determined to be a part of this wedding. The photographer is racing to get plenty of pictures, including the dog. His video caught the squirrels and he's determined to include every little nuance, not knowing what to expect next.

Carla's pastor grins broadly, glancing down at the dog, and steps forward standing in front of Carla and Larry. Larry turns and signals Missy to join them and she runs to stand next to Carla. Carla turns and hands her bouquet of clear pink Gerbera daisies with lavender roses, burgundy carnations, and white Stephanotis flowers to April.

"We are gathered here today," the pastor begins.

The dog's ears perk up and its tail twitches. Missy leans forward to peek at the dog and Carla nudges her with her hand.

The pastor continues with their vows and glances down at the little dog before asking, "Do you, Larry Mathew Dunn, take this woman, Carla Rose Bloom, to be your lawfully wedded wife until death do you part?"

"I do," Larry says, looking deeply into Carla's shimmering eyes.

"Do you, Carla Rose Bloom, take this man, Larry Mathew Dunn, to be your lawfully wedded husband until death do you part?"

"I do," Carla whispers as a tear trickles down her cheek.

The pastor looks at Missy. "Step between Carla and Larry," he whispers to her.

Missy quickly steps between Carla and Larry. The pastor grins broadly then looks at her seriously and asks, "Do you, Melissa Grace Bloom, accept Larry Dunn as your new daddy and to obey and honor him?"

Missy grins brightly, looking up at Larry and proudly states, quite loudly, "I sure do!" Everyone laughs and tears flow throughout the guests.

"Then I hereby pronounce Larry and Carla as man and wife. You may kiss the bride."

The little dog scoots to the side, barks once, and happily dances in a circle and suddenly plops down waiting for the next happy union.

Kay's pastor steps forward as Carla, Larry, and Missy stand quietly.

The little dog looks up at Kay and Rick then to the pastor.

"We are gathered here today to join these two in holy matrimony," the pastor begins. He goes through the usual wedding vows and as before, when he announces them man and wife and the newlywed kiss, the little dog barks once and dances in a circle.

Cheers and laughter echo through the trees and across the lake. Several boats have slid in close to watch the ceremony and as the cheers fill the air, they blink their lights, clap, and holler congratulations. Larry, Carla, and Missy walk back down the aisle with hands joined as everyone congratulates them. Rick and Kay follow behind with the little dog happily bouncing along behind them. The dog's owner stands quietly at the end of the aisle waiting to snatch the dog up. As soon as Carla and Larry have stepped onto the grass, the owner profusely apologizes. Both are laughing and assuring him that the little dog just added to the festivities and really was rather cute.

"Please join us, Sam," Carla tells the dog's owner, who is a neighbor three doors down.

"Oh gosh, I'm not dressed for a wedding party." He replies, reaching out for the little dog.

"You're fine! Come on. Take Bubbles home and bring Mary with you and come join us." Carla insists.

"Are you sure?" he asks.

Larry replies, "We're sure. You're already part of the party." Larry laughs, reaching over and petting the little dog.

People have gathered around the couples and someone yells, "If you want a seat, grab a chair and bring it with you."

Sam leaves, carrying the little dog and the reception begins.

* * *

As the sun sets, the lights from the pool shimmer off the floating plastic water lilies. Small delicate clear lights twinkle in the branches of the many patio floras and music fills the air. A friend of Rick's has agreed to help out with the bar. The brides' fathers each give a toast to the couples and Larry and Carla stand on one side of the cake with Kay and Rick on the other side. Each couple holds a knife and as "hear, hear" is shouted by the guests, they cut the cake. The night is filled with laughter, dancing, and champagne. At midnight, the guests have gathered in the front of the house. Kay's car as well as Larry's has been decorated with streamers and "Just Married" written across the back windows. Carla and Kay stand side by side holding their bouquets while all the women have gathered together to hopefully catch the tossed bouquet.

Carla glances over her shoulder with her back turned to the crowd and yells, "Are you ready? Here goes." She throws her bouquet as high in the air and as far as she can and quickly spins around to see who catches it. Becky is near the back of the crowd of women and screams, "It's mine!" as she jumps in the air grabbing the bouquet. Cheers fill the air. She races forward holding the bouquet high above her head looking like the lead runner in the Olympics displaying proudly the torch. Carla hugs her laughing.

Kay steps forward laughing and yells, "Whose next? You better be ready." She turns her back to the crowd and yells "Here it comes," throwing her bouquet high and wide. The bouquet soars through the air, missing the crowd of women by twenty feet. One woman races for it and like a championship quarterback tackles the bouquet just before it hits the ground, screaming, "Gotcha!" Everyone roars with laughter.

Larry and Rick join their wives and suddenly the people form two lines, making way for the newlyweds to walk down a human-lined lane to their cars. "Congratulations," "Have fun," "Best wishes," and "Goodbyes" are all shouted as rice is thrown over the couples. They each enter their cars and Carla and Larry drive to the large, newly built hotel that overlooks the lake as the first guests of the honeymoon suite. Their flight to Acapulco isn't until noon the next day. Kay and Rick drive into Atlanta to spend their first night in the honeymoon suite of a large hotel. They leave for the Bahamas at nine. The crowd disperses with much laughter, hugs, and statements of "A beautiful wedding," "The brides were beautiful," and comments about the squirrels and dog.

Berta has her arms around Missy as Missy cries. "But how long will they be gone?" she asks through her tears.

"They'll be back before you know it," Berta says, turning Missy gently and guiding her into the house. Jenny had fallen asleep but Missy insisted on staying up until they left.

* * *

The flight from Atlanta to Acapulco, Mexico, takes Carla and Larry most of the day due to having to change planes in Miami, Florida. Sitting in the backseat of a speeding taxi, with speeding cars and blasting horns all around them, it winds its ways through the streets of Acapulco. This taxi ride is an experience all unto itself. Carla is praying while hanging on for dear life to Larry's arm while watching the scenery flash by. With a prayer of thanksgiving, she and Larry finally step into the honeymoon suite. Standing on the private balcony, they look out over the Pacific Ocean. They can see the rugged Sierra Madre Mountains to the east and Acapulco Bay to the west. A telescope is fastened down tight on the balcony and Carla looks through it. "Oh, wow, Larry, look at this." She says, grinning. Larry leans over and looking through the telescope can see for miles out across the water. "This is awesome. We can stargaze tonight." He steps back from the telescope and adds, "That is if we can't think of anything else to do." With a mischievous twinkle in his eyes he grins broadly and winks at her. Carla blushes.

The room has a king-sized bed, a large flat screen TV attached to one wall, a sofa, table with two chairs, and in the luxurious bathroom, a large heart-shaped pink spa takes up one end of the room. Larry leans back against the pink tub wall and Carla leans back against his chest, resting her head on his shoulder while the steaming hot water swirls around them. "It is so beautiful here," Carla says in a dreamy voice with her eyes closed and Larry's arms wrapped around her waist. They are silent for several moments. Larry kisses the side of her head and remains quiet. "Larry?" Carla whispers and when there's no answer, she begins to chuckle quietly. From behind her, she hears soft snores. Larry has fallen soundly asleep.

* * *

They spend their days swimming, snorkeling, touring, and trying their hand at wind surfing. At Coyuca Lagoon, they watch exotic wildlife and Larry laughs when he sees a sign directing them to the mud baths. "How about a mud bath?" He grins.

"I don't think so." Carla laughs and they continue to walk along paths lined with coconut trees and palm trees.

"We better head back to the boat for the rest of the tour," Carla says.

Once on the boat, with several other passengers, a lady sitting across from them smiles brightly at them. "You look like newlyweds," she says.

Carla grins broadly and glances up at Larry. "Yes. We've been married five days."

"Oh, that's wonderful. Congratulations. My Henry passed last year and we always wanted to come here so I said I'm going to come for the both of us."

"I'm sorry. Are you traveling alone?" Carla replies.

"Yes. Well, no. I know my Henry is with me."

Carla isn't sure what to reply so merely nods.

"I understand we're having lunch at the Isla of los Pajaros," Larry says.

"Yes, we are. That's the bird sanctuary. I can't wait to see the marabous. I've never heard of that bird so I'm excited to see what they look like," the lady states.

The boat docks and everyone disembarks. Larry and Carla take several pictures of the black and white herons, various pelicans, storks, and finally the marabou stork. Carla shivers. "That has to be the ugliest bird I've ever seen," she tells Larry, aiming the camera. The large bird has a bald, pinkish-colored head and neck with a large rough bill protruding out. Its feathers are black and white. The bird she's watching suddenly dips its head and grabs something in its bill. Making clapping sounds with its bill, it throws its head back and quickly swallows it. Carla snaps the picture just as the bird spreads its wings out. Larry looks at the information sheet they've been given and says, "Wow. That sucker's wing span is nine to ten feet from what it says here." Carla shivers and states, "Let's go. That thing is just too ugly for words." Laughing, Larry places his arm around her shoulders and they walk away.

* * *

At Zocalo, they walk around the tree-lined plaza and enter souvenir shops, eat freshly caught seafood under a palapa-style roof, and stand among several tourists watching the cliff divers risking their life as they dive headlong down a cliff into the churning waters. Returning back to their hotel, they decide to walk along the beach. Small children dressed in dirty underpants and barefoot approach them. "Dolla, por favore," they beg. Carla took pity and gave the two children some change on their first day on the beach. After that, when she and Larry appeared, the two begging children suddenly turned into six and each time they appeared, the group got larger. They learned very quickly not to fall for the large sad brown eyes of the small Mexican children.

Those sad eyes were a begging ploy and the children would race away laughing to the next couple and stare sadly up at them begging for change.

They've visited many open air restaurants, taken a glass-bottom boat tour, and tonight, being their last night, decide to go on a sunset cruise. The boat takes them out far enough to see the night lights of Acapulco. While standing at the boat's railing, Carla leans against Larry's shoulder, "This is just so beautiful. I can't believe we've been here a week already."

Larry smiles down at her. "It does seem like it's flown by."

"It's been wonderful." She smiles up at him.

Larry takes her in his arms and kisses her passionately. Releasing her, he grins. "Well, Mrs. Dunn, how do you like married life so far?"

"Hmmm." Carla leans into him and pulls his face down to meet hers. "I love it!" she says and kisses him in a long lingering kiss.

* * *

Rick and Kay sit eating the spicy native food of Nassau. Rick gulps down a glass of water. "Wow, is that spicy!" he says, placing the empty glass on the table and laughing.

"I'd like to go to swim with the dolphins," Kay replies.

"We can do that. Why don't we plan on doing that in the morning and go to Lucayan National Park after we finish eating? I'd like to see those caverns. Since we're not expert divers, they may not let us see them but I'd like to try."

"We can snorkel there even if they don't let us see the caverns," Kay says.

"Yeah and you like lighthouses. The brochure shows that there's one there."

"Oh good. I hope we can find some sand dollars. I'd like to take a few home as souvenirs. I'll bet Missy would love a sand dollar."

Rick lays his napkin on the table. "Are you ready to go? If we're going to the Lucayan National Park then we need to see if we can take the water ferry there."

Rising from her chair, Kay grins. "I love riding those. It's almost like being in Italy with the gondolas."

* * *

Kay has been able to take pictures of starfish, collected four sand dollars, and they do a little snorkeling. They weren't able to visit the caverns since they are deep underwater and only expert divers are allowed to visit them. Rising early the next morning, Kay and Rick have their bag with masks, fins, snorkels, and towels. As with most of their day trips, they wear their bathing suits under their clothes ready for any opportunity to play in the crystal clear waters. They've opted to go out into the Caribbean ocean on a boat and swim with the dolphins in their natural environment. The boat takes them out into the deeper turquoise clear waters. Even though the water is deep, they can see the bottom and Kay is absolutely thrilled. Suddenly, dolphins are playing and jumping a short distance away. With the other tourists, they quietly slide down into the water from the boat and swim away from the boat. The dolphins begin to swim amongst them and playfully twirl and twist, some close enough to touch, and perform acrobats by shooting up and out of the water. A professional photographer films Kay and Rick as they swim with the dolphins. Kay is able to pet one gently for a second and it's all caught on film. The photographer assures them they will have it all on a DVD to take home with them.

Their last couple of days is spent touring the Pirates Museum, the geologic formations at Ben's Cave, shopping in the International Bazaar, and visiting the "the Surge." Rick wants to fly through the tunnels of the Surge in the water park and with Kay sitting in front of him, they twist and turn, fly around corners, down slopes, and finally shoot out of the large tube into the clear ocean waters. Rick is laughing. Flying through the air, Kay's scream mingles with the screams of others jettisoning out of the tube. Rick shoots to the surface, coughing. He swallowed water when he neglected to stop laughing when he made a huge splash upon landing.

Grabbing Kay, he kisses her. "Do you want to do it again?" he laughs.

Kay swipes at the water in her eyes and pushes her wet hair back away from her face. "No. Let's go lay on the beach," she says, making her way out of the water.

They spend the rest of the afternoon sunning and talking about their future.

* * *

Once back home, both couples are busy completing their moves. Larry helps Carla hang pictures and Rick moves the last few items to Kay's house and helps her to rearrange furniture and set up his office in a spare bedroom. Missy has seen the DVD of Kay and Rick swimming with the dolphins and pesters Carla and Larry about wanting to go swim with the dolphins. "Missy, we can't do that right now. Maybe we can go next summer for vacation. Now please, quit pestering us about this!"

"But that's a long way off!" Missy insists.

"You will be in school in another couple of weeks. We haven't even gotten settled in yet," Carla states while scooting an armchair to another position in the den.

Larry walks into the room. "Oh, honey, let me do that!" he rushes over and takes hold of the chair.

"Mr. Larry, can we go next summer to swim with the dolphins?" Missy asks.

Larry stops what he's doing and turns to look at her. He slowly walks toward her and kneels down in front of her looking her in the eyes. "Missy, do you know how much I love you?" he asks gently.

Puzzled, Missy looks at him and nods her head yes.

"Do you know that now that we're a family, you don't have to call me Mr. Larry?"

"But what will I call you?" Missy replies softly.

"Well, what would you like to call me?"

Missy thinks for several moments then a big grin spreads across her face. Carla is quietly watching this exchange. Larry says nothing as Missy thinks.

"Can you I call you 'Daddy'?" Missy finally exclaims.

Tears well up in Larry's eyes and Carla gasps placing a hand over her mouth as tears flood her eyes. Larry can hardly speak and finally grabs her in a hug and says, "You sure can! You're my little girl now and it would make me very happy if you called me Daddy." He swipes a tear and releases her.

Missy grins broadly. "Okay! Daddy, can we go swim with the dolphins next summer?"

Carla and Larry burst out laughing while drying their tears. "I will do my very best to take you to swim with the dolphins next summer." Larry assures her and stands looking down at her. He looks at Carla, points to Missy, and grins broadly. "That's my girl!" he states and returns to the chair he was moving.

Epilogue

Five years later.

"Go faster!" Missy yells as Larry speeds across the lake. Carla sits in the boat facing the back with their three-year-old daughter, Alexis, sitting on her lap. Carla smiles down at "Lexie." "Hold on tight." She tells her. Lexie grins broadly and points toward Missy.

Missy is now very proficient on her single ski and has joined a waterskiing group that performs during the summer for special events at the lake. It's unusual to have an eleven-year-old girl standing at the top of a three-tier pyramid shooting across the lake on skis but the lady that heads the group saw Missy skiing and immediately knew the child was a natural and asked Carla and Larry if they would allow her to join the group. Missy begged and begged until her parents finally gave in, only after watching the group's performances several times.

This is a special Fourth of July weekend show and Missy is practicing before tomorrow's show. She still has to ski with double skis on occasion but her favorite is on the slalom. She and Larry have skied together as well as her and Rick. They have taught her several tricks on the slalom and in the upcoming show, the leader has told her she will be doing a solo performance. Missy is nervous but excited.

"I can't turn fast enough if you don't go faster," Missy yells at Larry then suddenly falls. Larry spins the boat around and slowly pulls up beside her.

"Daddy, I can't twirl around like I'm supposed to unless you go faster. That's why I fell," she says, swiping at the water on her face.

Larry gives her a few pointers then adds, "You're doing great. I can't speed up too much, Missy, or you'll get hurt. I'll go just a little faster but you have to concentrate on placing your hand properly when you switch hands."

"Okay," Missy replies, shoving her feet in the ski pockets.

Larry slowly stretches the rope out and when Missy hollers "Hit it," he speeds off with Missy flying across the wakes and whooping it up.

* * *

The next day, Rick, Kay, their two-year-old son John, Larry, Carla, Lexie, Dr. Anderson, and Berta sit in the front row of the stands. April, Jenny, and Alex have come for the long weekend and sit watching anxiously with the others. As the ski group pass in front of the crowd, Jenny screams, "Yeah, Missy!" and the crowd claps. Three teenage girls are on the bottom row of the pyramid with two girls standing on their shoulders. Missy is on top holding the ski rope in one hand and the American flag with the other, waving above her. The Star Spangled Banner is playing through the loudspeakers and the crowd is standing. Tears flow down Carla's face as she watches her daughter proudly carry the flag. At the end of the song, the boat pulling the performers disappears behind a large curtain. The crowd goes wild clapping, whistling, and shouting.

Larry looks at Carla with tears welling in his eyes. "Can you believe that's our kid?" He says to Carla, wiping a tear. Carla can hardly speak. She hugs Lexie close to her chest, kisses her cheek, swipes at a tear, and replies, "That's definitely our little girl!"

April leans over to Carla and Kay, "I can't believe how she can stay up there without falling! Man, she's good!" April laughs.

The loudspeakers suddenly announce, "Now, for a special solo performance by the youngest skier this group has ever had. Please welcome, Miss Melisa Dunn!" The crowd erupts into applause and from behind the curtain a boat roars out. Missy is on double skis dressed in a bikini of red, white, and blue. Ribbons of the same colors whip in the wind from her hair. She has a gold star above her head and in her right hand, she holds a flaming torch lifted high above her head. America the Beautiful plays through the speakers as Missy passes past the crowd, smiling brightly. Carla, Larry, Rick, and the whole crowd are on their feet singing. Missy makes two more passes in front of the crowd then throws the torch to someone near the curtain and the boat roars across the water. Missy jumps wakes, twirls in circles, and skis so close to the side of the boat that the crowd gasps. She laughs and shoots out sideways away from the boat. Suddenly, the boat disappears out into open waters in the distance.

Carla watches, handing Lexie to Larry. The crowd is standing with hands raised, shading their eyes. Slowly a ramp rises out of the water. Carla gasps. Larry looks at her with a puzzled look. "What's going on?" he asks.

Carla shivers. "I don't know. Was that the end of her performance?"

Rick looks at Kay then glances at Carla and Larry. He leans to Kay and whispers, "They better not do what I think they're going to do!" he exclaims.

Suddenly, the boat begins appearing. The roar of the engine is heard before the boat is fully seen. The roar increases and when the boat flashes past the ramp, Missy flies up and across the ramp, flying high in the air and does a summersault in the air before landing on the water. The crowd goes wild, except for Missy's family. She loops around and heads toward the shore jumping off the skis before hitting the beach. She runs up to Larry and

Carla, laughing and smiling the biggest smile a human can make. She grabs Carla in a hug, then Larry and quickly turns and runs back out into the water and waves at everyone, shouting "Happy fourth of July," and bows several times.

Her family stands transfixed and in shock watching her. Missy trots off to the side and as the crowd continues to clap, her leader tells her to go take another bow. She runs back out into the water in front of the crowd and bows several more times before running off to change her clothes. Rick is livid, Carla stands shaking and thinking about the danger her daughter was in by doing that trick. Larry is still too shocked to get mad and the others are flabbergasted.

* * *

After the show is over and they're all gathered back at Carla and Larry's home, Missy has gotten chewed up one side and down the other by Rick. Larry has had to step in, grabbing Rick's arm and dragging him outside.

"Aren't you going a bit overboard, Rick? She's just a kid," Larry states.

Rick looks at him, shaking his head and trying to calm down. "I just keep seeing her laying in a hospital in a body cast. I can't help it. She could have been killed doing that stupid stunt!"

"She's all right, buddy. We've talked to her and she's promised not to do it again. It's something she's always wanted to do and now she's done it. Really good, I might add."

"Who taught her to do that? You!?" Rick asks angrily.

"No. They have a professional skier that works with them and you know Missy, she can talk anyone into just about anything. She talked him into teaching her."

"I want to talk to him!"

"Rick, you need to get a grip. She's fine, praise God. Now, let's have the barbeque and get past this," Larry says gently.

Rick takes a deep breath and paces a few steps. “Yeah, you’re right. It’s over and done with. I guess I should go apologize to her for yelling at her.”

“She’s probably in her room,” Larry says and walks back into the house.

* * *

As the summer wears on, there’s more family gatherings and they have been to Ivy a few times since Carla and Missy moved back to Gainesville. She and Larry decided to sell the Ivy house to Alex’s parents since they loved it so much. When they do visit, they have always been welcome to stay with April and Alex which pleases Missy and Jenny. The two girls are now talking and giggling about boys instead of dolls and board games. They’re both in the sixth grade and attending middle school. They talk on the phone several times a week and most vacations are spent together if possible.

Carla is talking on the phone when Missy bursts through the door carrying a handful of mail and her backpack. “Mom, I’m home,” she yells and tosses the mail on the dining room table while running to her room.

“I’ll talk to you later, April. Missy just got home. Maybe we can come down over Labor Day. I’ll talk to Larry about it,” she says into the cordless phone.

“Okay. Give Missy a hug for us. Bye.”

Carla hangs up and carrying the phone into the dining room, she picks up the mail and thumbs through it. The last piece is a letter and looking at the return address, she doesn’t recognize the name. She glances at the address again to make sure it is to her and not a delivery mistake by the mail carrier. She slowly tears the envelope open and unfolds the letter and begins reading.

Dear Mrs. Dunn:

You don't know me but I have been working with Carol McPhee these past five years. I am part of a prison ministry sponsored by my church. Carol asked me to send you the letter enclosed and I agreed with the stipulation that she allow me to read it first. She has and that is why you have received it. I hope it will be an encouragement to you.

Blessings on you and your family;
Mrs. Frazer.

Carla takes a deep breath and rereads the letter. *Maybe I should wait and read it with Larry.* She thinks laying the two letters on the table and staring at them. *Lord? What should I do?* "Read it," the Lord replies. Carla reaches for the letters with shaking hands. She rereads the first one again and slowly places it on the table. She begins reading Nancy's letter.

Dear Carla:

There is so much I want to say and I hope you will read my whole letter. I'm not even sure where to start. I guess I'll start with having to be in this place. I hate it here but I know that had I not been sentenced to this place, I would still be doing the things I was doing for all those years. I'll be in here for a long time. But you already know that. I want to say that you put me here but I know that's not right. I put myself here. That's hard for me to admit. It's been a long learning process. Please hear me out. When I first came here, I hated you and everything you and all Christians stand for. I got into so many fights and spent a lot of time in solitary confinement. That's when I met Mrs. Frazer. She said she told you she's with a church prison ministry. Anyway, she wouldn't leave me alone. That woman can talk more than any human being I've ever known! I kept telling her to get away from me but she kept coming back. She didn't preach or anything like that. I probably would have killed her if she had. After a while, I started talking to her and gradually she started encouraging me to go to the prison church services. I didn't go for a long time but then out of sheer boredom, I started going. The stuff the preacher talked about made no sense to me but I continued to go and she continued to visit me all the time. Then the preacher started visiting me and he gave me a Bible. There's not a lot to do in these places so I started reading it, just a little. It contradicted everything I believed and I almost threw it away several times but something wouldn't let me. I know that doesn't make sense but it is true. Every time I'd start to throw it in the trash, something stopped me. Then one day, they had a program where a woman spoke and they sang all these spiritual songs and prayed and all that. We were required to go. I didn't want to go but I had no choice. When they started praying, I started to get up and leave. I know you already think I'm nuts but this really happened. I don't understand it even now. Anyway, I got partway up from my seat when I felt a hand on my shoulder shove me back down on the chair. I thought it was a guard but when I looked there was no guard close by. I started to stand again and it happened again. No guard was anywhere near me and the other women weren't paying any attention to me. They all had their heads bowed and praying. After the prayer, this woman started speaking. I couldn't believe she had the same beliefs as me! She said she worshipped Satan for a long time and then started telling about some of the things that she did and stuff that happened to her. Then she started talking about Jesus and how He helped her. I didn't believe all the Jesus part helping her but after that program was over, the guards let Mrs. Frazer bring her to my cell and we talked. I'm rambling, I know, so bear with me. Like I said, I know you think I'm crazy but please believe me. For three days after that, every morning I would be woke up hearing my name whispered. My cell was flooded with this glowing kind of light. I'd hear "Carol" then a minute later I'd hear it again. It did it three times and then the light would fade. It did it each morning at dawn. Nobody was around! Everyone else was still asleep! It was just plain weird. I still haven't figured that out. The preacher said it was God calling me but I don't know if I believe that. Anyway, the last three years I have been getting counseling. The preacher that comes every week and a psychiatrist comes twice a week. What I'm trying to say is that I'm sorry for all thc pain I causcd you and Melissa. The psychiatrist showed me the documents that your husband had in court proving my baby died. That's still hard for me to accept even now. With the preacher's help, I've learned that it was all part of what the devil was doing. He was making me believe what he wanted me to believe. I could write a book about that so I won't go into it here. I do want you to know, Carla, that I am so sorry for all that I put you and Melissa through. It's taking a long time to realize some things but with God's help I'm getting there. Yes, you read right. Last month in one of the church services, I asked Jesus to be my Savior. The pastor is helping me to renounce all the satanic stuff I was into and the Lord has revealed to me the depth of the darkness I dwelled in. It's still hard for me to believe the hold that Satan had on me but God, in all His mercy, has forgiven me and my prayer is that someday you can also forgive me. Please forgive me and if you can find it in your heart to come here someday I would like to tell you I'm sorry in person.

Carol

P.S. I don't go by Nancy anymore.

Carla has tears streaming down her face as she lays the letter gently on the table. She's unaware that Larry has come home and is standing in the doorway watching her quietly while she's been reading the letter. She wipes her tears and suddenly realizes she isn't alone.

Larry walks to her, sits on a chair next to her, and looks at her. "Bad news?" he gently asks. Carla shakes her head no, slides the letter in front of him, and lowers her head on her folded arms on the table and sobs. Larry reads the letter and when finished lays it on the table. His eyes are filled with tears. Carla sits up and throws her arms around his neck and sobs into his shoulder. When she can contain her tears, she releases him. Larry says nothing. Carla swipes at the remaining tears and says, "God has answered my prayers." Larry looks at her with a questioning expression, so Carla explains. "Larry, I've never told anyone but I have prayed Nancy would find the Lord for all this time. I didn't know if it would ever happen or not because she was so lost but I kept praying for her." Carla begins crying again.

Larry picks up the letter looking at it.

"I want to go see her," Carla suddenly states.

"Are you sure?" Larry asks surprised.

"Yes! I want to go see her. I need to go see her."

"When?"

"I don't know. I just know I need to see her in person."

"Are you going to answer her letter?" Larry asks.

"No. I want to tell her in person."

"Tell her what? Honey, you aren't making much sense."

"Do you remember when I went to see our pastor before we got married about the dream?"

"Yes. What about it?" Larry asks puzzled.

"I forgave her then. Now I want to tell her in person," Carla replies.

"Oh. You didn't tell me that."

"I know. That was just a really hard time for me, and for Missy."

Larry leans over and takes her in his arms. "You are an amazing woman. God has blessed me so much with you. You decide when you're ready to go see her and we'll go together." Larry releases her.

"I'll pray about it and we'll know when it's God's time for me to go."

"Okay," Larry says, standing. "Where're the kids?" he asks, walking toward the kitchen.

"Missy is doing homework and Lexie is still taking a nap."

* * *

Three months later, Larry and Carla pull into the prison parking lot. Carla sits looking at the wire strung along the top of the high cement walls. Her hands are shaking. Larry looks at her. "Are you sure you want to do this?" he asks.

Carla glances at him then back to the prison walls and nods yes.

"I'll go in with you," Larry says.

"No, I think I want to go alone," Carla replies, quietly staring ahead.

"Honey, I don't think that's a good idea. You've never been inside a prison."

Carla looks at him and tries to smile. "I'll be okay. The Lord's with me."

"Okay. I'll wait by the front door." Larry reaches for the door handle. "I really wish you'd let me come with you."

Carla steps out of the car and Larry meets her in front of the car and they walk to the prison entrance. "I'll be fine," Carla says, pushing the door open.

She goes through security, fills out the paperwork, and takes a seat to wait. Others sit along benches waiting to be escorted to where they can visit their loved ones. Carla clasps her hands in her lap trying to stop the shaking. Soon she's led to a seat with a small window facing her and a small partition on each side giving the semblance of privacy. A telephone hangs on the partition to her right. She sits down. Nancy walks to the chair on her side of the glass and with a surprised look, she sits down. The two women sit staring at each other without speaking. Nancy's hair is back to its natural brown and her face looks drawn and tired. She's lost weight and is wearing the prison orange jumpsuit. Her hand shakes as she points to the phone on Carla's side of the window, indicating for her to pick it up. Carla removes it and places it to her ear as Nancy does the same.

Carla is about to replace the phone and run out. Seeing Nancy this close, her mind is flooded with the memories of the terror this woman caused her and her daughter.

Nancy speaks, "I didn't know you were coming. How are you?"

"I'm fine. How are you?" Carla replies hesitantly.

"I'm okay. I'm glad to see you," Nancy says cautiously.

The conversation is sporadic and each seems to be lost for what to say. Nancy finally asks about Missy.

"Missy is fine. I'm not here to talk about Missy," Carla states emphatically.

Nancy gazes at her for a long silent moment then finally asks, "Why are you here, Carla?"

Carla takes a deep breath before answering. She looks through the glass directly into Nancy's eyes and says, "I came to tell you in person that I have forgiven you."

Nancy begins to cry.

"I forgave you a long time ago." Carla continues.

"Thank you. I'm so sorry."

"Nancy—ah, Carol. I got your letter. God has answered my prayers for you if what you said in the letter was true."

"It's true," Nancy says, wiping tears off her cheeks.

Carla feels emboldened now and continues. "I have prayed for you for a long time and praise God he has answered them. I forgive you, Carol, for all that you put us through and I will continue to pray God will strengthen you and grow you in Him. That's what I came here to tell you."

Nancy can't speak for sobbing. Carla gently replaces the phone on its receiver. She stands looking at Nancy for a long moment then walks away from the window. Larry is standing beside the door when she walks out. He looks at her, not knowing what her reaction will be after being inside a women's prison and talking face to face with the woman that caused so much pain. Carla wraps her arm around his waist and smiles up into his face. "I'm good. God's good, now let's go home."

They walk arm in arm back to the car. Larry says nothing but leans across the seat and kisses her. He shakes his head in wonder of this wife of his, puts the car in gear, and drives out of the parking lot.

If you would like to ask the Lord Jesus to be your Savior, pray:
Lord, I come to You in Jesus Name.
I believe You are God's Son
and You died and arose
for the forgiveness of my sins.
I ask you to forgive me of my sins.
Cleanse me, Lord.
Come into my heart
as my Lord and Savior.
In Jesus Name, Amen.

Biography

After completing my education at Arizona State University, I joined Eastern Airlines as a flight attendant and made the friendly skies my career, making Georgia my home since 1968. My husband of eighteen years went to be with the Lord in 1993 and I gave my life to Christ soon after his death. I have since given my life over to serving my Lord and Savior, Jesus Christ. In 2003, I founded Elah Ministries, Inc. It is a nonprofit 501(c)3 Christian ministry offering hope, healing, and deliverance to hurting souls. All profits from the sale of my books support this ministry. This is my fifth published book and I give all glory to the Lord for He is the ultimate Author. I merely type the words.

My novels include beach scenarios because that is the ultimate relaxation for me. Listening to the waves, the sea air, reading a good book, and letting the salty waves wash over me, it can't get any better than that. If I can't go to the beach, I love working in my yard, playing in the dirt. I thoroughly enjoy good Christian novels and hope that my readers will be blessed by reading mine.

For more information: www.elahministries.com